GLITTER STREET

GLITTER STREET

Tim Sullivan

Rawson, Wade Publishers, Inc.
New York

Library of Congress Cataloging in Publication Data
Sullivan, Tim D
　Glitter Street.
　I. Title.
PZ4.S9518G　　[PS3569.U3592]　　813'.5'4　　78-72897
ISBN 0-89256-095-9

Copyright © 1979 by Tim Sullivan
All rights reserved
Published simultaneously in Canada by McClelland
and Stewart, Ltd.
Manufactured in the United States of America
Composition by Dix Typesetting Co. Inc.,
Syracuse, New York
Printed and bound by R. R. Donnelley & Sons Co.,
Crawfordsville, Indiana
Designed by E. O'Connor
First Edition

*For my wife, Dawn, and
my children, Tyrone,
Stephanie, and Brendan*

Acknowledgments

No book is written without the help, advice, and encouragement of many people. I wish to thank the following in order of appearance: James Patterson, Peter Skolnik, Kennett and Eleanor Rawson, Sandi Gelles-Cole, Betty Spisa, Robert Bishopric, Dom Rizzo, Maureen MacMullen, Sharon Morgan, and Thomas Deinet.

GLITTER STREET

Prologue

St. Ignatius's auditorium was unusually hot even for an August evening, but no one would let the priest turn on the fans or the air conditioning. The hum of the fans and the whir of the air conditioners made it hard to hear the call.

The serious players went to St. Ignatius. Mistaken calls were met with verbal abuse. Slow calls were met with unanimous grumbling. And nobody ever took a bladder break unless his or her boards were covered.

Mary Osborne dabbed the perspiration from her forehead with a dainty lace handkerchief and then set it on the table next to her boards. She had her usual five boards across, three rows deep, fifteen boards in all. Mary was one of the gifted ones. She didn't put down chips or pennies on her boards. Just a quick run of her fingers across the numbers, a brief check of the electric board on the stage, and she knew the position of every call on her fifteen boards.

Mary Osborne sighed. This was one of her last Wednesday Bingo games at St. Ignatius. She would miss it dearly. She had been a regular for five years. Rain or shine, hot or cold, she could be found sitting in the same place, the second row, first table, first seat, right near the refreshment stand, and a short trot from the ladies' room, if nature's call ever came during a break, of course. Every Wednesday night she was at the door at seven o'clock sharp. In her seat three minutes later.

St. Ignatius had the best game in town. The real players came here. The people who ran the game did it for the school, and they were a nice lot. Mostly working people, as she herself had been until forced to retire from the insurance company five years ago.

Well, that was yesterday, she thought. Today had its own decisions to be made, and she had made hers.

"B seven," an Irish accent echoed over the sound system. Mary glanced at her boards and smiled. She picked up a little silver bell and rang it. That was her lucky number, and it had been called on the seventh call in the seventh game. A very good sign. A bell on the other side of the room rang. Mrs. Feld, Mary thought.

"An omen, Biddy," Mary shouted.

"*Mazel*, Mary . . . *mazel*," was the reply.

Mrs. Feld was a nice Jewish lady. Mary would miss her when she left the country.

Mary Osborne's eyes never left her boards, but she touched each of her treasures, which were lined up neatly at the top of her bonus Bingo sheets. There was a china owl. A holy picture of Mary. A tiny pewter statue of John F. Kennedy. A bronze baby shoe. Rosary beads. A tiny bottle with a 1908 penny in it. And finally, a one-carat diamond measuring one quarter of an inch in diameter and weighing one forty-second of an ounce. It was flawless, colorless, and worth all the grand prize Bingo winnings at St. Ignatius for the next year if sold in the subwholesale marketplace.

1

West 47th Street/New York City

"We're ready to start shooting when you are, Sean."

Sean O'Keefe glanced at the watch his ex-wife had given him before their divorce two years ago. It was almost six o'clock in the morning. The damn watch always ran slow, just like his ex-wife. Even at that ungodly hour, it was already hot and muggy as hell. A typical New York August.

"Okay, Cal. Get the gentlemen on their marks by the Exchange. I'll be right there."

O'Keefe looked up and down the empty street. The street was usually alive with people, hurrying, dealing, and talking with their hands. Hands that reached to the heavens in exasperation. Hands that clasped their owner's head in chagrin. Hands that shook one another firmly, followed by a *"mazel und broche,"* Hebrew for luck and blessings. When you heard that, you knew a deal had been made. That was all. No contracts. No lawyers. No pieces of paper. No IRS man with a tape recorder. Just a handshake based on trust and faith in the same way it had always been done. The words were more binding than any legal paper. A commitment, and whether a million was made or lost, the deal was binding on both parties.

Sean O'Keefe had walked this street many times. He would walk from window to window studying the contents carefully, fascinated by the array of glittering diamonds that caught the reflection of the sun and exploded into a thousand dazzling lights. Some of the old-timers remembered him as a kid. One of the men he was interviewing, Ben Levi, the honorary mayor of Forty-seventh Street, used to let him run errands at his newly opened shop back in the forties. Others remembered him as the beat cop walking the three hundred and eighty-two steps along the street that probably housed more cut and polished diamonds than any place in the world.

Sean smiled as he glanced at Sid Fine's shop on the right side of the old arcade. When he had returned from the Marine Corps and started as a detective, Sid had sold him Linda's engagement ring and their wedding rings. Sid had carefully explained the four C's of the diamond business—color, carat, clarity, and cut. Sean had studied the diamond carefully with Sid's loupe, unable to see more than an oval diamond ring with two tiny baguettes.

"Awkish *goy*," Sid had jokingly called him. Sid had never liked Linda, smart old Jew that he was. He had tried to talk Sean out of the marriage, but Sean had been horny for Linda's fantastic body. Sid had told him in a fatherly tone, "Sean, you're thinking with your crotch not your heart, and certainly not your head." But lust won out, and it had been an exhausting and satisfying year. The next two years were miserable. Linda was a closet pot head, then a graduate of pill popping, and finally a roundheeled, flatback pushover for some of the grubbiest misfits Sean had ever seen. The stranger they were, the more they turned Linda on. At last report she had switched to girl friends in the sack. At first Sean had been angry, then hurt, but now all he felt was pity, even if she had taken everything that wasn't nailed to the floor. Later he got hit with the alimony.

That was three years ago, when he was still on a cop's salary. Now he was making pretty good money, thanks to an old marine buddy who convinced a local station that it would be a real image booster to have a cop as a news reporter. So he had quit the force and had become a minor TV celebrity of sorts. Linda was still getting her cut of the action, and then some. The only good thing that happened was that she took her engagement ring back to Sid to sell. He screwed her royally, and split the difference with Sean. "The least I could do for a friend, even if he is an awkish *goy*," Sid had said between bites of a corned beef sandwich.

Sean O'Keefe knew the street better than any *goy* in the city, and he also knew that he probably knew less than the most down-at-the-heels Jewish polisher. But Sean was both respected and liked in the district, as a cop and a TV reporter. It was this relationship that had helped him to expose the ring of killers who were plaguing the district. They had turned out to be Arabs, the street's name for young Israelis, usually polishers and cutters. There was a growing resentment between the old-timers, mostly conservative Orthodox Jews, and the newcomers. Sean had been doing a story on this friction of Jew against Jew when the killings started. It was his initial investigation that helped the police make their arrest of two young men from Tel Aviv who couldn't get work, and had decided to get what they wanted with a gun.

This morning Sean was doing the final segment of the story: an interview with Ben Levi and two other members of the Forty-seventh Street Diamond Council. The unofficial governing body of the street. A sweep shot of the area, and then back to the editing room where it would probably be cut to two minutes tops. Not a hell of a lot of time for a story that took almost six months out of his life and nearly got him killed.

"Hey, Sean, I'm going to need a level," yelled Fred Coyle, the unit's soundman.

Sean joined the three men standing by the chalk marks on the sidewalk. The unit's assistant handed Sean the microphone. He blew into it. A look of ecstasy appeared on Coyle's face as he put his hands to his earphones. "Stop that, Sean; you know blowing into my ear turns me on."

Sean smiled, a slow easy smile that had helped to raise his local, non-network station a couple of rating points on the six o'clock evening news slot. "You're a dirty old man, Coyle."

"I'll have you know that I resemble that remark, O'Keefe. You're level, you can start any time."

"Okay, here we go," O'Keefe said as he positioned himself next to Ben Levi.

"Ben, I'm going to make you a superstar."

Ben Levi laughed. "Smartass *goyim* kid."

"Hold it," yelled Stan Zimmerman, the cameraman. "Sean, we gotta get that damn mail truck outa the way if you want to shoot them in front of the Exchange."

Sean looked around. There was a mail van parked near them and two more across the street.

"Shoot from another angle," Sean yelled.

"It won't work. Either move the truck or shoot somewhere else."

Sean frowned slightly. Zimmerman should have had this set up before they got ready to roll. Sean couldn't care less if the damn truck was in the frame or not. He had a suspicion that Stan had been smoking grass on the job lately, but he would let it ride. Zimmerman had been one of the best cameramen in the business until he started messing with drugs. He was supposed to be clean now, but Sean knew he wasn't. He also knew that if he said anything, Zimmerman would be out of the business. Sean didn't want that. The guy had enough problems.

"Can't, Stan. Mister Levi would like it in front of the Exchange."

Sean made a quick decision. He had to do the interview before the street got crowded. Already the early birds were starting to arrive. Sean turned to the young black assistant, Cal Long.

"Cal, you're from Brooklyn. Think you can hot-wire that mail truck and move it back a little?"

The young man smiled with satisfaction. "Does the Pope say his beads?" The smile faded slightly. " 'Course, if I get busted, it's a federal rap."

"Screw 'em! They shouldn't be parked here in the first place."

Cal grinned and strutted off toward the truck.

Sean watched him open the door and swing into the front seat. Strange that these mail vans were even parked here, especially unlocked. Mail vans on this street usually carried merchandise and had armed guards. He shook his head. Still thinking like a cop! He began talking to Levi and the other men.

Cal squeezed under the dashboard looking for a way to start the engine. Something hard stuck into his buttocks. He looked annoyed as he lifted his head, only to see a hand holding a .45 between the seat divider. Cal felt the blood rush to his head as he stared at the gun. A face appeared wearing an Arab headchord. Only the eyes were visible. "You'll remain in that position for two more minutes . . . if you move, I'll blow your ass all over the front of this truck. Do you understand?"

Cal tried not to move his eyes any more than possible as he said yes.

2

6th Avenue

At the corner of Forty-fifth and Sixth Avenue, Patrolman Charlie Russo thumped the side of his blue and white with his foot. His partner, Jane Doyle, leaned over from the driver's seat and opened the door. Russo had their breakfast from Burger King in two bags. He slid his two-hundred-pound frame into his seat and started sipping his coffee noisily. Doyle frowned. It was the same look his wife gave him when he slurped coffee. Russo sipped his coffee more quietly and asked what was up.

"I think this shift is starting to get to me, Charlie. I could have sworn I saw three armored trucks go by with no markings. They were barreling up Sixth."

Russo slurped his coffee loudly again. Unmarked armored trucks traveling in groups of three? Something wasn't kosher.

"And are you ready for this?" Doyle asked.

"There's more?"

"I could swear one of those drivers looked like an Arab."

Russo spilled some coffee in his lap. "What's an Arab look like? Coulda been Jewish . . . even Italian."

Doyle frowned. Russo was putting her on again. "It wasn't his face, you twit. He was wearing one of those things on his head, you know . . ."

Russo grinned. "A *yarmulkah?*"

Doyle sighed and shook her head. "I'm going to call it in."

Russo got serious. "You head up Sixth. I'll call it in."

5th Avenue

At 6:08 A.M. Father Terrance McCord was about to cross Fifth Avenue. He had been up all night at a bargaining session with lay teachers from Manhattan's parochial schools trying to avoid a September strike. The priest was deep in thought. He didn't notice that the light was against him. He wasn't even aware that he was in the street until he heard a horn blare, and looked up to see an armored truck bearing down on him. There was a moment of agonizing pain on impact. The priest's body sailed through the air and landed in front of two horrified old women coming from early mass at St. Patrick's. Three silver armored trucks continued to speed down the avenue. Father Terrance McCord had the dubious honor of being the first victim of the liberation. There would be more.

West 47th Street

At 6:13 A.M. a dark face peered through a small hole in the side of one of the mail vans parked on Forty-seventh Street. Eyes watched the TV reporter talk to three men in front of the Diamond Exchange. A small crowd of people were standing around the fringes, waving at the camera and trying to get into the picture. The face withdrew from the peephole and glanced back at his five sweaty companions, all of whom wore headchords, olive drab fatigues, and carried M-16s.

One of the men in the back of the van peered through a partially painted window. Suddenly he let out an ear piercing whistle, and hollered, "Now!"

Six men burst from each of the three mail vans as three silver armored trucks sped onto the street. The armored trucks made a quick left and uniformly blocked Forty-seventh Street from the Fifth Avenue approach. Three more armored trucks repeated the same maneuver on Sixth Avenue.

For the next two days the area between these armored trucks would be a no-man's-land.

3

West 47th Street

Within two minutes the street was sealed off from the adjoining avenues. Gawkers, early birds, and passersby were caught up in an escape-proof trap.

One small Hasidic Jew tried to run between two of the armored trucks, and was cut down by a burst from an M-16.

With the reflexes of a good newsman, Stan Zimmerman turned his camera on the attackers. A hail of bullets smashed his camera and face with simultaneous accuracy.

Cal Long was pushed violently from the cab of the mail van. As he tried to get up, one of the attackers hit him on the head with a rifle butt.

Sean O'Keefe's stomach churned and his heart pounded violently. He concentrated on concealing his fear. He remembered the advice of the head of the New York Hostage Squad, when he had been involved in a hostage negotiation. "For God's sake, O'Keefe, don't get the turkeys pissed off at you." O'Keefe had been decorated for heroism by both the United States Marine Corps and the New York City Police Department, but he didn't feel like a hero today. He was as terrified as the three Jewish diamond merchants standing next to him.

Two men from the mail van across the street were giving most of the orders in what sounded like Arabic.

To calm his shaken nerves, O'Keefe focused on the terrorists' movements. His instincts told him what he saw might be useful later. If there was a later.

Sean's eyes moved quickly along the street. Each end was blocked by three armored trucks. There was one man in each cab . . . total six. Two men exited from each armored truck . . . twelve. Six men from each mail van . . . eighteen. About thirty armed men in all, if Sean's count was accurate.

The men from the armored trucks quickly set up metal shields between the trucks, forming a solid metal fortification across both ends of the street. Two men returned to each of the armored trucks. The remaining men took up positions behind the shields.

The terrorists from the mail vans quickly rounded up the frightened people on the street—fourteen in all—and forced them into the middle of the street at gunpoint.

All the terrorists were dressed in fatigues and headchords. All appeared dark skinned, ranging from tan to ebony. All spoke some Arabic tongue. All were well trained and performed with the military precision that could only come from many hours of well-planned practice.

Sean almost panicked when he saw what happened next. Several men quickly brought out sections of a steel cage. They assembled the cage easily, herding the hostages roughly into the temporary holding pen. Two of the terrorists rigged the north and south sides of the cage with dynamite. Then they set lines and strung them out to the building entrances on the north and south sides of the street. They connected the wires to detonators behind the steel shields like the ones at the ends of the block. Two men got behind each of the shields and trained their guns on the cage.

A man who appeared to be the leader used hand signals to motion his men into various buildings within the fortified perimeter. Sean's alert ears caught a good old American "motherfuck" as one of the terrorists tripped and fell on the curb. They don't all speak Arabic, Sean thought.

He was very uncomfortable in the cage. He had been in a similar cage in Vietnam, and the close confinement had driven him to attempt his successful escape. But this cage, with the explosives and four guards, wasn't like a bamboo cage. For his own sanity, he continued to take mental notes.

The armored cars were positioned slightly past the subway entrances at the west end of the street, and past the two large buildings at the east end of the street. The small most important buildings in the middle of the block were under the attackers' control.

The entrance routes from the Fifth and Sixth avenue stores and the subways were covered by guns from the armored trucks. If the police used the tall buildings, they would see nothing but the hostages in the cage and the empty mail vans.

The leader and one of his men were looking at the cage, and Sean had a very uncomfortable feeling that they were talking about him. He looked away purposely and noticed Cal Long, who had been forgotten by the terrorists. Cal had regained consciousness and was trying to crawl into the entrance of one of the buildings. Sean saw one of the M-16s behind the shield turn quickly, pause, then fire. Cal stopped crawling and sunk to the pavement with a hole in his head.

The leader glanced at the lifeless form of the young black assistant and then continued talking to his second in command as if nothing of importance had happened.

Sean felt a surge of violent anger. Miserable, ratfuck bastards; they didn't have to kill the kid.

The leader lit a long cigar and surveyed the street

casually. He seemed to approve of what he saw as he glanced at his watch. Then he walked over to O'Keefe's cage and looked directly at him. Sean's stomach churned but his face remained impassive.

The leader's voice was clear and quiet with a slight accent.

"You're an extra bonus for us, Mister O'Keefe. I plan to solicit your help in this little media event."

"You can get stuffed if you think I'll do a damn thing to help you degenerates." Sean had forgotten the warning from the hostage negotiator, but was so angry he didn't care if he got them pissed off or not.

Sean's anger didn't seem to move the leader one way or the other.

"You'll help, Mister O'Keefe." Then he spoke loudly so the people in the cage could hear him. "And if any of you put one finger on the dynamite charges, my men will shoot your hand off."

The color drained from Sean's Jones Beach suntan.

4

6th Avenue

Officers Russo and Doyle approached Forty-third Street after getting radio clearance to cruise the area. There had been no reports of trouble with armored cars.

Doyle drank her coffee with one hand and skillfully maneuvered through the early-morning traffic with the other.

"You think I've gone bonkers, don't you, Charlie?"

Russo bit into his ham and egg sandwich and brushed off a bit of yolk with a coffee-soaked napkin.

"We're investigating, aren't we? Hey, there seems to be some sorta tie-up around Forty-sixth."

Doyle craned her neck to look. "Seems pretty early for that sort of thing."

Russo took another bite of his sandwich and washed it down with the remainder of his coffee.

Doyle turned on the siren and maneuvered to the front of Forty-seventh. Russo muttered something under his breath as Doyle stopped. He got out of the car with his sandwich in hand, his head down. He didn't hear Doyle yell his name because her voice was drowned out by the sound of gunfire. Russo fell to the ground, sandwich still in hand.

As bullets smashed through the car's windshield, Doyle dove out of the door and landed on all fours on the street. It was a nightmare for the slender young officer. Cars zoomed past her or came to a screeching halt. The cars that passed in front of Forty-seventh were riddled with bullets. Some crashed into nearby buildings or other cars. A Ford nearly ran Doyle over, but she quickly rolled back near her car, cutting herself on the broken glass from the windshield.

Cars were quickly abandoned on the avenue as motorists scurried to the buildings. Some were shot. Most made it.

Doyle peered cautiously under the car. She saw Russo's hand still holding the sandwich. She wriggled farther under the car and slowly pulled the large man partially under the car, but his bulky body got stuck. She was close to exhaustion when she noticed that half of Russo's face was missing.

Patrolman Charles Russo, twenty-seven, with a wife and two children just getting up in Staten Island, was dead. So were ten motorists and three pedestrians.

Officer Jane Doyle put her head down on the street and retched violently.

911 Control

At 6:45 A.M. the switchboard at 911 was hit with a barrage of calls. This was usually known as the "quiet time." The muggers weren't up yet, school traffic hadn't started to flow, and most of the early-morning car commuters didn't have phones in their cars.

Officer Fred Kovac was nursing a bad hangover from too much good booze last night at a new singles bar in Shirley, Long Island. He had looked forward to the "quiet-time" duty, and he wasn't prepared for the onslaught of calls.

"Officer Kovac speaking . . ."

"Hey, man, some dudes just wasted a cop, man . . . shot him dead as shit . . . zapped the shit outta his car, too . . . 'n' blasted a lotta cars an' citizens. And there's another cop kissin' concrete . . . looks like a broad . . ."

Kovac blinked rapidly, trying to clear the cobwebs from his head. "Where is this, please?"

"Sixth and Forty-seventh . . . man, you mothas betta bring a fuckin' tank, 'cuz those dudes doin' the shootin' have got themselves a bunch a armored cars blockin' the whole street, man."

Kovac was very alert now, and he felt his pulse rate quicken. "What's your name, sir?" The phone went dead.

Kovac looked over at the other officers in his section. They were all busy on the phones. Kovac quickly typed an "officer down" card and sent it to dispatch on priority.

"Nine-one-one, Officer Kovac . . ."

"I don't believe it. I'm sitting here at the window, and I don't believe it."

"What, sir?"

"They've blockaded the whole street."

"Where, sir?"

"Forty-seventh . . . they've got it blockaded at both ends with armored cars. And they've got people locked in a cage . . . right in the middle of the street. Hey, are they making a movie or something?"

Kovac glanced at his "happenings sheet." No movie shootings were scheduled for the day. "What's your name, sir?" Kovac started typing again as he talked, and each click of the typewriter ricocheted through his ears.

"Martin Shapiro."

"Where are you, sir?"

"I'm in the building on the northeast corner of Fifth and Forty-seventh."

"Thank you for calling, sir." Kovac turned to the older black officer next to him. "Man, the shit's hit the fan on Forty-seventh."

The black officer shook his head. "You're tellin' me! This is my sixth call."

"Nine-one-one, Officer Kovac . . ."

"Those damn dogs have been crapping in front of my building again, and my little girl stepped . . ."

Kovac was speechless for only one second, then he exploded. "Lady . . . we've got an officer shot . . . people getting killed, and you call about dog shit? Fuck off, you stupid bitch . . . call the mayor, not a goddamn emergency number!" He slammed down the receiver.

"Nine-one-one . . ."

As Kovac typed up the next call about the Diamond Street, he tried to remember if he gave that dumb broad his name. Probably. Fuck it. These were times that tried men's souls.

Manhattan South Precinct
West 51st Street

Fred Browning, the desk sergeant at "M" South, burst into the muster room just as Captain John Dixon was inspecting the morning contingent. Dixon and his men did a double take, because Browning had never been noted for his speed.

The heavyset sergeant started gesturing wildly with his hands as he blurted out what he had to say. "Captain . . . riot gear . . . everyone . . . orders from the top. Diamond Street's been hit big . . . armored trucks . . . Arabs . . . one officer down . . . lots of citizens hurt or dead . . . hostage situation!"

The captain gulped slightly and tried to remember what was in the pounds of contingency plans for various emergency situations. Thousands of maps, diagrams, and words flashed in his head. He drew a deep breath, said a silent "Hail Mary," and turned to his men. "You heard it . . . haul ass . . . cordon off that street. Bernstein and Schmid, block Sixth Avenue at Forty-fifth. O'Brien and Fox, block off Forty-seventh at Madison. Pelleterri and Patterson . . . get those people on Sixth the hell out of there. Keep out of the line of fire. Hold any action until the brass get there. Seal the street. Nobody goes in or out. Browning . . . have all duty personnel stay put for orders."

Captain Dixon rubbed his temples with his index fingers. Why the hell did this have to happen now, he thought. Just three more months until retirement. A nice pension and a job offer to be the police chief in a small Vermont town.

West 91st Street

Brian Hamlin, the newly appointed police commissioner, was at home trying to rationalize the mayor's latest budget cuts. Many heads had rolled, and there were to be more. This pained Hamlin, because he was an up-from-the-ranks cop.

He had started thumbing through the personnel readouts when the phone rang. His wife, Linda, answered it. He didn't like the look on her face.

"Brian, it's Jim Conrad. He seems very excited. He says it's urgent."

Hamlin looked worried. Jim Conrad, his chief inspector, did not get excited. It must be major trouble.

The voice on the other end of the phone spoke quickly, without emotion . . . this was the Jim Conrad Hamlin knew.

"Brian, it's happened. I don't know all the facts yet, but it looks like Arabs have just hijacked the Diamond Street. They control the whole street with armored cars . . . people have been killed, including a cop."

Hamlin clenched his teeth. He had known that sooner or later some terrorist group would do a number on New

York, and now it had happened. He tried to match the chief inspector's calm tone, but his worry and fear were obvious.

"You know what to do, Jim. Make sure Washington and the FBI here are alerted. I'll be right down to Command Central."

Hamlin hung up and took a deep breath to try and control his emotions. He looked at the personnel readouts of potential police cuts. He picked up the stack of papers and hurled them across the room. "Fucking stupid political bastards!"

East 87th Street

Special Agent Hugh McBride had just finished walking his dog at seven o'clock. He had risen at six, as usual, and gone through the exercise routine that kept his fifty-year-old body lean, wiry, and hard. He was pouring a glass of prune juice when the phone rang. He picked it up quickly so it would not wake his wife, who was home sick with the flu. The voice on the other end was Tim Kelly, head of the New York FBI office.

"It's happened, Hugh." Kelly's voice had a slight quiver to it.

"What and where?" McBride asked.

"The diamond district . . . armored cars . . . hostages . . . people killed."

McBride's jaw tightened. "Any input on who?"

"They think it's Arabs."

"Beautiful! The Middle East moves to New York. Well, it was bound to happen sooner or later."

"I talked to Conrad. We're all meeting at Command Central. I've sent a car for you."

The apartment intercom rang. "I think it's here already. See you at police headquarters."

He hung up the phone and gulped down his prune

juice. He hated the stuff, but he had been constipated lately since the newspapers had been on his back about his methods of infiltrating terrorist groups.

Arabs? He had six different Arab groups under surveillance. Only one had the capability of pulling something like this, but it only took one.

5

Under West 47th Street

A subway train rolled into the Rockefeller Plaza Station at 7:10 A.M. sharp. Right on time. A handful of passengers got off the front car and headed toward the stairs that lead to the exits on Forty-seventh Street. There were a few jewelers, polishers, cutters, a handful of businessmen, two shopping-bag ladies, and some Puerto Rican youths.

Fred Williams, the conductor, was just about to close the doors when the motorman yelled over the intercom, "Get those people back in the cars. There's big trouble up on Forty-seventh Street. This is going to be a passby stop."

Williams stuck his head out of the window. "Hey, you people . . . get back on the train. There's trouble on the street."

A couple of people automatically obeyed. The rest continued on. One of the Puerto Ricans yelled back, "Your motha." One of the shopping-bag ladies sat down on the steps and urinated. Twenty people headed up the stairs to the upper level where there was a change booth with one attendant, and a Nedick's stand with two attendants, who were just opening up for the morning. Most of the passengers headed toward the tunnel to Rockefeller Concourse. The rest walked toward the Forty-seventh Street exit on the southeast corner. A black woman in the change booth yelled, "Don't go up to the street!"

José Rodriguez gave her the finger and slapped hands with his buddies. José patted the pocket of his jacket proudly. "Nobody's goin' mess with this child 'cause I got my own 'nine' now."

"Right on," said a short pimply-faced boy about fourteen. "Nobody messes with a dude with a 'nine.'"

"Who's that jive mama think she is . . . tellin' us we can't . . ." He was cut off in midsentence at the top of the stairs as a M-16 bullet smashed the glass light over the entrance. José, in a reflex action, pulled his "nine" from his pocket as he and his friends retreated down the stairs. This was a big mistake. Seven transit cops, with guns drawn, were heading for the stairs. The first thing they saw was a gang of Puerto Ricans rushing toward them. The second thing they saw was a Belgian-made 9-mm automatic pistol that could shoot fourteen high-velocity bullets in four seconds with more force than a Thompson submachine gun. All seven cops fired in unison at the amazed José. All seven bullets found their mark and the "nine" hit the ground, followed by José Rodriguez. José's friends quickly hit spread-legged positions against the wall in hopes there would not be a second volley from the police.

More police joined the others. This section of the subway was now top priority because it led directly to the concourse, leading to every major building on the west side of Sixth Avenue, all the way up to the J. C. Penney Building at Fifty-third Street, six blocks away, and to the underground concourse under Rockefeller Center. It would take a small army of police to patrol the maze of tunnels and entrances.

The transit police quickly lined the youths up against the wall near the change booth. José's body was put near some baggage lockers. The gates on the northeast, southeast, and southwest subway entrances to Forty-seventh Street were closed and locked. The blue steel door to the tunnel leading to Sixth Avenue and Rockefeller Center buildings was closed and locked. The underground area was secure and guarded by twenty heavily armed transit policemen.

On the street

Police cars rode along the sidewalks with loudspeakers blaring, "If you cannot move your car, we're asking you to abandon it and clear out of the area until traffic can be rerouted. We repeat, if you cannot get your car out of the area, abandon it . . . this is a dangerous situation."

New Yorkers and commuters weren't about to abandon their cars on New York streets. As one commuter would say in a TV interview on the six o'clock news, "Leave my car in the middle of a New York City street? . . . You gotta be kidding, man. If the strippers missed, the cops would probably have it towed away and charge me a bundle to get it back. No way am I ever going to leave my car."

Most drivers felt the same way, so traffic was hopelessly snarled on both Fifth and Sixth avenues up to the Sixties and down to the Thirties. The avenues and streets were one big twenty-square-block parking lot.

In the air

Officer Ted King, "Sky King" to his fellow officers, maneuvered his police helicopter over the avenues and shook his head as he called in his report to Command Central. "Forty-seventh between Fifth and Sixth has three armored trucks and steel shields at either end of the street. Guns are pointed east and west from the trucks. Armed men are behind the connecting shields. Two solid fronts. Hostages are in a metal cage in the center of the street guarded by men behind shields in doorways. Looks like the cage is wired with explosives."

An emotionless, steady voice came through King's earphones. "Are they on the roofs?"

"No, sir."

"What's the traffic like now?"

"It sucks, sir."

"Be more specific, Officer King."

King had forgotten that he was talking to a chief inspector. "Forty-seventh from Sixth to Broadway is clear. Back to First is a mess. Sixth is screwed up back to the Thirties. Fifth is fuc— fouled up to the Sixties. There is clearance from Forty-seventh to Forty-fourth on Fifth. Side streets are all blocked."

"All right. Report any unusual activity. Keep your eyes on the roofs, and if there is any activity . . . get out of range fast. I don't want you shot down."

"Neither do I, inspector."

Command Central

Chief Inspector Jim Conrad was a very methodical and pragmatic man. He had mentally broken the situation into two objectives. Keep the terrorists contained. That was the easy part. Get them with the least amount of bloodshed. That was the hard part.

Conrad changed the frequencies on the special Command Central emergency radio control panel.

"Lieutenant Cole . . ."

A voice came back over the receiver. "Yes, inspector."

"Are you and your men ready?"

"We're ready, sir."

"There are two clear areas. Two blocks north and south on Sixth and Fifth. It will be tight, but get your people in there. Dispatch the armored units parallel to Forty-seventh and wait for further orders."

At 8:30 A.M. two blue and white converted Sea Stallions landed on the avenues with two combat-equipped SWAT teams, two hostage-negotiation units, and two converted fully armed marine amtracks.

47th Street

Sean O'Keefe and his fellow hostages had been expecting to hear the scream of police sirens; instead they heard the roar of heavy Sea Stallions overhead, accompanied by heavy gusts of prop wind that caused many of the hostages to panic. The guards showed no trace of emotion. O'Keefe guessed that they were expecting the helicopters. Their main concern appeared to be rounding up anyone inside the buildings. New prisoners were brought out at gunpoint and put in the cage. They were mostly maintenance people and security guards, but all the hostages did a double take when two fat older men and a plump black hooker were marched out in their underwear. Even the stone-faced terrorists seemed amused.

The cage had become overcrowded and there was no room to sit. Some of the older men were starting to get sick. The leader and two of his men walked by. O'Keefe yelled out that there were sick people in the cage, but was ignored. The leader pointed to Ben Levi and the two men Sean had been interviewing. The guards unlocked the cage and dragged the three men into a nearby store. This caused a great deal of fear among some of the older Jews. Sean had a feeling that they knew why Levi and the others had been taken away.

There was some shoving and cursing behind O'Keefe. He turned to see a wino pushing his way toward O'Keefe's side of the cage. O'Keefe hoped that the bum wasn't going to throw up all over everyone. The temperature was beginning to rise, and the last thing they needed was the smell of vomit.

"O'Keefe!" The wino didn't sound like a wino, and as he inched forward Sean recognized him.

"Sean, it's me . . . Sid Stern . . . from the Seventeenth. I was working decoy. Thought I'd start early today, fuck the luck."

Sean grinned, acknowledging the artistry of Stern's disguise.

"Your wife must love your new assignment, Sid."

The cop shook his head. "We split. She went back to Dallas with the kids."

Sean nodded knowingly. "Do you have a piece?" he asked.

"Sure, but I'm not about to John Wayne it. I'm scared shitless, if you want to know the truth."

A third man joined O'Keefe and Stern. It was the soundman, Coyle. He slipped something into Sean's pocket.

"Tape," Coyle whispered. "I was rolling when the headman was talking to you. His voice should be there."

"And what the hell am I going to do with it?" O'Keefe asked.

"I think he likes you. Besides, I don't want to get caught with it on me."

"You're all heart, Coyle."

Suddenly the old man next to Coyle started to moan.

"Christ, I think this old guy is having a heart attack," Stern yelled.

As O'Keefe and Coyle tried to calm the old man there was a sound of heavy equipment moving on the avenues. Two blue and white amtracks appeared at either end of the street. They turned and faced the armored cars with their guns. Then there was an eerie silence.

The leader and two other terrorists quickly appeared

on the street. It was as if they had been waiting for this moment. The leader had a battery-operated bullhorn in his hand. He spoke into it, and the sound echoed throughout the street.

"We have liberated this street from the Zionist Fascists. We have hostages. If you fire on us, we will immediately start to kill them. We will be releasing three prisoners and three corpses as an act of good faith. One of the prisoners will act as liaison and negotiator. We will speak to no police officials, FBI agents, religious or government people. The person we have chosen to negotiate will return here in exactly fifteen minutes, or we will kill one hostage for every minute he is late. Also . . . you may take the time to redeem the dead and wounded on Sixth Avenue. We will release three hostages and the dead in two minutes. The negotiator we have chosen will return in fifteen minutes . . . or we will kill hostages. Is that clear?"

Two voices echoed back from the amtracks. "That is clear. We understand."

O'Keefe had a very uncomfortable feeling that he knew who the go-between would be.

The leader and two of the terrorists approached the cage. One of them opened the door.

"You're it, O'Keefe."

"I was afraid you were going to say that," O'Keefe said, trying to keep his voice from shaking.

The leader pointed to two men in the cage, a jewelry polisher and a store owner. "You and you go . . . but each of you is to carry a body with you. They'll start to smell in this heat. O'Keefe, you can take your cameraman's body."

Sean was trying to control the anger that had replaced his fear. "What about this old man? I think he's on the verge of a heart attack."

The leader shrugged. "If he can walk out, he can go. If he can't . . . he stays."

The old man nodded that he would try to walk out.

"What do you want me to tell the police?"

"Tell them that our demands will be presented later today. Tell them not to overreact by trying to infiltrate our liberated territory."

Sean scowled at the revolutionary rhetoric, but prudently remained silent.

Sean picked up the body of Stan Zimmerman. He could feel the rage burning inside as he walked toward Fifth Avenue. He was followed by the polisher carrying the Hasidic Jew, and the store owner carrying Cal Long. They were followed by the stumbling old man with the heart condition. It was a sad sight that was captured on film by an English photographer with a telephoto lens from a Fifth Avenue building. The picture would hit the front page of every major newspaper later in the day.

6

Police Headquarters

Command Central was the largest room in police headquarters. It was used only during emergency operations. It had its own generator system so that it could function during blackouts or a sabotage of power facilities.

The room looked like a World War II strategic operations center. Large maps covered the walls. The center of the room was dominated by a big illuminated table where area maps could be projected and personnel movements could be monitored. Special phone switchboards, radio transmitters, and a radar unit stood against one wall.

Command Central had been placed on full alert twenty minutes after the first 911 call. Now it was crowded with police and FBI personnel.

Hugh McBride showed his identification to the officer at the door and was directed to the center of the room where Chief Inspector Conrad and some officers were studying a map.

Conrad was a short muscular man in his mid-fifties and a tough, smart street cop who didn't rattle under pressure. He looked small next to McBride's lean six-foot frame.

McBride and Conrad had worked together before and got along well. McBride was an exception to the usual "suits" at the Bureau. McBride worked *with* the police, gave them credit when it was due, and had the instincts of a street cop.

"What's going down, Jim?" McBride asked as he glanced at the map section of the diamond district and the surrounding area.

"We've got them bottled up, but there's no way to get to them without buying it for the hostages. We've got spotters in the buildings on the east side of Fifth . . . not on Sixth because the angle of observation is off."

Conrad motioned for McBride to follow him. They stopped at a group of small light boxes. Conrad flicked on the lights to reveal a series of maps.

The first map showed what was under the street.

"The subway is sealed off. No way out and the trains are bypassing the stop. The surrounding tunnels and concourses to the buildings on Sixth and Rockefeller Center are sealed off. We have men with listening devices in the cellars of the adjoining buildings on Forty-sixth and Forty-eighth. We have men covering the sewer exits and entrances. All the phones on the street are being monitored by our people."

"I sure as hell hope you got the proper papers first," McBride said bitterly.

"Still getting flack about the civil rights of terrorist groups from the press?"

McBride shook his head. "And they're right, but sometimes you can't play by the rules or the other guys will shove the rule book up your ass."

Conrad smiled knowingly. "You're damned if you do, damned if you don't."

"What are these areas leading away from the north and south sides of the streets?"

"According to the city maps, those shaded areas are solid rock that couldn't be messed with. Something to do with a fault connecting to the rocks on Fourteenth Street."

McBride scratched his nose. "They run in straight lines from the street."

"I noticed that, too. I stationed men here at Forty-eighth west of Sixth, and more here in the concourse under the McGraw-Hill Building."

They moved to another light box which showed an artist's sketch of both the north and south sides of the street.

"What's this here in the middle of the block?"

"An arcade that goes through the building to Forty-eighth."

"Can we get through?"

Conrad shook his head. "No, there are locked steel gates at either end, and they've got a guy right here watching it." Conrad pointed to a doorway on the south side.

"Any plans to get on the street?"

"We're bringing in some equipment to see if we can tunnel into a building from Forty-eighth."

"You'd better take over the buildings on the four corners of Fifth and Sixth in case they have spotters."

Conrad nodded his head in agreement. "We already did. We caught a female photographer coming out of one of the buildings with pictures."

"Jesus, I hope you didn't confiscate her pictures."

"No. We made a deal. A couple of detectives went home with her. One set of pictures for us. One set of pictures for her."

McBride smiled. "Congratulations. You saved the mayor a few bucks in photography costs."

Conrad shrugged. "Well, considering that she said she was a police photographer . . . that's impersonating an officer, you know . . . let's just say we struck an agreeable bargain."

The men continued to examine the maps. They were interrupted by a female sergeant. "Inspector, some of the hostages were released to carry out the dead. One of them is to return to act as a liaison. It's Sean O'Keefe."

Conrad nodded and a concerned expression appeared on his face. "Thank you, sergeant." The woman left and McBride shook his head. "I'll never get used to having women around."

Conrad smiled. "I hear you're getting quite a few in the New York office now."

"Yeah, and each one tries to outmacho the next."

"You're just a hardnosed chauvinist, McBride."

"Probably, but the day they bring some female over me is the day I pack it in."

There was a pause and then McBride asked, "Who is Sean O'Keefe? From the expression on your face, I'd guess you know him."

"I do," Conrad said. "He's an ex-cop who turned TV reporter. I was his rabbi. I grew up with his dad, Jim O'Keefe, a district leader in the Tenth."

"Good cop?" McBride asked.

"One of the best," Conrad answered. "He had some marital problems and traded his shield for a press pass and a bigger paycheck."

"Think he can handle the liaison?"

"If he doesn't lose his temper, he should be okay."

"Hothead?"

"No, but he doesn't take kindly to being pushed around."

"Who does?" McBride joked.

The two men returned to the maps. They had the terrorists holed up. The next move was up to the Arabs.

Stanton Street/Lower East Side

Miranda had been accompanied home by two detectives who were now sitting in the living room of her top-floor loft apartment. They were waiting for copies of the pictures she had taken of the siege of the street.

Miranda studied the series of enlargements she had made. There were long shots showing the overall situation of the street, and her specialty, close-up shots—telephotos of the armored cars, the hostages in the cage, the mail trucks, and some of the terrorists. But the shot that stood out was the one of Sean O'Keefe carrying the body of Stan Zimmerman, followed by two other men carrying bodies, and the old man with the heart problem.

Miranda had done a special blowup of the picture of O'Keefe with the men in a staggered line behind him. Their faces had the same dazed expressions she had captured in many war photos. All except O'Keefe's. His face showed anger, rage, and hate tinged with pity and fear. Miranda wasn't sure if it was tears or sweat running down his face, but her intuition leaned to tears because of the pained look in his eyes.

In her own little memory file she would call this picture *Man in Emotional Pain*. It was a prize picture and she knew it. It was a bloody shame that the pictures that gained the most attention were the tragic pictures. The natural disasters, the child burning from napalm, a man shooting a prisoner in the head, a beheading of terrorists in some Middle Eastern country, and Sean O'Keefe carrying his cameraman between two armored trucks.

Miranda was tired. For the last six of her twenty-nine years she had been taking pictures like this all over the world, and she was sick of seeing what people could do to one another. She needed a rest, and she looked forward to her mother's arrival tomorrow for a visit. They would talk and laugh, shop at good stores and visit the best restaurants.

She wrapped up a set of photos for the detectives and called a messenger to deliver the other set to her agent.

She knew he would agree with her assessment of the O'Keefe photo. It would bring in top dollar and top distribution. At this point she didn't care. She just wanted to sleep until tomorrow when she would meet her mother at the airport.

7

Kennedy Airport

A sleek military transport jet glided into Kennedy Airport, touched down, and was immediately guided to an empty hangar by an airport jeep. The heavy metal doors to the hangar were quickly closed as the plane taxied in. Stairs were hastily moved toward the plane, but before the ground crew could get there, the door at the side of the plane opened and six men jumped out in a single file, pausing only to straighten their legs after impact with the ground. They were all over six feet tall, lean, muscular, and agile. They walked quickly toward two black limousines where two men in suits waited for them. The six men were dressed in crisply pressed fatigues and wore the symbol of their outfit cocked over one eye. They were the Black Berets, an elite antiterrorist force flown in from Fort Stewart, Georgia. Technically, the Black Berets were not to be used in a domestic terrorist engagement. This was the job of the FBI's special terrorist units in local offices. But this was an exception and had been approved by the White House. The operation was still under the control of the FBI and the NYPD, but what each of the six men carried in their locked shoulder bags gave them a special edge when the action began again.

The man in the lead nodded to the two men in the suits. There was a certain tolerant scorn in his expression.

"Captain Frank Carter, reporting as ordered." There was a slight smile as he emphasized the word *ordered*.

Suit One nodded, well aware of the inference to the White House intervention.

"Captain," Suit One said coldly, "I'm Agent Brady." He turned to Suit Two. "That's Agent Finnegan." Suit Two nodded civilly. "My orders are to escort you to a meeting at police headquarters with the FBI and the police command." He pointed toward the other five men. "Agent Finnegan will take your men to the perimeter of the action. I will return you to the perimeter after the meeting."

The captain nodded curtly. He turned to his men and spoke to the officer next to him. "Lieutenant, you and the men will accompany the agent to the designated area. I will join you as soon as possible."

The young lieutenant gave a snappy salute. Carter returned an equally sharp one. The Black Berets quickly got into the limousines. The FBI agents slammed the doors slightly harder than necessary.

The long black cars started up and headed toward the steel doors. The two ground crew men quickly opened the door and the limos sped out toward the runways with their sirens blaring.

The two ground crew men closed the door, then looked at each other.

"Shit, sure is cold for August."

The other man nodded in agreement. "A few frosted balls heading for town."

"Think they'll get those terrorists on Forty-seventh Street?"

"Yep . . . if they don't get each other first."

West 47th Street

It sounded like every alarm on the street had gone off at once, and they probably had. Sean and the hostages watched in amazement as a group of terrorists began to smash in the doors to the jewelry stores. Small explosions echoed throughout the street, and soon the terrorists began carrying jewels out, casually tossing them into large mail carts.

Inside the cage some of the men began to curse in Hebrew and Yiddish. Sean recognized some of the words. None were complimentary.

"Jesus," Coyle said, "they're going to strip the place clean."

"That's just the little stuff. The really good stuff is in those triple-doored steel mothers in buildings fifteen and thirty," Sid Stern said.

Sean leaned against the bars of the cage and closed his eyes. "And five will get you ten they're saving that for the finale."

"Why the hell don't the cops do something?"

"What the fuck do you want 'em to do, Coyle?" Stern yelled. "They as much as break wind and we'll be blown all over the midtown area."

Coyle's face reddened slightly. "God, I forgot about the dynamite on the cage."

"I'm glad the cops have better memories," O'Keefe said.

Coyle tried to sit down, but there wasn't room. "My feet are killing me." He turned to Sean. "Do you think they can get anything out of the tape I gave you to take out, Sean?"

"I don't know, maybe. I just hope . . ."

Sean stopped in midsentence, cut off by a rifle shot. One of the terrorists standing by the mail van near the cage grabbed his face as blood gushed between his fingers and splattered on the front of his shirt. His hand fell away and part of his face fell with it. He hit the ground with a thump.

The color drained from Coyle's face and he covered his mouth and started to gag. Sean shook him. "Don't you dare throw up on me, Coyle, or so help me God I'll piss all over your sound equipment."

The remark was so out of context with the reality of what was happening that Coyle forgot his stomach and started to laugh.

Sean put his hands on the soundman's shoulders. "You're okay, buddy . . . just don't puke, for God's sake."

The terrorists had all scattered for cover. There was another shot, but it only hit the side of the building.

Loudspeakers boomed from both ends of the street.

"We are not firing . . . repeat . . . we are not firing . . . sniper . . . there is a sniper in the area . . . do not overreact . . . this is the police . . . we are not shooting . . . repeat . . . we are not shooting."

There was an eerie silence, then an answer came from the leader over his bullhorn.

"You have fifteen minutes to get that sniper . . . or we'll start shooting at the hostage cage. That shooting came from Fifth Avenue . . . probably the building on the northeast corner. You have fifteen minutes to bring the sniper to the corner of Fifth Avenue so we can see you have him in custody . . . fifteen minutes starts now."

A SWAT team and a dozen uniformed officers rushed into the building. A frantic floor-to-floor search turned up two men. Aaron Schwartz, a member of a Jewish Defense League splinter group, and a young black with a pair of binoculars and a walkie-talkie. The black was hustled off in a squad car directly to police headquarters for questioning. Aaron Schwartz was marched in front of the amtrack on Fifth Avenue. Two SWAT officers held his arms.

Sean and the hostages watched as the leader emerged from one of the doorways. He had the bullhorn in one hand and a .45 in the other. He walked quickly to the armored trucks blocking the street at Fifth Avenue. He stared at the man being held between the two policemen, raised his gun and fired once. The bullet smashed into Schwartz's right knee. He fell forward and was caught by the two shocked officers, who reached for their sidearms instinctively with their free hands. Before they could draw their weapons the leader spoke into the microphone. "Don't draw your weapons. This is a warning . . . don't let this happen again. Now get the Jew out of here." He paused for a moment. "And tell your men to stop their tunneling operation on Forty-eighth Street."

The leader put his pistol back into his holster and walked calmly back to the center of the street. A motion of his hand brought the terrorist back on to the street, and they continued to sack the stores. Two of the men conferred with the leader, then dragged the body of their dead comrade into the nearby delicatessen and placed it in the refrigerator, where it wouldn't spoil in the hot midday sun.

Outside Police Headquarters

McBride held a soft drink can next to his head as he paid the hot dog vendor. He stared vacantly at the new police headquarters building across the street. A lot better than the old place, he thought to himself.

"Headache, or heat got you, Hugh?" asked a voice that came from below McBride's waist.

The tall man looked down at the small figure standing next to him smoking a pipe.

"Both, Eric, and a case of constipation to boot."

The dwarf was Professor Eric Clayton, a leading speech therapist and language expert. Clayton had the uncanny ability to determine a person's nationality and background by listening to the voice.

Long ago, when Clayton discovered that he would never grow past his present four-foot stature, he decided he would have to excel at something to compensate for his handicap. He had become an expert in his field and often worked on cases with McBride, much to the Bureau's dismay. Washington liked to do their own investigations and McBride's use of outsiders cast a shadow on the efficiency of the Bureau. They also felt that McBride was a loner, not a team player. But he got results, and that overshadowed the noses that were out of joint in Washington.

McBride believed that an individual generally could get faster and better results than a bureaucracy. McBride had used Clayton numerous times to help with everything from a kidnapping to obscene phone calls to a senator's wife.

"Well, who are they, Eric?"

"Irish," Clayton said.

"Bullshit."

"Irish," Clayton repeated stubbornly.

"You sure?"

"Of course. Their spokesperson is definitely Irish, maybe spent some time in England. I hyped the volume on the background voices and I came up with Gaelic."

"Gaelic?" McBride interrupted. "You mean Irish Irish?"

Clayton puffed at his pipe. "For a great many centuries, my friend. There was some Arabic, but it's Brooklyn black Arabic, probably picked up from one of the black movements with the Muslim connections."

"No real Arabs?"

" 'Fraid not."

"Irish," McBride muttered incredulously.

"And some Brooklyn blacks," Clayton added.

"What the hell are Irish and blacks doing teaming up?"

"It would appear that they're stealing everything that isn't nailed down."

McBride scowled again. "Correction, Eric. They're gathering up everything that isn't nailed down and they're not going anyplace with it."

"I certainly hope not. They'd be richer than the Arabs the way the price of diamonds is going up."

McBride sighed. "Jesus, I've got to go up to that meeting at police headquarters and tell Irish cops, Irish FBI agents, and probably an Irish Black Beret that Irish terrorists are holding a New York City street in a state of siege."

Clayton suddenly got serious. "It won't be the first time the Irish have killed blacks and other Irish in this city. During the Draft Riots in the Civil War, the Irish were getting the shitty end of the stick. They started killing blacks, even burned an orphanage. Then they got the hell kicked out of them by the state militia and the police, most of whom happened to be Irish."

"I sure as hell hope that history isn't going to repeat itself."

"Depressing thought. Well, I have to be on my way. I have a class to teach up at NYU. Give my best to Rose and the kids. Everyone's well, I hope."

McBride nodded. "Rose's arthritis is still giving her trouble, and the kids . . . well, they'll all be in college this year."

"Four in college. Now I know why I never got married."

McBride cleared his throat awkwardly and Clayton stared at the ground for a moment.

"Well, Eric, I'm in your debt as usual," McBride said after an uncomfortable pause.

"We'll call it even when Rose is feeling better and is up to a good home-cooked meal."

McBride smiled. "You work cheap, Eric."

Clayton returned the smile. "Old and dear friends can never be measured in monetary considerations, Hugh."

McBride blushed slightly. "Give me a call when this mess is over, maybe we'll go out and get drunk." McBride turned and walked away, waving his hand over his shoulder as he went.

Clayton stood by the hot dog wagon puffing his pipe. He felt a hand on his shoulder and turned to see the Italian hot dog vendor.

"Irish?" the man asked.

"Irish," Clayton said.

"Jesus," the vendor said.

Command Central

The conference room off Command Central was small. The air conditioner was broken, and the room was full of smoke. The men inside looked tired, frustrated, and angry.

"What the fuck do you mean they're Irish, Hugh?" Commissioner Hamlin bellowed. McBride had never heard him swear before. There were similar utterances from Chief Inspector Don O'Neil, head of uniform patrol, Chief Inspector Jim Conrad, who never lost his temper, the New York office agent in charge, Tim Kelly, and Agent Bill Brady. The only one who did not show any emotion one way or the other was the Black Beret officer who sat against the wall with a black leather shoulder bag in his lap.

"That's what I said," McBride answered.

"Where the hell did you get that from, Hugh . . . our people?" Tim Kelly asked.

"No, Tim. One of my people."

"Come on, Hugh . . . you know procedure."

"Screw procedure. The man I used on those tapes was the same one who worked the Goldman kidnapping and that number with the senator's wife and the heavy breather."

"We would have gotten the information with a little more time," Kelly yelled.

"That's the magic word . . . time . . . we may be running out of time."

"So, these guys are all Irish?" Jim Conrad asked.

"No, some of them, maybe most of them, are black."

The men stopped talking and looked at one another.

McBride stared at them. "What did I do, say the magic word or something?"

"They've got a black down on the fourth floor and they rounded up four more in buildings around the area. Spotters for the terrorists. They're all kids . . . under thirteen. That means Family Court, and they know it."

"Probably won't get anything out of them."

"They're blacks not Irish, Hugh," Bill Brady added.

"How many blacks do you know that can speak Gaelic, Bill?"

"Gaelic?"

"That's right. The mother tongue."

"What the hell are the Irish doing here?" Commissioner Hamlin asked.

"Stealing diamonds by the basketful," McBride answered.

"How the hell are they going to get the stones off the street? We have them sealed in."

"They must have something going for them that we don't know about," McBride said.

"Are you sure, Hugh?" Kelly asked.

46

"I'm sure."

Hamlin frowned. "God, the Jews and the Irish have gotten along in New York for years. They'll be at each other's throats when this gets out."

"Well, you can bet that it will get out. You'd better get some cops on the synagogues and Catholic churches . . . parochial schools, too," Conrad said.

"Might be a good idea and good PR to put Irish-Jew teams together."

"It makes sense," Hamlin agreed.

"Gentlemen." A voice came from the side of the room. "I would like to be able to tell my men what our function in this operation will be."

All the men turned to look at the Black Beret captain.

Tim Kelly looked slightly embarrassed. "I'm sorry, captain. This Irish thing has thrown us for a loop. As you can gather from what we've said and from our surnames, we're all Irish."

"That hadn't escaped my attention, Agent Kelly. I'm Baptist myself."

Kelly cleared his throat uncomfortably. "I'll be honest with you, captain. I don't know what the hell to do with you. We've got police SWAT teams and FBI teams all over the area. I don't know what you could do that they couldn't."

The captain smiled and patted the leather bag on his lap. "I think we might have a bit of an edge."

"Oh, yeah," McBride said. "Those special toys that your fellas at the Pentagon came up with. Do you think they would be effective against the terrorists in the street as the situation stands now?"

The captain shook his head. "I don't believe so. There are too many intangibles. The distance would be too great, and I couldn't guarantee the safety of the hostages."

"Captain," Commissioner Hamlin said, "we're setting

up a subcommand unit in the lobby of the Time-Life Building. We would appreciate it if you and your men would come there. And, of course, you would be involved in planning any operation against the terrorists."

Captain Carter nodded. "Thank you, sir. We'll be glad to help in any way we can when the time is right."

McBride stared at the leather bag that the captain had now slung over his shoulder. "Captain, I don't suppose you could tell us what the hell it is you have in that black bag of yours."

The captain smiled at McBride. "I'm sorry, I'm not allowed to. Presidential orders, sir."

Interbureaucratic grabass, McBride thought to himself. He was just about to say so in couched terms when the phone interrupted him. Commissioner Hamlin picked it up. He frowned then hung up.

"More trouble about to hit Forty-seventh Street," he said. They all quickly left the small conference room and headed for the Command Control room next door.

5th Avenue and 47th Street

Fifth Avenue was blocked by barricades at Forty-ninth, Forty-fifth, and the cross streets in between. The same pattern was used on Sixth Avenue. The buildings on the four corners of Fifth and Sixth were closed and the entrances were guarded by police. The same had been done for all the buildings on the north side of Forty-sixth and the south side of Forty-eighth between Fifth and Sixth.

The sightseers were kept to a minimum, and most of them left of their own accord when they found that they couldn't see anything on Forty-seventh Street.

At five thirty chanting was heard on Fifth Avenue and Forty-second Street. At five forty-five more than five hundred Hasidic Jews stood behind the barricades at

Forty-fifth Street yelling for revenge and the death of the terrorists, especially the blacks.

When the news broke that the terrorist spotters were black youths, the Jews in the Williamsburgh section exploded. For years there had been bad blood between the blacks and the Hasidim in this Brooklyn community and it had often resulted in violence. Today the Hasidim spilled into the streets and headed to the black section of the police precinct known to the local cops as Fort Apache. Most of the police were white Gentiles who felt surrounded by hostile warring tribes. The police managed to separate the two groups, but fifteen people had to be taken to the hospital. The still-frustrated Hasidim decided to take on the terrorists next. They boarded the subway en masse. Command Central and the units at Forty-seventh were immediately notified.

Captain John O'Brien was ordered to report immediately to Forty-seventh and Fifth. His squad car got tied up in traffic and the Hasidim beat him there by ten minutes.

O'Brien got his orders from a communications van on the corner of Fifth. The orders came directly from Inspector Conrad. "I don't care how you do it, O'Brien. Get those Jews the hell out of there."

O'Brien walked slowly toward the barricade. A line of helmeted policemen were standing ten yards from the screaming, chanting Jews. O'Brien walked past the line of police carrying a bullhorn. He glanced at the faces. Many were familiar from long hours of negotiating and arguing. He was looking for one face in particular. He finally saw it, and put the bullhorn near his mouth. He spoke to them in perfect Hebrew. Some of the cops on the line did a double take. O'Brien had learned to speak Hebrew as a kid. His father had been a ward leader on the predominately Jewish Lower East Side. The voters were Jewish so the Irish pols learned both Hebrew and

Yiddish, and even went to *shul* with *yarmulkahs* on their heads. At his father's insistence O'Brien had learned Hebrew along with Latin at the nearby parochial school. It wasn't a matter of choice, just good Democratic politics. His knowledge of Hebrew was one of the reasons he was given the Fort Apache command. That and the fact that his wife was black. He also knew how to deal with and use power without abusing it.

"You all know me." There was a rumble from the crowd and a few obscene gestures.

"Same to you, *shmuck*," he said returning the gesture. "Now I'm going to tell you some hard truths, and if you've got half a brain under those stupid-looking beaver hats you'll listen to me."

The insults coming over the bullhorn stunned the crowd.

O'Brien continued. "In three days I'm retiring, so I really don't give a shit what you fuzzy-faced assholes think of me. And that goes for that pack of black turkeys back in the district, too."

There was a low murmur from the crowd, "Now that's the first half of the cold cruel truth, and you can believe it. Now comes part two. If you *shmucks* get past the police to the terrorists, which I doubt, they'll slaughter those hostages, and probably most of you. On the other hand, if you want to stand here and pull men off the street, that could increase the chances of the terrorists giving us the slip with the diamonds. So, it boils down to this . . . if you don't get the hell out of here, I'm going to order these officers behind me to start kicking your asses all the way back to Brooklyn, because as I said before—I don't give a shit."

There was more mumbling from the crowd, and then they split into small groups and talked excitedly among themselves. After a moment one of the Hasidim came forward to meet with O'Brien. It was the face that

O'Brien had been searching for, Rabbi Solomon Cohen. O'Brien and Cohen had known and liked one another for years. They had both achieved prominence in the Williamsburgh section at the same time. O'Brien as the precinct commander. Cohen as the rabbi of the powerful synagogue. The two men quickly got together with a local black minister who became less hostile to O'Brien once he discovered O'Brien's wife was black. The three men had cursed and damned each other in public, but in private they had worked together to keep the lid on the neighborhood. It had worked for three years.

The rabbi reached O'Brien, shaking his fist in O'Brien's face, but his voice was calm. "You pulled that 'I'm retiring' bit two years ago . . . and what's this about stupid beaver hats?"

"They are stupid-looking. You couldn't stop 'em, Sol?"

The rabbi shook his finger in O'Brien's face. "No way. It was either this or back to slugging it out with the blacks. I figured they'd get your fat Irish tail up here somehow."

"And now I'll have to sit in the mayor's office and get the ethnic respect lecture."

"I'm going to have to scream for your hide again."

"What else is new. You think you can get them back home?"

"It shouldn't be a problem. They've got you to hate now."

"*Shalom*, Solomon."

"Take care of yourself, Irish."

The rabbi threw his hands up in exasperation and stormed back to the crowd. He talked with animated gestures to some of the men. The new plan of action quickly spread through the ranks and soon they were marching back to the subway shouting, "O'Brien must go."

O'Brien watched them go, then turned and walked

back to the communications van. "Tell the inspector that the Hasidim are headed home, and so am I. I'm getting too old for this shit." Maybe I will retire this time, he thought.

47th Street

By 8:00 P.M. the street was quiet. The battle lines were firmly drawn and both sides settled in for the night. As the sun started to drop in the horizon the twilight rays picked up the reflection of the diamonds and other jewels piled high in the mail carts. The carts were lined up neatly near the curb in the middle of the street as if on display. A rough estimate would place the combined weight of the jewels at about three tons. If one were to hazard a guess, which is a dangerous thing to do in the diamond business, the rough wholesale value of the six carts' contents would be roughly a billion dollars. At retail value the price could easily double.

"They'll never get all of those rocks out of here," Coyle said as he stared at the glittering contents of the mail carts.

"It doesn't seem to worry them too much," Sean said as he tried to find a more comfortable standing position.

"And that's just the stuff from the stores. They haven't touched the big vaults yet," Stern added.

"Oh, oh," Coyle whispered. "Here comes trouble."

Sean and Stern turned around to see four of the terrorists heading toward the cage. The other hostages apparently noticed them also because there was a sudden nervous shuffling of feet.

The leader reached the cage, produced a key from his pocket, and opened the cage door. He pointed to the large delicatessen on the north side of the street. "You will move single file to that restaurant where you may use the facilities and eat if you wish. You will be guarded, and any attempts to escape will result in immediate execution."

A voice came from the back of the cage. "Since you're inviting everyone into my delicatessen would it be too much to ask if I could prepare the food?"

The leader motioned the man forward. A short heavyset bald man wormed his way to the front of the cage.

"Since it's your establishment, you may enter first. There will be a guard with you at all times just in case you should try to smuggle any knives back with you."

"If I brought a knife back it would just be to slit my wrists over a whole day of lost business."

There was a trickle of laughter as the man was led away to the deli.

At nine thirty everyone had finished eating and taking care of the bodily functions. Inside the deli there was an almost festive atmosphere. The owner had been a gracious host and would not allow anyone to pay, not that anyone had offered. His altruism prompted a few good-natured requests for outgoing orders.

Ben Levi and the other two council members had been brought in, but they were segregated from the rest of the hostages. Sean gave Ben Levi a questioning look with his eyes. Levi just shook his head and shrugged his shoulders in bewilderment.

Coyle tapped gently on Sean's shoulder. "I hope this isn't the last meal for the condemned."

Sean scowled. "Don't give them any ideas." He looked around the room at the ring of guards. Their bodies seemed relaxed, but their eyes were alert. Then he noticed that all the guards had black hands. He tried to recall the leader and the three men who were always with him. They all had white hands. Black foot soldiers. White leaders. It was getting harder to believe that these guys were Arabs. Maybe some loose group of multinationals for some nutsy cause. But what cause? They hadn't made any real demands, just revolutionary anti-Semitic rhetoric. They seemed more interested in getting the diamonds than anything else. Maybe this was just a good old-fashioned heist with an updated theme.

At nine thirty spotlights went on at both ends of the street. The cops wanted to make sure they saw every move clearly. The diamonds in the carts picked up the light and scattered it in a million tiny prisms. The hostages were marched back to the street, but now instead of one cage, there were two. This delighted everyone except O'Keefe, who noticed that the explosives had been removed from the cage and placed between the two cages. Also, besides the detonating wires running from both sides of the street there were now connecting fuses for igniting. Sean remembered Coyle's comment about the last meal and began to feel very uneasy.

Kennedy Airport

The BOAC flight from London had just landed as Miranda hurried to the passenger debarkation area. She had slept most of the day and felt fully rested. The cab from her apartment on Stanton Street in the Lower East Side had gotten tied up in traffic because the siege on Forty-seventh Street had caused vehicle rerouting all over Manhattan.

She knew that her mother would be the first one out because she would only require a cursory customs check, if that, because of her status. She was right. Her mother came barreling into the terminal carrying two large suitcases. She was hard to miss. There weren't too many two-hundred-pound, six-foot-three women who wear Halston originals and carry their own bags.

47th Street

At midnight the street was silent, but the spotlights made it look like the middle of day. The two cages gave the hostages enough room to lie down. Most of them were sleeping or dozing.

Sean O'Keefe sat propped against the cage trying to figure out what the terrorists were up to. And if, in fact, they were terrorists at all. He was pretty sure that the revolutionary rhetoric was just an act and that the real purpose was a simple heist, but he couldn't figure out how they intended to get the diamonds off the street.

The leader and two of the other white men had gone into building fifteen about twenty minutes ago. Two more terrorists followed a few minutes later. One was white, the other black. He wondered what they were up to now, and within seconds he had his answer.

A gigantic explosion deafened the hostages. Some screamed. Others began to pray. Stern and Coyle jumped to their feet at the same time and looked around in panic.

"Don't worry. They didn't set off the dynamite on the cage," Sean said quietly. "They're blowing the triple doors to the vaults in building fifteen. They'll probably go after the vault in building thirty next."

"The vaults . . . they're blowing the friggin' vaults?" Stern exclaimed.

O'Keefe sat down again. "It's going to be a noisy night because sure as hell nobody is going to stop them, and it'll probably take most of the night to get through those doors."

8

Building 15/West 47th Street

It took two hours to blast through the three steel doors to the vault in the basement of building fifteen. Such an operation would have normally taken much longer, but the terrorists didn't give a damn if the police heard them or not, or if they blew off the whole side of the building, which they nearly did.

Four men waited for the smoke and dust to clear, then stepped through the wreckage of some of the world's most sophisticated detection equipment to the diamond cabinets behind the third set of steel doors.

The smallest man, who looked like a frightened mouse, was Sidney Katz, the inside man who knew the street and its secrets. The man who knew diamonds. Logan, a massively built man with a red beard, watched Katz closely. Logan had grown up on the Belfast streets and was in charge of the explosives and the muscle. Fred Stone, a slender black man with a wiry muscular body, stood next to Logan. He was the commander of the black street troops. The last man through the door was also tall and slender. A handsome man just short of being pretty. Michael Duggan, the leader. The brains of the operation. The man the IRA was depending on to bring this bizarre operation to a successful conclusion.

Sidney Katz was in charge of this part of the operation. He knew the diamonds. Duggan, Logan, Stone, and young O'Leary, the senator's son who was still on the street, would see nothing more in a diamond than a crystal form of carbon that was worth a lot of money. Katz saw magnificent beauty. Beauty was the reason that he was involved in the heist. Sidney Katz adored beautiful women, but his meek appearance and personality didn't attract the kind of women he so admired. For that he needed money. He and his father had a successful diamond business, but it was not enough to satisfy Sidney's expensive ladies. He had tried gambling his way to riches and lost heavily. Then he had tried to cover his debts by cheating three different dealers on the street. He broke the law of the street, and in turn the street broke him. He was expelled, and to a diamond dealer that was death.

The shame of Sidney's expulsion had caused his father to have a heart attack. Sidney could still remember his father's delirious rantings on his deathbed. It was part of that seemingly incoherent babbling that led Sidney and the Irish to the planned escape routes.

After his father's death, the loansharks closed in when they discovered that the elder Katz had left the business to Sidney's brother. Sidney was left flat broke. Without money he was a marked man.

When Duggan and Logan dragged him pleading and screaming from the arms of one of his women, an ungrateful bitch who had sold him out for a couple of hundred bucks, he thought he was a candidate for the Flushing Meadows or the Jersey marshes. Instead he discovered that they had purchased his freedom from the loanshark for a tidy sum. In effect, they owned him.

For the Irish, it had been a bargain because Katz not only knew his diamonds, he also held the key to their escape, although he didn't realize it at the time. The months of briefings, the days of training in the Catskills, and the endless repetition of details were bad enough, but the idea of dressing up like an Arab and carrying a loaded M-16 terrified him.

The Irish and the blacks were the warriors, and he was no more than a male camp follower taking orders. In the diamond counting room, however, he was the man. They had to depend on him. His decision would make or break the operation.

"Hurry up, Sidney, we don't have all night," Logan growled.

The slender little man whose neatly combed hair craftily concealed his receding hairline, whirled around, his eyes ablaze with his sudden and obvious power. "Don't push, Logan. You're in my game now, so shut the fuck up," Katz snapped.

Logan tensed and started to move toward Katz, but Duggan and Stone restrained him.

"Easy, Logan, this is his forte. We could pick glass and never know the difference. Let him do his job and earn his money," Duggan warned.

Stone patted Logan on the shoulder. "Michael is right, Dennis. Let Sid do his thing. You wouldn't want him to get pissed and give us a bunch of lemons, would you?" Stone asked.

Logan glared at Katz. "He'd better not," he said ominously.

Katz tried to hide the panic he felt in the pit of his stomach. Logan scared the hell out of him.

"Do your job, Sidney. It'll be all over this afternoon, and we'll be out of here with what we came for."

Katz smiled at Duggan. Duggan was a gentleman. He never bullied or threatened. He always asked. Logan, Stone, and even the American kid O'Leary had no class, no breeding. Duggan was a man of some refinement.

Katz cracked his knuckles, a habit that got on everyone's nerves, turned and walked to the large metal cabinets against the wall. There were ten large metal cabinets with approximately twenty four-inch steel drawers marked with the dealers' names. Katz glanced at the drawers and smiled as he pulled one open. The drawer contained diamonds of one of the dealers who had him kicked off the street. Katz had promised himself that the accusing dealers and the members of the council would be the first people from whom he stole.

The drawers were lined with row after row of neatly folded pieces of tissue. Each folded tissue contained a diamond or group of diamonds. The diamonds were classified by carat, color, and clarity. There was a slide file of classifications at the left of the drawer, but once the tissues were opened Katz's skilled eyes told him what he wanted to know. As he unwrapped the packets the light caught the glistening gems.

There were brilliants, the round diamonds that were the favorites in engagement rings. Emerald cuts in rectangles and squares, with facets polished diagonally across the corners. Marquise, a pointed boat shape that made the finger look longer and slimmer, a favorite with Katz's ladies, probably because it cost slightly more than a brilliant of the same size and quality because of the additional labor in cutting. There were ovals and pear shapes like the world's largest cut diamond, the Cullinan, mounted in the British royal sceptre. It is a 530.20-carat white stone and on display at the Tower of London.

Katz put his loupe in his right eye, quickly plucked a packet from the drawer, and unwrapped a large white oval. He shook his head as he glanced at the classification. "And they called me a thief," he muttered. "This has more faults in it than the whole state of California." He threw the gem over his shoulder with careless disregard and it landed on the floor.

After ten minutes he chose two large stones and ten small ones which he placed on top of a Diamondlite that was used for closer observation. When he had finished he would check them again with the Diamondlite to ensure quality.

Katz moved to the next drawer. His eyes gleamed with the same approval he gave the body of a beautiful woman. He sighed in ecstasy. "Fishbein, you're a *momzer*, but you do have taste."

Within fifteen minutes the take from Fishbein's drawer was four times the previous drawer and was added to the growing piles.

Stone glanced at his watch. "Sidney, baby, how long you gonna be? We've got another vault to blow tonight."

Katz gave a little grunt of disapproval. "Stone, I'm pricing diamonds not piece goods."

Stone scowled at the abrupt answer, but Duggan waved Logan and Stone outside. "Sidney, we have things to take care of on the street. We'll be back in a couple of hours." Katz did not answer. He was too engrossed in peering into every nook and cranny inside the glittering gems.

The three men walked upstairs to the ground floor. Logan stopped and looked back. "Are you really going to leave that little twit in there by himself?"

"Of course. He's a man in love. He's doing something he hasn't been able to do in months."

"How do we know he won't screw us and take only the good rocks for himself?" Stone asked.

Duggan shook his head. "It's important to him to be right. He's lost his reputation on the street. He wants to prove himself more than he wants to screw his associates."

"I don't trust him," Logan grumbled.

"I don't trust him either, but I trust his ego. This makes him the most important man in this operation. He likes that."

"I think we should have dumped him as soon as he showed us how to get out of here."

"And would you have graded the diamonds for us?" Duggan asked.

"I gotta ride with Duggan, Dennis. The Jew knows those rocks. If we just snatched and ran we could end up with one hundred pounds of shit."

Logan grunted. Duggan checked his watch. Two o'clock, slightly behind schedule.

47th Street

Sean watched the three men walk out of the building. Where was the fourth man? They left one man with all the diamonds? Why? What was he doing?

Sean stared at the mail carts with the jewels. Six carts. How many pounds . . . tons! How much were they worth? Millions? Billions? How the hell were they going to get all that stuff out of here? If they were planning a fast getaway somehow, they would have to travel light.

The leader approached the cage. He examined the sleeping figures, then unlocked the cage.

"Come with me, Mister O'Keefe."

Sean got up. His body was sore, his eyes were tired, and he was soaked in sweat from the humid night.

"What do you want? You haven't killed anyone so it can't be another body detail," O'Keefe said wearily. He walked out onto the street and Duggan relocked the cage.

"Thought you might like an exclusive story."

"Why me? You've got most of the news cameras in the city out there on the avenues somewhere. Why not do a number for them? They'd love it."

"Unlike many of my so-called revolutionary brethren, I do not crave media exposure. There'll be enough of that when we're gone."

"Gone?" Sean stared at him. "You really think they're going to let you walk away from this?"

"Oh, they'll try to stop us. We'll lose some people, but we will get away."

"Empty-handed if you do."

"A debatable subject, O'Keefe, but time will tell."

"Why do you want to talk to me?"

"Perhaps because we have something in common."

"Not bloody likely."

"We're both Irish. The strain is watered down a bit on your side, though."

Sean stared at the tall lean man in the sweat-soaked fatigues. "What about all those guys with the black hands . . . they're black Irish, right?"

"Observant. I've been watching you, O'Keefe. Your eyes never stop. You have probably determined that four of us are white and the rest black. The blacks are mercenaries, very expensive ones. The rest of us are Irish . . . with one exception."

Sean stopped as they reached the armored cars blocking Fifth Avenue.

"And could the exception be a rogue Jew up there picking the cream of the crop in diamonds?"

"You are observant, O'Keefe."

"Why are you telling me you're Irish when you've gone to all this trouble to play an Arab?"

"That was merely a tactical move. It struck an immediate emotional chord on the street . . . instant fear and believability. But now it must come to an end because the ploy has been discovered and it is known that we are Irish."

"How'd you find that out? You haven't been off the street, and any radio transmission or phone calls would have been detected."

"Quite true. But if you will notice"—he pointed toward Broadway—"that building down the street with the light. That lights goes on and off . . . a code. During the day we use mirrors in that building"—he pointed east to another building—"and that building. We have people keeping us informed about what is happening."

"Irish cops?"

"Let's say sympathetic Irish Americans."

"Beautiful."

"I take it the Irish situation doesn't interest you."

"Of course it does, and so does the Palestine situation, and the Lebanese situation, and the situation of the Jews in Russia, and the blacks in South Africa and the Orientals in Uganda. But when you start planting bombs in department stores and restaurants or shooting some poor son of a bitch in the knees or gunning down some poor workingstiff in Belfast, then shit on you and your cause . . . because it stinks."

"You believe in a gentlemanly war, the blue coats against the gray coats charging across each other's picket lines."

"You want to know what I believe, mister? I believe a twenty-year-old black kid who wanted to be the next Walter Cronkite, and was his mother's only son, is dead. A pill-popping cameraman trying to keep his soul together is dead. Some old Jew who probably wanted nothing more than to earn an honest day's work is dead. And I want to know why they are dead . . . for Ireland? What the hell did they have to do with Ireland? To them Ireland is just a parade up Fifth Avenue with a bunch of people in green hats heaving their cookies on Eighty-sixth Street about nine o'clock that night. Go tell their families that they died for Ireland. Go tell the families of the victims in the Fraunces Tavern bombing that they died for Puerto Rican independence. I'm sure that will make everything just swell."

"You self-righteous American ass," Duggan snapped. "You've bought the whole Irish-American myth. All priests are Bing Crosby or Pat O'Brien . . . not so. All revolutionaries are Errol Flynn. What are the Irish to

Americans . . . cops, poets, drunks, writers, priests, politicians. But world revolutionaries . . . no, not the Irish . . . too provincial . . . too backward. They just go on killing one another until there are none left. Yesterday, that was true . . . today, no. What's happening here is just the tip of the iceberg."

"You're going to get your own nuclear bomb, right?"

"It is a possibility, my sarcastic friend. Enough of this. I shouldn't have wasted my time on you."

Duggan marched Sean back to the cage and locked him in. Sean sat down among the sleeping hostages and continued to watch and think. Now he knew why, but he couldn't figure out how.

Building 15/West 47th Street

Sidney Katz grinned happily as Logan, Duggan, Stone, and O'Leary entered the vault. It was four in the morning.

"Come on, Sidney, we're going to start blowing the doors of building thirty," Duggan said a bit impatiently.

"It won't be necessary," Sidney said smugly. "We have all we need right here."

The four men stared at the Diamondlite and the thirty-three piles of diamonds. If piled all together they would probably fill a decent-sized cookie jar.

"That's it? A billion and a half worth of diamonds . . . that's it?" Stone asked.

"So what were you expecting, a giant treasure chest? That's one of the things that makes diamonds better than money. Besides their stability, you can walk around with a king's ransom in your pocket . . . and they only go up in value. After we get away they'll probably be worth even more."

Duggan walked over to the diamonds and studied each

pile. Three piles of ten-carat diamonds worth over five hundred million dollars each. Total, one billion, five hundred million dollars. These were to be carried by the three Irishmen for the revolution.

Next there were twenty-five smaller piles of one-carat stones for the blacks. Each pile was worth one million dollars, except for three piles for those involved in the forthcoming diversion. Those men would receive a million and a half. All twenty-five black mercenaries would be instant millionaires after the escape.

In another pile there were one- and two-carat diamonds worth five million dollars. This was Fred Stone's payment. Stone and the other blacks were receiving the small stones because they would be easier to sell. Katz and the Irish had larger stones. Katz would know how to get rid of his in the underground diamond world, and the Irish would be making deals for weapons with people who thought that anything below ten carats was an industrial diamond.

Katz's pile contained one- to ten-carat diamonds, valued at ten million dollars. The last three piles were one- and five-carat diamonds, two million for the personal use of each of the three Irishmen. The grand total, close to $1,547,500,000 in first-rate diamonds.

"I don't like to sound greedy, but I do believe we could all carry a bit more without getting ruptured," Stone said.

They all looked at Duggan. He shook his head. "We have what we came for. We set a limit because we have to travel light and there's no sense in blowing the other vault when we have what we came for right here."

Katz opened the top drawer quietly. Thirty-three more groups of diamonds glistened on the black velour without the protective tissue wrapping. "We could double our take," Katz added.

There was a moment of silence, then Duggan nodded

his head. "All right, as Fred said . . . it wouldn't rupture anyone. The price of the haul just went up to over three billion dollars."

O'Leary emptied a box of money belts. Each had a coded number. In one hour the belts were filled. The five men put on their belts. The Irish had two each. Stone and Katz each had one. The twenty-five belts for the blacks were put back in the box.

"It does seem a bitch to leave behind all those carts full of diamonds plus a full vault," O'Leary said.

"It would be a bigger bitch to get away with them."

"It would be impossible," Duggan said.

"The impossible dream," O'Leary quipped. "If we had all those diamonds, we wouldn't have to drive the English out of Ireland, we could just buy them out, and get a couple of English cities to boot."

They all laughed, except for Logan, who never laughed.

9

West 47th Street

Twenty-four hours after the takeover Sean O'Keefe had not slept. He stayed awake all night waiting for them to blow the doors of the second big vault. The explosion never came.

The blacks wheeled three carts of jewels into the small lobby of building fifteen. They moved the other three carts into the lobby of building thirty. Sean watched them. Window dressing, he thought. They had no intentions of taking those jewels out. They were after the cream of the crop in the vaults. He was sure of it. They probably scored big in the first vault, so they didn't blow the one in building thirty. The police would probably expect something spectacular now, but Sean was pretty sure that the actual escape was going to be very low key.

Time-Life Building

Mobile units were clustered all around the entrance of the Time-Life Building. Various command units were set up in the lobby. In the front section of the building Command Central was set up in a smaller separate unit.

Inspector Conrad, McBride, and other FBI agents gathered around a large map of the street.

"They've moved the carts of jewelry into those buildings," Conrad said.

"What about those explosions early this morning?" McBride asked.

"I think it was one of the big vaults, the one on the south side of the street. There was no heavy street activity involved."

McBride pulled out another map and looked at it. "Are you still guarding those solid areas on the map?"

Conrad nodded. "Yeah, one is right near some gay hotel. The other is somewhere around the McGraw-Hill Building. Any special reason for asking?"

McBride shook his head. "No, it just bugs me that there's nothing there. One of the busiest sections of the city, and no pipes, telephone cables, just rock."

"There's a similar thing on Fourteenth. Blasting the rock would be dangerous. It could collapse the surrounding buildings . . . at least that's what they say. Besides, we're not interested in what was, we're interested in what is."

"Maybe so," McBride said as he glanced at his watch. "I've got to go. I have an appointment at church."

The other men stared at him. "I don't think this can be prayed away, Hugh," Conrad said with a certain amount of sarcasm in his voice.

"Neither do I, Jim. I'm meeting someone there who might be able to shed some light on these turkeys, heaven withstanding."

47th Street

Sean noticed that the blacks were going to buildings fifteen and thirty in groups of two. He also observed that some of the men kept touching the front of their shirts after they emerged again, as if to make sure something was still there. It was a reflex action of New York males on the subway. Check the wallet and make the pickpocket's job easier.

Coyle had noticed the activity, too. So had Stern.
"What are they up to, Sean?" Coyle asked.
"I think it's payday."

Building 15

Sidney Katz watched the men come in, get their money belts, and smile at the news that they had been given a million-dollar bonus each. If they made it out, half of them would probably get caught trying to fence the diamonds, Katz thought.

It was almost over. A few more hours and he would be on his way out of town. Then a few weeks laying low, and then Brazil, with all those diamonds to lavish on those lovely Brazilian women and their magnificent pampered bodies.

Katz was sure they would get away because the only people who knew how they would escape were being guarded in a bookstore across the street. The three members of the Diamond Council knew what his father had known when he was a member of the council. A secret he took with him when he resigned because of the shame of Sidney's expulsion. The secret revealed in a fit of delirium on his deathbed with only Sidney to hear. A secret that Sidney did not understand until he shared it with Duggan.

Sidney had been telling Duggan about his father's experiences as a fighter in the Warsaw ghetto. Duggan was intrigued because he was a military buff and was interested in defense tactics. Sidney told him about the tunnels under the ghetto that Sidney's father and others had used to escape to America. Many of the street's dealers were victims of concentration camps or had family who were. They were very suspicious people and believed it possible that they would have to escape again.

The old diamond district had been on the Lower East

Side near the first European immigrant community but the Holocaust survivors had opened for business on West Forty-seventh Street, fearful and suspicious of the *goyim*. So they did what they'd done in Europe. They tunneled. Two large tunnels leading away from the street. One from building fifteen. One from building thirty.

It cost a fortune to accomplish and maintain, but each council throughout the years had continued to pay over ten million in bribes each year to keep the secret. The bribes went to city officials who had altered maps, construction people who had built the original tunnels and then rebuilt the tunnel into the basement of the McGraw-Hill Building when the old building was torn down.

Katz's father's babbling about tunnels under the street had been interpreted by Sidney as ranting about the Warsaw ghetto, but Duggan had had him repeat every word over and over. Then Duggan, Logan, and O'Leary had posed as sewer maintenance men and had followed one tunnel to the old bathhouse on Forty-sixth Street, and the other tunnel to the basement under the McGraw-Hill Building on the west side of Sixth Avenue. The Jews had planned this as an escape should another holocaust occur, but it would be used instead by Irish revolutionaries and black mercenaries.

47th Street/A bookstore

Ben Levi and the two men with him weren't sure why they had been segregated from the rest of the hostages until they looked out the window and saw the increased activity around the building next door and building fifteen across the street. Their first thought was of the vaults in the two buildings. Their next thought was of the tunnels. But how could the terrorists know? They had paid bribes for years. In fact, most of the original people involved were dead.

Suddenly without warning one of the guards ordered the three men away from the window. They were shoved to the back of the store in front of the bookcases. Levi and the other men thought it was just to get them away from the window. They were wrong. The two guards opened fire with M-16s. Levi and the other two men crashed into the bookcases and the shelves collapsed on top of them. The guards, satisfied with their job, left the building.

St. Patrick's Cathedral/5th Avenue

Hugh McBride entered the Fiftieth Street side door of the cathedral, dipped his finger in the holy water, crossed himself, and slid into a front pew next to a tall distinguished man with white hair.

Senator Ted O'Leary turned as McBride sat down.

"Why did you want me to meet you here, Hugh?"

McBride's face was cold and expressionless as he spoke to the man he has known most of his life.

"Remember when we were kids, Ted? Whenever I wanted to know if you were bullshitting me, I'd drag your ass into church. You could never lie with the Virgin Mary watching you."

The senator scowled. "What's this all about, McBride?"

"I want to know about those Irish terrorists holding Forty-seventh Street."

The senator's face reddened slightly. "What Irish terrorists?"

"Come on, Ted, you've seen the papers. Don't play dumb with me. There isn't a damn thing that goes on in the Irish community from New Orleans to New York and all points west that you don't know about. I know you're helping the IRA because you've made no secret about it. You've worked with them, you know who they are and which ones are active around here. I don't have a lot of time and even less patience . . . I want some names."

"I'm not about to turn over good men without . . ."

"Can the crap, Ted. I don't want to hear any of your speeches. I want the names of the guys who you think are into this thing, or I go to the press and put you in cahoots with those jokers and ruin your ass with every Jew in the state."

"You wouldn't . . ."

"I would. Names, Ted. Not your organization. I know they wouldn't go for this shit. Give me the hard numbers. The ones you think would try a stunt like this."

O'Leary's facial muscles tightened. "Would you believe I've been debating all night about coming to see you?"

McBride could see the hurt in the man's eyes and softened his tone slightly. "You never lie in church, Ted."

"There were two fellows from Belfast. We raised a lot of money . . . the money disappeared and so did they, along with one of our people."

"Names, Ted."

"Michael Duggan, Dennis Logan"—he paused and his eyes began to tear—"my son, Kevin."

McBride sensed the man's hurt and worry. "Kevin?"

"I think so. This guy Duggan was always talking about some dramatic gesture to make Americans aware of the Irish situation. He always seemed to have bigger things on his mind."

"What are these guys like?"

"Duggan's well educated, a good talker. Logan's big and mean, a street fighter."

"Are there any other Americans helping them?"

"I think so."

"Any ideas how they'll get the diamonds out of there? Out of the country?"

"I heard Kevin say something about an underground network, but I never picked up anything on it."

McBride got up. "I'll be talking with you again, Ted."

"I didn't know anything else about this, Hugh."

"I believe you, Ted. You're a lot of things, but not this. Not murder and terrorism."

"Neither is Kevin, Hugh."

"If he's on that street he is, Ted."

10

5th Avenue

An extra contingent of police had been moved to the barricades on Fifth and Sixth avenues. At first, the early-morning crowds had consisted of curious office workers from the area, but now the crowds had taken on a new dimension. Mostly young, blacks, and Hispanics. The police could sense something was in the making, but they didn't know what. The unnerving thing was that they were not boisterous, unruly, or disruptive. They were quiet, as if waiting for something to happen. Something that would involve them.

Time-Life Building

"I sent the Black Berets over to the McGraw-Hill Building," Conrad said. "They're beginning to get edgy sitting around, so I told them we had a tip that something was going down over there."

McBride nodded. "I just took a look at what's happening on the avenues. We might need them there if things get tough."

"I thought of that, but if they used those new toys of theirs on those kids, we'd be fried alive. Terrorists, yes. Those people at the barricades, no."

"What do you think the crowds are up to, Jim?"

"I don't know. They could storm the street, but most of them would be killed. No, it's something else."

"What's happening on the street?"

"It's relatively quiet. Some activity in and out of buildings fifteen and thirty. We heard gunshots earlier, around seven thirty, but it was inside. We can't tell what happened, only guess."

"Have you had any reports of noise from your men with the listening devices?" McBride asked.

"Rats scurrying, that's all. You got anything?"

"Not much. We've checked the numbers of the mail vans that your spotters gave us. They were stolen about a week ago. Some postal employees are also missing. Probably a tie-in. We're checking it out. Nothing on any armored cars being stolen. We've talked to some diamond dealers to see if we could pick up anything. And my trip to church paid off with a few names, but nothing concrete, just a few possibles," McBride said as he paced back and forth.

"Looks like the next move is up to them."

"I'm afraid so, and the way things are moving . . . it should be very soon," McBride added.

47th Street

The hostages were all extremely nervous since the gunshots were heard in the bookstore. They had seen the guards leave the shop and were sure that the three council members were dead.

Sean felt sick to his stomach. He knew and liked Levi and the two other men. He was sure they had been brutally killed. More victims of the glorious revolution. With a searing rage, he swore that if he got out of this mess in one piece he would get the leader and his men no matter what, even if he had to go to Ireland.

5th Avenue

Officer Fred Schwartz was on the twentieth floor of the office building on the northeast corner of Fifth Avenue and Forty-seventh Street. The same building the sniper and the black spotter had been in. Schwartz watched as the terrorists got into the cabs of the mail vans and backed them up to buildings fifteen and thirty. He spoke into the walkie-talkie in his hand. He shook it, cursed it, and then threw it across the room against the wall.

"Cheap broken-down crap they give us," he yelled.

His partner, at the window, was scanning the street with binoculars.

"It's broken again?" he asked.

"Still! What the fuck do they want us to do, send smoke signals?"

"We'd better call it in on the phone. You got the number they gave us in case of emergencies?"

"No, I thought you took it down."

"Wonderful. Call the precinct and have them relay to command."

The other officer picked up the phone and dialed. He slammed the receiver down. "The line is busy."

"Shit. Call Nine-one-one. I'll head downstairs and try to spot someone with a walkie-talkie."

47th Street

Sean, Coyle, and Stern also watched the vans back up to the buildings. From their vantage point they saw what the spotters couldn't see: that nothing else was happening.

"If the cops are watching this act, they'll think the terrorists are loading up the carts of jewelry that were stashed in buildings fifteen and thirty earlier," Sean said.

"What the hell are they up to?" Coyle asked.
"More games probably," Stern answered.
"I think they're getting ready to make their move."
"Sean, they're not going to just drive off."
"Have you seen the top dogs around lately?" Sean asked Stern. "I have a feeling they're already on their way out, somehow," Sean added.

And he was partially right.

Duggan, Logan, O'Leary, and Katz had discarded their fatigues and Arab gear and were dressed in business suits. They had exchanged their M-16s for 9-mm pistols worn in holsters underneath their jackets. There were still traces of dark makeup on their faces, but it was not noticeable from a distance.

"It's ten forty. We move."

They all checked their watches and squatted quietly before the open door to tunnel one. They all held large flashlights and carried the bulk of the stolen diamonds strapped to their waists.

11

Time-Life Building

The command unit at the Time-Life Building was in a state of full alert. Messages were starting to come in from all over.

"This is Eagle Two. The vans are starting to move away from the buildings. I don't know if they have the carts of jewelry or not."

"What are they doing, Eagle Two?"

"Just driving in circles in the middle of the street."

"Groundhog here. We're picking up sounds from under the street . . . not rats . . . running feet."

"Location. Repeat location!"

"South side of the street moving toward Sixth Avenue."

McBride slapped his hand on the map. "Tunnels. Those rock areas are tunnels. Alert the units at Forty-sixth and at the McGraw-Hill Building."

West 46th Street

The mobile unit in front of the Tudor Baths Hotel held ten very bored SWAT officers who were no longer amused by the comings and goings of the homosexuals seeking early-morning pickups at the gay hotel.

At one time the Tudor had been a respectable bath and steam club for the area's businessmen, but hard times and fancier competition drove it out of business. The new owners had seen the advantages of catering to the homosexuals who drifted around the Broadway area. It was a sleazy place with small cubicles where screams were seldom investigated. Anything was allowed as long as the money was up front.

"Mobile Forty-six here."

"Seal off the street . . . units on the way. Anyone comes out of that fag hotel . . . or any other building near it . . . stop them."

The SWAT captain turned to the others. "Well, you heard the man, move. Block off the street. Nobody on or off. Dibbs, Black, west end . . . Peters, Mankowitz, east end. Everyone else spread out on the street. Keep your eyes open."

McGraw-Hill Building
Lower-level lobby

The Black Berets watched an out-of-town school group troop past, staring at the men as if they were from outer space. The children were headed for the New York Experience, one of the biggest tourist attractions in the city. The lower-level entrance that connected to the Rockefeller tunnel was sealed off, but the building itself was open to the public. At nine o'clock, office workers had streamed into the building and now people were arriving for the eleven o'clock show at the New York Experience.

The Black Berets sat in the lower-level plaza outside the building. A young lieutenant approached Captain Carter with an annoyed expression on his face. "Captain, I feel like a damn fool. Everyone stares at me as if I'm an advertisement for this New York Experience thing."

The captain tried to conceal his anger. "I think we're getting screwed."

"Captain." A sergeant approached carrying a radio unit. "You're wanted on the radio. Some FBI guy named McBride."

The captain grabbed the mike and yelled into it. "Look, McBride, I'm getting tired of being jerked off. Screw political niceties, I want some straight . . ." He paused and the anger left his face.

"Where? But there are citizens around here . . . all right . . . all right . . . we'll do what we can."

Carter gave the mike back to the radio man and motioned to his men who ran forward with the black leather bags swinging from their shoulders.

"Get into the building and clear all the civilians out quickly. Set up a perimeter in front of the New York Experience entrance."

"But the theater is full of people, captain," the lieutenant said.

"And if McBride is right, it could be filled with terrorists in a few minutes."

"Unlock weapons and secure the area," the lieutenant yelled.

47th Street

Sean's heart began to pound as the two circling mail vans turned and sped directly toward the armored trucks blocking Fifth and Sixth avenues. It looked as if they would crash into the armored vehicles, but at the last minute the armored cars quickly pulled out and the vans raced through to the avenues. The armored cars quickly reversed gears and wheeled back into place. The terrorists driving the armored cars ran to building thirty. The guards who had been watching the cages got up from their fortified positions between the two cages and lit the fuses to the dynamite. The hostages in the cages started to scream and beat on the sides of the cages.

5th Avenue

The amtrack could not turn fast enough to get a shot off at the mail van. The van turned right and headed for the barricades at Forty-fifth Street. The back door of the van opened and three mail carts containing jewels were dumped on the street. The van then cut sharply and crashed deliberately into the building on the west side near the barricades. The driver rolled out the door, crawled under the barricade and merged with the crowd. The man in the back jumped out of the van and was shot by a SWAT sharpshooter. Fred Stone, the driver, was the first terrorist to escape.

On Sixth Avenue the same action was repeated, but both men were killed when the police shot out their tires. The jewels scattered all over Sixth Avenue.

Building 30/Basement

The black terrorists stripped off their fatigues as they rushed toward the basement tunnel that led to the McGraw-Hill Building. They tossed away their weapons and picked up tool kits containing a pistol and ammunition. Then they rushed, single file, into the tunnel with flashlights.

47th Street

Sid Stern took out his pistol and carefully aimed and shot at one of the fuses burning toward the dynamite. He missed.

"Shoot the fucking lock off, Sid," Sean yelled.

"Are you out of your mind, Sean? This isn't a John Wayne movie. A bullet would ricochet all over the place."

Sean grabbed the pistol and fired at the lock. The bullet did ricochet . . . into Coyle's foot.

O'Keefe pushed the cage door open and rushed out toward the burning fuse which was about fifteen inches from the dynamite coming from the north side of the street. Stern headed for the fuse coming from the south side of the street. Both men grabbed the fuses inches from their goal. Both men screamed as the flesh on their hands burned.

Tudor Baths/West 46th Street

Duggan, Logan, Katz, and O'Leary quickly climbed the basement stairs of the Tudor Baths and quietly entered the lobby. There was only one person there, a tired-looking little man reading a newspaper behind the desk. The man glanced up as Duggan, Katz, and O'Leary swished by. Logan couldn't swish if his life depended on it.

Duggan blew a kiss to the desk clerk. The effeminate man made a suggestive motion with his tongue.

"Next time we're in town, sailor," Duggan said.

The man giggled, batted his eyes, and returned to his newspaper.

"Bloody pufta," Logan snorted. He opened the door angrily and stormed out into the street followed by Katz and O'Leary. Duggan stopped inside the lobby to close the door. It was his good fortune that he did.

Three SWAT officers spotted Logan, O'Leary, and Katz at the same time. "Hold it right where you are and get your hands up."

Logan screamed some ancient Gaelic curse and drew his pistol. O'Leary did the same, almost as a reflex action from the intensive training he had received from Logan. Katz put his hands up immediately, trying to disassociate himself from the other men. The police fired their automatic weapons. Logan was nearly split in half. O'Leary was hit in the chest and groin, but made it back to the lobby and collapsed in front of Duggan. Katz was only hit once, right through the heart.

Duggan ran back into the lobby and slammed the door. The man at the desk dropped his newspaper and screamed in a high-pitched voice, "Jesus, what's happening?"

Duggan drew his pistol. He did not see a popeyed little man. He saw a witness who knew his face. He fired only once, killing him instantly. Duggan, unlike Logan, did not like to see men suffer needlessly. He felt pain was a punishment. Quick death was an act of kindness when it was necessary to kill.

The little man fell forward on the desk without a sound of protest.

Duggan quickly ripped open O'Leary's shirt and pulled off the money belts. Then he rushed up the stairs to a large room surrounded by enclosed cubicles. Some of the doors were open, and Duggan noticed small beds and nothing else. He knew it was only a matter of minutes before the police would be all over the place. He looked at the stairs to the next floor. The sign said Cruising Floor.

Duggan ran up the stairs as he heard the police charging through the downstairs doors. He walked quickly down the hallway with doors on each side. The rooms appeared larger than the ones downstairs. Men could be seen lying naked on the beds in some of the rooms. They made remarks like, "How's about a kiss, luv?" . . . Hey, guy, come on in." . . . "You into S and M, cutie?" . . . "Rough trade?"

Duggan clenched his teeth in disgust. At the end of the hall there was one more open door. He looked in. A pimply-faced youth with greasy hair was fondling a pathetically small penis. The pasty-faced youth looked up and smiled. Duggan smiled back. The young man got up, holding his organ in his hand, stroking it as he walked. "Let's get down, good-lookin'."

"Right on, sweetcakes," Duggan said as he entered the room and quickly closed the door behind him.

The young man extended his arms with lips puckered and eyes closed. "How about a get acquainted kiss?"

The young man's eyes flew open as Duggan smashed four knuckles of his right hand into the homosexual's windpipe.

"No moral judgments, friend, just an unfortunate necessity," Duggan said as he carried the lifeless body to the bed and arranged it face down on a pillow, knees bent and ass up.

Duggan showed his distaste for what he intended to do by gagging as he stripped off his clothes. He unfastened the money belts with the diamonds and put them with O'Leary's two belts and his pistol on the floor, covering them with his clothes.

He was just about to take off his socks when he heard the screams and curses in the hall, and the shouted commands from the cops.

Duggan looked at the corpse, grimaced, and straddled the body.

Officer Jud Fredericks kicked open the door and frowned at the two men on the bed. He holstered his gun and walked into the room, shaking his head with disgust as he grabbed Duggan by the shoulders and pulled him off the bed.

"Okay, girls. No more playtime." Fredericks grabbed the young man by the legs and pulled him off the bed. "You too, sweetheart." Fredericks noticed Duggan's naked body to his left and started to rise, but was met by a deadly karate chop to the neck.

Duggan quickly turned the body of the policeman over and stripped off the uniform. Then he strapped all four money belts around his waist, put on the policeman's shirt, slipped on the pants, strapped on the pistol, and put on the hat. It was not a perfect fit but close enough. He put on his own shoes, which were a little more fashionable than the policeman's, but were at least black.

He picked up his pistol and wiped off the fingerprints, then tossed it back on the clothes. He looked at the two wide-eyed corpses. The cop looked ridiculous in his underwear and black socks and shoes. The young man just looked pathetic. Duggan walked calmly down the hall. The occupants of the rooms had been taken to the floor below. The second floor was bedlam. Police and homosexuals were fighting all over the place.

Duggan grabbed a homosexual in blue bikini shorts threw a hammerlock around his neck and lifted him off his feet. He pushed and half carried the man down the stairs, across the crowded lobby and into the street where cops were herding the Tudor's clientele into a police paddy wagon. Duggan waited his turn, then tossed the man into the back.

The street was full of police vehicles. Duggan walked toward Seventh Avenue. Just another blue uniform.

Patrol cars blocked the street backed up by a contingent of helmeted police. Duggan was aware of a strange whirring noise. A glance to the left revealed a group of Japanese tourists clicking off pictures as fast as their motor driven cameras would operate.

Duggan turned his head the other way. He smiled as he approached one of the helmeted policemen at the barricade. "What a mess," he said.

The cop returned the smile and nodded. "Yeah, and what do you wanna bet the gay rights and civil rights lawyers beat the paddy wagons back to the precinct."

Duggan nodded. "I know what you mean." He continued walking toward Seventh Avenue, turned, took a deep breath and headed for Forty-second Street.

5th Avenue

There was an eerie silence on Fifth Avenue.

From curb to curb, the streets were covered with jewels twinkling in the bright August sun.

Close to five hundred young men stood transfixed in an almost hypnotic state as they gazed at the wealth scattered before them. The answer to a thousand dreams. The escape from a thousand horrors.

In front of them, about fifty very anxious cops formed a human barrier. Their hands twitched nervously on their guns.

Miranda and her mother had just emerged from Saks Fifth Avenue, loaded with packages, when the mail van broke out on to the street. Curious spectators, mostly shoppers, were gathered at the Fifth Avenue barricades. Miranda took one look at the cops and the hostile crowd in front of them, stuffed her packages into her mother's already overcrowded arms, and grabbed her Minolta camera from her bag. Running toward the barricade, she climbed a light pole and began clicking off shots.

The crowd began shuffling their feet and muttering. The cops stood their ground. Each group seemed to be waiting for the other to make a move.

Sergeant Tom Turner, six two, and thirty pounds overweight according to police regulations, slid his hands over his sweaty billy club as he stood on the east sidewalk of Fifth Avenue. This is one bad scene, he thought as he and the double line of police moved forward about half a block.

He looked at the gems surrounding him. He wouldn't mind if one of those goodies happened to slip into his size-twelve shoe. He moved forward a little and there was a crunch under his foot. A crunch? Diamonds don't crunch. He lifted his foot. There was granulated glass all over the heel of his shoe. He picked up some of the loose stones and looked at them, then threw them on the sidewalk and put his full weight on them.

CRUNCH!

Lieutenant Joseph Flynn stood by the amtrack with a bullhorn, his face glistening with sweat. He was trying to think of something to say to calm the crowd, but the words wouldn't come. He was about to speak when Sergeant Turner grabbed the bullhorn out of his hand and ran through the line of police, stopping about twenty feet from the crowd.

"Hey, turkeys, what the fuck you think this is . . . Christmas?" Turner's voice echoed from building to building.

The crowd cheered. "You better believe it, baby. Right on, fuzz. You ain't goin' to stop us, man." The crowd started chanting, "Christmas . . . Christmas . . . Christmas."

"Your ass turkeys . . . we've all been had . . . screwed . . . you . . . me . . . everybody here. 'Cause that shit in the street is nuthin' but shit!"

"You're jivin' us," a voice yelled and the crowd shouted in agreement.

"Jivin' you, huh?" Turner picked up some of the clear sparkling stones and walked over to the sidewalk.

"Look at this!" He jumped on the stones and ground them into tiny fragments. He picked up the pieces and scattered them in the air with a sweeping gesture.

"Shit! Glass!"

He picked up a handful of the stones and threw them to the crowd.

"Here. Take 'em home to your ladies and see how fast they tell you to stuff 'em."

The other cops followed Turner's lead and started throwing the stones into the crowd.

The officers on Fifth Avenue communications got the

drift of what was happening and radioed the units on Sixth Avenue to do the same thing.

Reinforcement units rushed in from the side street and formed a wall of police behind the crowd.

"Now if you want to be good citizens and save the city a few bucks in sanitation costs, you can clean up this mess for us. We'll move the barricades back two streets and you can pick up what you want. Or, if you want to cause some trouble because you're pissed off . . . you can look at the sea of blue behind you and give it another thought."

The crowd grumbled, but everyone knew it was a no-win situation. They began breaking up into small groups and drifted away down the side streets, followed by clusters of cops in case of sporadic trouble.

Turner sat down on the curb and breathed a sigh of relief. He noticed a pair of black shoes in front of him. He looked up and smiled nervously at the lieutenant he had grabbed the bullhorn from.

"Are you through with the bullhorn, sergeant?"

Turner held it up in the air. "It's all yours, lieutenant. Am I in deep shit?"

The lieutenant took the bullhorn and sat down next to Turner. "I admit I was pissed off, but more at myself than you. To be honest I was scared to death."

"Don't feel like the Lone Ranger," Turner said.

They both sat and stared very quietly at the stones covering the street. The only sound was Miranda's camera clicking off shots before two police officers politely carried her back to the barricades where her mother waited patiently with the packages.

McGraw-Hill Building

While the police were making their way cautiously along Forty-seventh Street, the blacks were silently slipping into the side of the theater called the New York Experience. The audience was completely enthralled with the multimedia effect on the large screen.

One-by-one the men quietly filed out of the theater into the small lobby which was an arcade with old-fashioned penny games that were all more than a penny. The ticket taker and the candy stand cashier did a double take as the group of black men in building maintenance uniforms started toward the escalator leading to the upper-level lobby of the McGraw-Hill Building.

One of the black men smiled broadly at the two theater employees. "Don't worry. We got the pipes all closed off, and you won't have to evacuate the theater."

The ticket taker and the cashier looked puzzled, but like all New Yorkers, they remained casual in the face of potential danger and steadfastly refused to plead ignorance of anything.

"Oh, good," said the ticket taker.

"Glad to hear it," added the cashier.

The black men waved as they passed by and headed for the escalators. Once on the top level they started to walk toward the side exits. Something was wrong. They all felt it. There were no people. No activity. They could hear the echo of their own footsteps.

"Hold it right where you are, or you're dead men."

The blacks froze as six men appeared from behind the building's pillars. They had strange-looking things on their ears, like earphones. And they were pointing weird-looking rods that were connected to black boxes strapped to their waists.

The terrorists collectively calculated that battling it out with only six men was worth the risks involved in escaping with over two million dollars. They pulled open their tool kits and grabbed their weapons, firing them almost immediately. One Black Beret corporal was hit and fell to the floor.

"Fire," yelled Captain Carter into a small microphone that was attached to his earphone. There was a high, shrill, piercing noise that reverberated throughout the lobby. The terrorists dropped their weapons and grabbed their ears. Blood started to trickle from their noses and eyes, and they fell to the ground in agony.

There was the sound of sudden cracking, but the Black Berets couldn't hear it because of the special protective headgear they were wearing.

Suddenly the large plate-glass window in the front of the building buckled and shattered into a million pieces, showering the lobby with deadly missiles of glass. The high-velocity sound from the Berets' weapons suddenly became their enemy, destroying the Berets as completely as the terrorists.

When the audience from the New York Experience came up the escalators to the main lobby something a million times more vivid than what they had just seen on the large screen greeted their eyes. Bleeding, moaning men. Glass all over the place. Dozens of police and medical personnel. The sight of this bizarre New York experience left them stunned and slack-jawed.

Police guided them to a side door as they looked in disbelief at the carnage. One of the crowd was more stunned than the rest. Willie Johnson, dressed in gray maintenance pants and a sweaty white tee shirt, moved numbly with the crowd. He had tripped in the tunnel and had reached the theater after the others had left. Not sure what to do, he sat down and watched the show. When the crowd left, he left with them. He had slipped out of his maintenance shirt and looked like any young black in a white shirt except for the bulge around his waist. He was the only terrorist to leave the building in one piece. And he was a very rich young man.

12

West 47th Street

"Take it easy, damn it," Sean yelled as the medic tried to wrap the gauze gently around his ointment-covered hands.

His hands hurt like hell. He looked over at Stern, who was getting his hands bandaged, then at Coyle, who was being placed on a stretcher.

"Coyle, I'm sorry about your foot," he yelled.

The cameraman put his thumb in the air and tried to smile. "Not half as sorry as I am, but it beats getting blown to hell."

The police were all over the street. Some were standing guard over the diamonds in the mail carts. A paramedic unit made its way through the crowded street to the bookstore. Sean followed it, afraid of what he would see. The medics rushed in. Sean was stopped at the door by a policeman. "It's not pretty," the cop said.

"All dead?" Sean asked.

"Two for sure, one is hanging in there . . ."

"Do you know who?" Sean asked urgently.

The cop shook his head. The door swung open and the two men from the ambulance rushed out with Ben Levi on a stretcher. They were in the ambulance and gunning the motor before Sean could say a word. The tears started to flow down his face as he clenched his fists, ripping the bandages. Sorrow had replaced pain, and he did something he hadn't done in years. He crossed himself and prayed for a friend who deserved better than this.

West 46th Street

Six bodies lay in a uniform line on the floor in the lobby of the hotel. They were covered with hotel sheets. Four of the sheets were bloodstained.

Inspector Conrad and McBride got the rundown on what happened from the SWAT officer who was in charge. The precinct police had transported the homosexuals to Manhattan South where they were being questioned. Police had come through the tunnel from Forty-seventh Street and the basement of the hotel had been sealed off to everyone but the detectives and the FBI.

"The four bloody ones were involved in the shoot-out. The other two were found upstairs. One's a police officer. The other's an unknown," Conrad said.

McBride went to the blood soaked sheets. He lifted the first one and examined the face. An old man with plucked and penciled eyebrows. He picked up the second sheet. This man was younger. He didn't look Irish. More like a Jewish accountant. The third face was definitely Irish. The next face was Kevin O'Leary's. McBride's stomach sank. He had known Kevin as a child, teenager, and adult. Senator O'Leary's only child. Ted O'Leary's worries were well founded.

"What's wrong, Hugh?" Conrad asked, noting McBride's expression.

"That's Ted O'Leary's son." There was a slight catch in his throat as he answered.

"Jesus," Conrad said.

"I want a make on the others, except for the cop," McBride said. "Did they have any diamonds on them?"

"Two of them did," Conrad answered.

The names Senator O'Leary had mentioned flipped through McBride's mind. O'Leary accounted for. Logan, tough street fighter . . . probably the big man with the beard. Duggan? The other bodies didn't match what he thought the man looked like.

"You think some got away?" Conrad asked.

"I think it's probable. Don't notify O'Leary about his kid; I'll take care of that," McBride said. He had two reasons for volunteering for the unpleasant chore. The news should come from a friend, and it was also an opportunity to get more information. McBride was not proud of the second reason, but accepted it as something that had to be done.

Grand Central Station
A subway platform

To the people on the platform Michael Duggan was just a cop waiting for a train. Some of the people, for their own reasons, walked as far away as possible. Others preferred to be close to the blue uniform.

A tall black man in green pants and a bulky NYU sweatshirt watched Duggan and grinned quietly. Fred Stone had walked away casually from Fifth Avenue. He had pulled off his headgear the minute he got behind the barricade. He had ditched his shirt as he made his way through the crowd, unbloused his pants from around his boots at the edge of the crowd and then walked toward Grand Central Station. Standing on the subway platform he looked like a slob, but the diamonds around his waist made him one of the richest slobs in the city.

Stone edged next to Duggan. "I always knew all you Irish were closet cops at heart."

Duggan's head did not turn, but his eyes shifted to the side.

"Congratulations, Fred . . . I didn't think you'd make it."

"I think I'm the only one. I hear they wiped out the brothers at McGraw-Hill."

Duggan turned his head. "I'm sorry, Fred. They did a good job."

"They knew the risks," Stone said quietly. "How'd you make out?"

"I'm the only one who got away."

The express train arrived and both men quickly entered. They didn't speak again. Each was lost in his own thoughts.

At Fifty-ninth Street more people got on and the two men separated. At Eighty-sixth Street Duggan got off. He glanced back, but couldn't see Stone. Just as well, he thought. He was alone again. He preferred it that way. No connections. No links. Lonely, but the path Michael Duggan had chosen fit his style. No friends. No associates. No emotional ties.

Duggan left the station and headed toward Fifth Avenue. A group of children in parochial school uniforms passed by. He recognized their emblems as being from St. Ignatius and smiled to himself. These children, carrying their little colored bus passes to and from school, had triggered his plan for getting the diamonds out of the country.

Each of the Irishmen had devised his own individual escape plan once they had left the hotel. Duggan was sure that both Logan and O'Leary had worked out something with the pro-IRA Irish-American movement, and he was sure they would probably have been caught once the FBI started rousting Irish sympathizers.

Duggan's plan was a little more complicated, but in the long run, much more workable. He would have to initially make use of the movement today, but tomorrow he would be using his own pipeline.

Jack Timmons, the doorman at the apartment building on the corner of Park Avenue and Eighty-sixth Street, glanced at his watch. Three twenty-five. He nervously felt the key in his coat pocket.

Like most of the luxury buildings in the so-called Silk Stocking District, the service staff was composed of Irish from top to bottom. Some were second and third generation, some were fresh off the boat. Superintendents, doormen, maintenance . . . all Irish. Timmons's father was a super over on Park. His brothers worked over on Seventy-ninth. Unlike the rest of the family, who were comparatively happy with their life-styles, Jack Timmons craved the things that the upper-middle-class tenants in the building had. He was too honest to steal and, by his own admission, not really smart enough to earn more than he was presently making. A frustrating state of affairs for a twenty-eight-year-old who had greater expectations from life.

The key was going to be worth twenty thousand dollars to him, and it was beginning to burn a hole in his pocket.

He was thinking about how he would spend his money, when a hand on his shoulder turned his thoughts to prison.

"Shamrock," said the policeman whose hand rested on his shoulder.

"Jesus," Timmons said. "I thought I was busted."

Duggan smiled. "Key and package."

Timmons handed Duggan the key from his pocket and then walked quickly to the lobby desk and pulled out a suitcase.

"Apartment Twelve-D," he said. "It belongs to some banker's girl friend. She's over in Europe for the summer."

"What time do you get off duty?"

"Eight tonight."

"Good. I'll be out of here before then."

"Ahhhhh . . . I . . ."

"You'll get your money when I leave."

Duggan walked toward the elevators. The doors opened and two children exited with skateboards. They stared at the policeman who brushed past them. They were still looking over their shoulders when they bumped into Timmons at the door.

"What's going down?" the ten-year-old girl asked.

"Who's getting busted?" her seven-year-old brother asked.

"You kids watch too much television. Just something to do with a stolen-car report."

The kids shrugged and walked outside. Timmons continued to think about what he would do with his money.

Command Central

Command Central was deserted except for Inspector Conrad and Commissioner Hamlin. The siege was over and the operation was shut down until the next city crisis.

"We have the street blocked off to all traffic except police and FBI personnel. The dealers are working with the detectives to try and piece together what's missing and who belongs to what."

"What about the tunnels?" Hamlin asked.

"They're sealed and guarded, both of them."

"Anything from the arrests at the hotel?"

"Lots of pending lawsuits."

The commissioner frowned. Just what the city needed, more lawsuits. "How about the McGraw-Hill situation?"

"They've cleaned up the mess. It was brutal," Conrad said. "Only two of the Berets and five of the blacks are expected to pull through."

"Carter?"

"A piece of glass cut off his head."

Hamlin sighed and shook his head. "Poor bastard."

"The bottom line is, did we get them all, and are there any diamonds missing?"

"We lost one on Fifth in the breakout. We're not sure about the hotel, but Hugh McBride thinks we missed one, and I think he's right. McGraw-Hill? I don't think anybody made it out of that slaughterhouse."

"Why does McBride think one got away from the hotel?" Hamlin asked.

"The dead cop's uniform is missing. Two of the terrorists had diamonds; the one that made it back to the hotel didn't have any. Where are the diamonds? Where is the cop's uniform?"

"Out the door, down the street, and God knows where by now."

"That's about it," Conrad answered. "McBride wants us to check with the officers guarding the street to see if anyone in uniform left."

"Follow it up. Give him any help he needs. It's his worry now. We've made it through this time. We'll take a look at the street, hold a press conference, and then pass the buck to the FBI."

"What do you think the IRA will do if they get those diamonds out of the country?" Hamlin asked.

"We both know what they'll do. They'll turn Northern Ireland into another Lebanon and England into an island of bomb craters."

Upper 5th Avenue

Hugh McBride was depressed when he left the senator's apartment building. It always upset him to see a man cry.

The news of his son's death stunned the senator, but

sorrow quickly turned to anger, then hatred. O'Leary gave a detailed description of both Logan and Duggan along with a personal promise to give any possible help.

McBride now knew for sure that Michael Duggan had escaped and probably had the bulk of the diamonds. He also knew that after much posturing and bullshit he would be assigned to get Duggan. And he would do it, as always, his way.

Waldorf-Astoria

Miranda's mother walked into the sitting room of her suite and looked at the small figure curled up asleep on the couch. She placed a blanket over her daughter and smoothed the auburn hair away from the young woman's face.

"You are a beauty, my love." She smiled as she studied her daughter's delicate features, then she picked up some of the eight-by-ten glossies that Miranda had spread out on the marble table. She studied the pictures carefully. Like her daughter she had a trained eye for detail, but a mind trained to calculate future implications as well. And the future promised trouble that would reach much further than just the Manhattan siege. The large woman sat down with a small notebook and started jotting notes in a shorthand that was legible only to her.

East 82nd Street

The police car dropped Sean O'Keefe in front of his building. He waved his bandaged hand to the doorman, who ran to push the elevator button for him.

"Glad you're okay, Mister O'Keefe. Me and the family lit candles for you."

Sean was not aware that he had become a celebrity after his picture had appeared in the newspaper. He smiled at the gray-haired man in the green uniform. Al had been his doorman through a marriage, divorce, and a change of careers.

"Were those guys really Irish, Mister O'Keefe?"

"As Paddy's pig."

"God, that's terrible, but I bet it was the blacks that put 'em up to it."

The Irish could do no wrong according to Al.

"Who knows Al . . . who knows?"

When Sean arrived at his door he could hear the phone ringing in his apartment. In his haste to get in he grabbed the doorknob and cursed as the pain from his hand shot up his arm.

Once inside he was immediately attacked lovingly by a spindly-legged dog of mixed origins. The dog leaped into Sean's arms and started licking his face. "Okay, Dog . . . enough."

Sean had done a story on animal shelters and ended up with Dog. He had not really wanted a dog, but the thought of the mutt ending up in a garbage heap had prompted him to bring her home. Sean was very seldom home, and the care and walking was delegated to a boy down the hall who probably spent more time in Sean's apartment than Sean did.

The phone stopped ringing. Sean put Dog on a stack of newspapers that had been delivered but never read. He picked up the top newspaper and stared at the picture on the front page. It was a picture of him carrying Zimmerman off the street.

"Shit, how did they get that shot?" he muttered.

The phone rang again and he picked it up. It was the station manager gushing about Sean's publicity and how the station planned to promote it to the advertisers. Sean slammed the phone receiver down and walked over to the couch in his small living room and lay down.

"Fuck 'em. Right, Dog?"

Dog jumped up and curled under Sean's arm. The phone started to ring again, but Sean didn't hear it. He was sound asleep after two days without sleep. Dog stared at the phone, barked at it, and then snuggled into Sean's body and went to sleep, too.

East 86th Street

Duggan stuffed the money belts with the diamonds into the suitcase sitting open on the frilly-covered bed. He had showered, shaved, and was now wearing a tailored business suit. He looked like a well-dressed WASP banker.

He had cleaned the apartment so there were no traces of his presence. The woman who rented the apartment must have an interesting sex life, Duggan thought after looking in the bathroom cabinets at numerous gels, stimulants, and devices. These and the Frederick's of Hollywood underwear marked her as a high-priced call girl or a free-lancer with an active imagination. Duggan would have liked to meet her under different circumstances. His sex life had been very limited in New York with the exception of that horse-faced telephone operator he had taken to the swingers club. That had been for the cause, not for himself. He thought about what he had seen at the club. His memories aroused him, and he wiped the thoughts from his mind. He had too much to take care of to get sidetracked now.

In the lobby, Timmons did not recognize Duggan until he handed him the key to the apartment along with an envelope containing twenty thousand dollars.

"Would you get me a cab, please?"

Timmons looked around quickly and stuffed the key and envelope into his pocket. The biggest tip he would ever get for hailing a cab, he thought.

In the cab Duggan checked his watch. Seven thirty.

"The Plaza Hotel, please."

The driver clicked down the meter and headed south on Park Avenue. In one more week Duggan would be back in Ireland with the diamonds, if all went as planned.

13

A mid-Manhattan office building

"What the hell do you mean you want to take a leave of absence," Fred Garthstein, the head of the station's news department, bellowed.

Sean watched the traffic from the window and tried to control his temper. He didn't like Garthstein, never had and never would. Garthstein was a *shmuck*. Smart as hell, but a *shmuck*. Sean turned slowly and sat down on the corner of Garthstein's desk. He knew that Garthstein hated people sitting on his desk. Garthstein's eyes narrowed and he began to tap a pencil nervously on the side of his chair.

"You're trying to annoy me, aren't you, O'Keefe?"

Sean smiled. "Of course."

Garthstein tugged nervously at his beard and ignored Sean's remark. "Let me get this straight, now. You want a leave of absence so you can go off and chase the bad guys, right?"

"Right!"

"And you are going to do what the FBI and the cops can't do?"

"Maybe, maybe not."

"Why?"

"I owe a few people. Zimmerman's dead. Coyle has a hole in his foot, and Cal Long's funeral is tomorrow."

"Who the hell is Cal Long?"

"He was the kid we were training," Sean said, no longer able to contain his annoyance.

"Oh, yeah, the quota kid. Was that his name?"

Sean dug his fingernail into his thumb. He didn't want to lose his job, but he couldn't let that remark pass. "That was his name, you insensitive prick."

Garthstein's tapping increased in tempo. "That's exactly what I am, O'Keefe. And that's why I'm here, to keep you bleeding-heart types from turning the news into a soap opera."

"I . . ."

"Shut up," yelled Garthstein. "I don't give a damn if you like me or not. If you liked me that would only mean I wasn't doing my job. Personally, I don't give a shit if you take off and never come back. *However*, whether I like it or not, you have a draw in the ratings. What happened on Forty-seventh Street will make you an even bigger draw."

"What if I quit?"

"You can't. Your contract runs another year. *However*, if this little crusade of yours could somehow benefit the station . . ."

"For example," Sean asked coldly.

"Sign a contract for another year."

Sean scowled and turned back to the window. "And I suppose you just happen to have a contract all drawn up."

Garthstein dropped his pencil, opened the desk drawer, and pulled out a multipaged contract which he shoved across the desk.

Without turning around, Sean reached back and picked up the document. He walked toward the door and paused briefly, his back toward Garthstein.

"I'll have my lawyer look it over."

"You do that, O'Keefe. As soon as it's signed, you can go play cops and robbers."

Sean started to close the door behind him.

"Oh, by the way, O'Keefe, we don't pay you when you're on a leave of absence."

Sean slammed the door.

Garthstein leaned back in his chair and smiled as he picked up the telephone.

"Grace, get Kupperman on the phone."

He hung up and walked over to the window that overlooked the building entrance two floors below. He saw Sean hail a cab, and he smiled to himself again. The phone rang. He walked back and picked it up.

"Good news, Mister Kupperman. I'm sure O'Keefe will go for another year. That's right, sir. Well, the guy looks on me as a father figure. He knew I was looking after his best interests. Thank you, sir."

Garthstein laughed out loud as he hung up the phone and contemplated the bonus he would be getting for convincing Sean to sign for another year.

New York City

Sean tossed the contract on the seat of the cab and momentarily debated tearing it up and tossing it out the window. That wouldn't do any good. Garthstein would just type up another. No, he'd be smarter to give it to his lawyer. Sean wasn't opposed to staying with the station for another year, it was just the way Garthstein had gone about it. He liked the work and the station. The recent publicity could probably help him land a network spot, but he wasn't sure that was what he wanted. He really wasn't that ambitious. He just wanted to do something that interested him and provided some excitement. TV paid well, but the money, at the moment, was only helpful in keeping his creditors and ex-wife off his back.

Hey, ain't you the guy that was all over the papers . . . yeah, the TV guy?"

Sean glanced at the driver's picture and name through the plastic safety partition. Alan R. Goldberg.

"That's me," Sean mumbled. "And I bet you're Alan R. Goldberg, the famous taxi driver."

Goldberg looked into his rearview mirror and grinned. "O'Keefe . . . Sean O'Keefe, right?"

"Right," O'Keefe grunted.

"Yeah, I've caught your newscast a few times. You're not bad. You don't get too cute, like some of those other guys. You used to be a cop, too, right?"

"Right again," Sean relaxing a bit.

"I used to be a brain surgeon," Goldberg said glancing into the mirror to catch Sean's reaction.

Sean sat up, peered through the partition and laughed. He and Goldberg spent the remainder of the trip trying to outdo one another with tall tales of their adventures and misadventures on the New York sidewalks.

When the cab pulled up to Sean's East Eighty-seventh Street apartment building Sean pulled out a ten-dollar bill and slid it into the change tray.

"Keep the change, Al."

"Hey that's more than a six-buck tip."

"Are you complaining?"

"Hell, no."

"Believe me, the trip was worth it. I needed that bullshit session just to get my head straight. It loosened me up better than a Swedish massage."

"Hey, if you ever get my cab again I'll tell you the story about a massage parlor downtown that will blow your mind." Goldberg reached into his jacket and pulled out a smudged business card. "I work radio pickups. Anytime you're in the mood and I'm in the neighborhood ask the dispatcher to give me a holler."

Sean took the card and dropped it into his jacket pocket.

"That's really nice of you, Al."

"So what's nice? You're a big tipper."

Sean said good-bye and headed into his building. He waved to the doorman, who didn't see him because his nose was buried in the *National Enquirer*. Sean's eyes sparkled at the thought that popped into his head.

"Lady, for God's sake . . . put your clothes back on. You can't walk through the lobby like that."

The doorman's eyes shot up from his paper in anticipation. He scowled good-naturedly as he saw Sean waving from the elevator as the door closed.

Sean tossed his jacket on the dining room table which was stacked with unread magazines, newspapers, and a few dirty plates. He looked around the junk-laden living room. It was a visual disaster. Maybe, he thought ruefully, it was time for his monthly cleanup attempt. Even a slob has some standards!

Dog came running in through a doggie entrance cut into the terrace door. She saw her master and went into yelps of delight, urinating slightly on the carpet as she ran and jumped into Sean's outstretched arms. Sean had learned the hard way that it was better to let her jump into his arms than to hit him full force in the groin with her paws. The thin brown and white dog immediately sat in the bend of his arm like a small child. "How have you been, Dog . . . miss me?"

Dog started to lick his face. "Cut it out. Did anyone call?"

The dog cocked her head. "Not talking, huh? I'd better check the service." He put Dog down and she ran after a cockroach which was her favorite sport.

"Kill," Sean shouted encouragingly, but the roach outran Dog by a good foot and slithered under the refrigerator.

"Fast little bastards." He dialed his service. "O'Keefe here, put Sarah on."

"You okay, Sean," asked a concerned voice after a moment's silence. Sean smiled when he heard her voice. Sarah Franklin was a large black woman with one of the greatest faces in the world. He knew what she looked like because he had gone to the answering service office to find out.

Sarah had been his operator for two years. They sent each other Christmas cards. Sean considered her a friend . . . even close to family.

"Sarah, I could have sworn I saw you turning tricks down on Lexington Avenue. You're not moonlighting on me, are you?"

There was a rich throaty laugh on the other end of the phone. "You're bad, Sean O'Keefe, bad."

"You better believe it, too bad to be let loose with a foxy lady like you for more than a couple minutes."

"All talk and no action. You Irish honkies are all the same." There was a pause. "Are you okay, Sean? I saw that picture in the newspaper."

"You and everyone else in the western world. I'm okay. Still a little uptight. How are things with you?"

"Got mugged the other day."

"Jesus."

"Oh, I'm okay. The mugger isn't in great shape. I shoved a hat pin up his nose."

"Good for you."

"You've had a lot of calls."

"My wife's lawyer, right?"

"Right."

"Anyone important?"

"Fred Klein from the *Daily News*."

"He wants a story."

"Your personal banker."

"I'm probably overdrawn."

"A man from the FBI, an Agent McBride."

"What did he want?"

"Don't know. He said it was important that you call him. He called twice."

Sean grabbed a pencil and an envelope from a pile of unpaid bills. Sarah gave him McBride's number. He thanked her, made kissing sounds into the phone and hung up.

Sean had seen McBride a few times when he was a uniformed cop. He had been impressed. McBride always seemed to take time to chat with the foot cops. And he never talked down to them.

He dialed McBride's number and waited for the operator to connect him.

"McBride here."

"O'Keefe here."

"I hear you want to join the chase."

"Where'd you hear that?"

"I talked to your news director when I couldn't get you."

"Mister Warmth?"

"He told me you were going to go it alone."

"Right."

"Wrong."

"Why wrong?"

"You're going to be working with me."

"That's nice to know. How much are you paying?"

"Nothing."

"You sound like Garthstein. Why should I work with you?"

"You might get a piece of the reward. Ben Levi just made the announcement from the hospital."

Sean smiled broadly. "I'm glad to hear he's okay. I knew that tough old Jew would make it, God love him. How many got away and with how much?"

"As far as we can tell just one. The take was big. Probably a billion, maybe more."

"How big is the reward?" Sean asked.

"Ten percent of all that's recovered. Could be enough to buy that TV station of yours and fire that clown I talked to earlier."

"I've already thought of that. Only I wouldn't fire the bastard, I'd make him sweat day by day. Do you have any idea who got away?"

"We think it's the main man," McBride answered.

"I want a piece of him."

"So do I, but I want to get those diamonds back before they cause a lot of people a lot of grief. Why don't you meet me on Forty-seventh in about an hour, and I'll fill you in on the rest of the details."

"I'll be there," Sean said.

He hung up and reached down to pat Dog. "How'd you like to be owned by a millionaire, Dog?" She gazed at him adoringly and rolled over, presenting her stomach to be scratched.

New Scotland Yard

Chief Superintendent John McCann and Chief Inspector Peter Stewart of the special branch in charge of antiterrorist activity were discussing the disappointing recruitment of black officers. They were also worried about the continuing number of police resignations.

"It's bloody discouraging, Peter."

"It's part of the times, John."

The intercom buzzed and McCann picked it up.

"There's an Agent McBride from the FBI in New York who wishes to speak with you, sir."

"McBride? Oh, yes, he was the chap who helped us on that art theft case. Put him on."

"McBride. How are you, old man?"

McBride's voice sounded like it was coming through a pipe.

"Fine, chief superintendent. I'd like some help from you fellows if possible."

McCann smiled at his chief inspector. "Always glad to help the FBI."

"Did you hear about the big diamond thing over here?"

"Our newspapers are having a field day with it. We've even increased security in our diamond district. Is it true the terrorists were Irish?"

"It's true."

"Could mean a big problem for us down the road."

"Quite possible. Could you check a couple of people out for us . . . a Michael Duggan and a Dennis Logan?"

"Certainly. We'll run them through our new computer and see what pops out."

"I don't suppose you could spare one of your men from the criminal intelligence branch?"

"Mmmmm. C-eleven is up to their proverbial ears right now with restaffing."

"Budget cuts?"

"Unfortunately, yes. Hold on a minute . . ." McCann smiled and winked at Stewart as he covered the phone with his hand. "Stewart, be a good chap and have Maudie check and see if Smythe-Houghton is in New York."

Stewart grinned. "I'll get right on it." He got up and left the room.

"Hello, McBride. You may be in luck. We have a chief inspector, no less, in your fair city I think. Used to be in C-eleven, but is working in the special reserve squad now."

"I really could use the help. Especially if he has some idea about the Irish operations."

McCann and McBride exchanged compliments on past cases along with police gossip. Stewart returned and handed McCann a piece of paper with writing on it. McCann smiled broadly.

"Luck of the Irish, as they say. Chief Inspector

Smythe-Houghton is on holiday in New York. Staying at your Waldorf-Astoria Hotel. I hear it's a very nice place."

There was a pause. "So do I, chief superintendent. It's a little out of my price range."

"Mine, too, I would imagine. Smythe-Houghton has independent means."

"Is he a good man?"

Now there was a pause from McCann. "Excellent, perhaps a bit eccentric, but aren't we all. Anyway we'll check out those names for you and send them right out."

"Thank you. If I can do anything for you . . . just give me a call in New York."

"I most certainly will. If you manage to nab those Irish fellows it will save us quite a bit of grief over here."

The two exchanged good-byes and McCann hung up.

Maudie Brown, sitting outside the chief inspector's office, stopped typing a personnel request and leaned her head toward McCann's door. She heard the sound of laughter inside; something she hadn't heard around here in months. Well, the poor lambs deserved a good laugh every now and then.

47th Street

All the windows on the street floors were boarded up and the glass had been swept from the street and checked for any loose stones. Only police vehicles, detectives, FBI agents, and dealers who could identify themselves to a committee at the barricades were allowed on the street.

Sid Fine was on the Fifth Avenue corner with two other men as Sean pulled up in a cab. Sid grabbed Sean in a big bear hug. "Sean, I heard you nearly got yourself killed. I saw the picture of you in the Vegas paper. I coulda bawled." He looked at Sean's bandaged hands. "They tortured you?"

Sean shook his head. "No, just tried to blow me and the rest of the hostages up."

"Bastards!"

"How bad were you hit, Sid?"

"Picked clean. All the street-level stuff was dumped in those mail carts. It'll take months to sort out . . . some of us will get richer . . . some poorer."

"I can't figure why they didn't dump the real stuff on the avenues instead of that junk jewelry," Sean said.

"That many diamonds might flood the market price. Not in the long run, but at first. If they wanted to fence the diamonds here in the city, they'd have to stand in line to do it."

"Makes sense."

Sid started to laugh. "You know those bastards did do us one favor with that junk jewelry. The stuff was really good. So good, in fact, we traced it back to the source . . . I should say the cops did. It was a phony jewel operation that's been operating around here. From what I hear the terrorists cleaned out their stock."

"How'd the cops pick up on the connection?"

"The stupid *shmucks* tried to claim it back from the police. They called some of our people, and they recognized a couple of the jerks. So the cops make them sign all sorts of things that the phony rocks belong to them. They sign, and the cops bust them on the spot."

"Beautiful."

"Nickels and dimes really, but a pain in the ass."

"What about the insurance on the real stuff?"

"Sure there's insurance, but who wants money when they can have diamonds. It's like offering to swap a book of matches for a Tiffany gold lighter."

"You heard the terrorists were Irish?"

Sid nodded. "And the *momzer* on the inside was a Jew, and the rest were black . . . pricks are pricks."

"So there was an inside man. I figured there was. Anybody make him?"

"Name's Katz. He got kicked off the street for screwing a couple of brokers."

"How'd the Irish get hold of him?"

"I heard he was into an Irish shy, but can't swear to it."

A police officer came up to Sean and Sid. "Mister O'Keefe, Agent McBride is in the vault at building fifteen. He asked me to bring you down when you got here."

Sean said good-bye to Sid and followed the policeman. "How'd you know who I was?"

"I recognized you from the picture in the paper."

Sean scowled. "I'd like to find that son of a bitch who took my picture and ram his camera where the sun don't shine."

They took the elevator to the vault in the basement. A cop was guarding the door and there were two more inside. Sean gave a low whistle when he saw the twisted metal of the steel doors.

McBride and some of the dealers were in front of the diamond cabinets. When he saw Sean he excused himself and came forward with his hand out.

"O'Keefe, I'm glad you're here."

"I really don't know why I'm here. How can I help?"

"I'm putting together a team to work on this."

"Unpaid, of course."

"Of course, except for out-of-pocket expenses."

"And how do you attract people, your warmth and lovable personality?"

"Hardly. I play on anything I can. Ego, pride, patriotism, greed, friendship . . . you name it."

"And what's my motive for being part of this?"

"Anger."

"Not the reward?"

"That's a bonus."

Sean walked over to the diamond cabinet and looked into the top drawer, which was open.

"They left all these?"

One of the men nodded. "They took only the best. They knew what they wanted."

"What's the bottom-line total?"

"Maybe a couple of billion . . . maybe more," said one of the men.

"Easily fenced?"

"Many, yes. Some more difficult, but possible."

McBride motioned to Sean. "Let's grab a quick cup of coffee. Then I've got to go over to the Waldorf. I want to talk to another possible member of the team."

"What's the guy's reason for helping you?"

"I'll find that out when I meet him."

"What's he do?"

"Scotland Yard."

"And staying at the Waldorf? They must pay pretty well over there."

"Independently wealthy."

"On the take, maybe."

"I don't think so."

"Would it matter to you?"

"Not in the slightest," McBride said.

14

A 47th Street deli

Sean and McBride walked into the same deli the hostages had used during the siege.

"O'Keefe . . . O'Keefe!" The voice came from the deli owner who had fed the hostages. The heavy man leaned against the counter with his hand extended.

Sean smiled and grabbed the man's beefy hand. "Hey, how you doin'? Still giving away free food?"

"For you it's on the house!"

Sean's face reddened. "Hey, I was only kidding. I wasn't putting the bite on you."

"What's to bite? If it weren't for you and the cop grabbing those fuses I'd be a pile of chopped liver in the middle of the street. Anything you want is on the house, that goes for your friend, too." He nodded to McBride.

Sean suddenly remembered that he hadn't eaten in a while. He ordered a corned beef sandwich. McBride did the same.

"You fellas go grab a seat. I'll bring it to you personally."

Sean looked around as they walked to an open table in the back. There were a few Hasidim, but the majority of the patrons were cops and FBI agents. A strange contrast to his last visit, he thought.

They sat down and a waiter immediately brought them two cups of hot coffee.

McBride leaned back and stared hard at O'Keefe. "Okay, you've got questions, so get 'em off your chest."

"How'd you know that I had questions?"

"I could hear your brain churning the minute you walked into the vault."

"Okay, I have questions."

"As long as it's off the record."

"Fair enough. Let's start with you."

"Fair enough," McBride answered.

Sean was about to speak when the owner came over with two of the largest, leanest corned beef sandwiches Sean had ever seen.

"Are these corned beef sandwiches, or what?" the manager said proudly.

Sean raised an eyebrow. "They look lean enough, but they're kind of puny, aren't they?"

The manager roared with laughter. "That's because you *goyim* are such light eaters. I even put it on white bread for you."

"You didn't cut off the crusts?" Sean asked.

They all laughed and the manager walked back to the counter with a satisfied grin on his face.

"All right, for openers, tell me how the hell you get away with bringing in non-Bureau people. That must put a lot of noses out of joint."

McBride smiled slightly. He was remembering the charade he and Kelly had pulled off at police headquarters. In public or at an official function they would always appear to be at odds about McBride's methods of operation. It was really all an act for Washington.

"This definitely has to be off the record," McBride insisted.

Sean nodded.

"You know that Kelly is a recent appointment to the New York office."

"Right. He's been reshaping the Bureau operation

here. No more chasing radicals or bank robbers. The order of the day is to go after organized crime and white-collar rip-offs," Sean said.

"And it's about time too. But with the majority of agents going after our domestic criminals, we're very shorthanded on the subversive end. Kelly is no fool. He knows there was a lot of bullshit in the past, but he also knows there are very real dangers from extremists on both sides of the fence. We had a good example of that day before yesterday."

"I'd say that was a pretty good example."

"Well, Kelly brought me back to New York from Los Angeles. I only have a handful of agents under me, but they're damn good and have lots of street smarts."

"And when you need some outside help the man looks the other way."

"That's it, and that's why I'm here in New York, at least until retirement."

"Is the cut still fifty-five?"

"Five years from now, in case that was your next question."

"It was."

The waiter came over and refilled their coffee cups, smiled at the sight of the empty plates, and left to report to the manager that the sandwiches had been a success.

"What's being done to catch that guy that got away, or even find out who the hell he is?"

McBride took a sip of coffee. "That's a tough one. If it had been Puerto Ricans, Arabs, Russians, Chinese, blacks, Cubans, or even Croats we would have had a handle on them. But Irish? Who the hell would have ever thought the Irish would pull off something like this?"

"That's what he said."

"Who?"

"The one that got away."

"Duggan."

Sean scowled at McBride. "You didn't tell me you had a name."

"You didn't ask."

"Don't stroke me, McBride."

"I'm not. It's just a name so far, nothing more."

"Are you sure?"

McBride finished his coffee. "I won't kid you, Sean, this is going to be a tough one. This guy Duggan is smart. For all we know he could be out of the country now, and we're just getting started at zero."

"I guess I don't have to tell you that Duggan has big plans for those diamonds."

McBride just nodded and finished Sean's coffee. "Let's get over to the Waldorf and check out Smythe-Houghton. Maybe between the three of us we can get a handle on Duggan."

Upper East Side

It had been a busy day for Michael Duggan. He had left parcels of diamonds with his three unsuspecting operatives. One in Manhattan. One in Staten Island. One in Queens.

He checked his watch as he left the hotel across the street from the Metropolitan Museum where he had been posing as just another young business executive. Two o'clock. His bus for upstate New York would be leaving in an hour. He hailed a cab and got in. As he traveled down Fifth Avenue he glanced to his left as he passed Sixty-fifth Street and wondered if anyone had found the policeman's uniform that he had dumped in the alley after he left the woman's apartment.

Duggan leaned back and closed his eyes. He was glad to be getting out of New York City for a while. He needed to relax. It would be good to return to a familiar place. A place that held fond memories from his childhood. It would be a pleasure trip even if he had some more business to take care of.

Waldorf-Astoria

McBride and O'Keefe walked the short distance to the Waldorf. McBride noticed a flag of one of the Arab countries hanging over the entrance on Park Avenue.

"Looks like some Arab big shot is at the hotel."

"He probably bought it," Sean said caustically.

McBride found the thought amusing, but too much of a possibility to rate a smile.

The two men went directly to the desk, making their way through a group of conventioneers from one of the big national social fraternities.

"Reminds me of college days," Sean said.

McBride edged his way to the desk and moved ahead of two men with fraternity badges on their coats who were trying to convince the desk cleark to join them for a drink.

"Excuse me," McBride interrupted. "Would you please ring Chief Inspector Smythe-Houghton and say that Agent McBride of the FBI and Mister O'Keefe are here and would like to come up if it's convenient?"

"Hey," one of the tipsy fraternity men pointed at Sean. "You're the guy carrying the stiff in the diamond thing. I saw your picture in the paper in Topeka."

Jesus, I even made the front page in Kansas, Sean thought. "Yeah, that was me."

"You still involved in that thing?"

"Indirectly."

"Don't quote me on this," the man looked around to see if anyone was listening, "but I don't think that was an Irish thing."

"No?"

"The Jews did it for the insurance."

McBride turned to face the two men, noted Sean's expression and intervened quickly.

"What's your name, mister?" he asked.

"Mahoney, what's it to you?"

"You staying here?"

"Yeah, so what?"

"We might just want to talk to you."

"Who the fuck are you?"

McBride smoothly pulled out his identification. "FBI. If you have any concrete information about the robbery I'll want to talk to you."

"I don't know anything, it was just an opinion."

McBride looked around quickly and lowered his voice. "I would keep a low profile on your opinions here. This place is a hotbead of Israeli agents. Do you get my drift?"

"God," the man whispered. "They're everywhere."

"Even in the FBI."

"No shit?" The man turned to his friend. "Come on, Mike, let's go to the bar. Thanks for the warning . . . Mister—?"

"Finkelstein," McBride said.

The man frowned and O'Keefe laughed. McBride took O'Keefe's arm and led him toward the elevators.

"You've got a pretty good sense of humor, McBride."

"I do not. I figured it would appeal to yours, and I wouldn't have to waste time breaking up a fight."

They took the elevator to the twentieth floor and headed toward the inspector's suite. Loud rock music could be heard inside. McBride looked quizzical. Sean laughed. "Obviously you don't share the inspector's great taste in music," he said. McBride grimaced and knocked loudly on the door.

An amazon of a woman in her early fifties greeted them. She was tall but very lean and muscular, with piercing green eyes, and jet-black hair sprinkled with a few wisps of gray. She wore a suede pants suit and Gucci boots. She had very little makeup on and her skin was in better condition than many women half her age.

"Mrs. Smythe-Houghton?" McBride asked hesitantly.

"That's right. Come in, I've been expecting you."

"You have?" McBride asked. His confusion was apparent.

The woman moved gracefully into the suite's sitting room. Rock music blared from a portable stereo. McBride raised his eyebrows as he looked at it. The woman anticipated his thoughts.

"Sorry for the dreadful music. I met that group at a party in Soho and wanted to hear if they were as strange on record as they were in person."

"And are they?" Sean asked.

"I'd call it a tie, Mister O'Keefe."

"Don't tell me. You recognized me from the picture in the newspaper."

"Partially."

"I'd love to get my hands on the guy who took that picture. I don't like the notoriety."

"I'm sorry that my photo has created problems for you, Mister O'Keefe."

Sean and McBride turned toward the unseen voice just as a black swivel chair spun around to face them. A young woman rose from the chair, smiled, and walked toward both men with her hand outstretched.

"This is my daughter, Miranda," Mrs. Smythe-Houghton said.

She was a petite version of her mother, with long black hair, large green eyes, and a smashing, lean figure. She wore a light blue silk shirt that accentuated her full firm breasts, and a pair of tight jeans.

Sean felt slightly dazed as he shook her hand. She was one of the most beautiful women he'd ever seen.

"You took that picture?" he asked.

"Yes." She smiled at him. "I hope you won't hold it against me. It's one of my best shots."

Sean and Miranda edged toward a corner of the room, talking quietly, while McBride turned to Mrs. Smythe-Houghton. He had a very uncomfortable feeling that he knew the answer to the question he was about to ask her. "Your husband isn't here?"

"I wish he were, but the poor dear is in London, working."

McBride cleared his throat. "I . . . then you're . . ."

"Inspector Smythe-Houghton? Yes, didn't McCann tell you?"

She laughed, a rich bawdy laugh that was neither raucous nor cheap. "He does love to play tricks on people every now and then. But I'm sure it doesn't matter to you that I'm a woman. You Americans are much more progressive than our rather staid English gentlemen."

McBride's face reddened slightly. "Well, I . . . I mean I . . ."

"Oh, dear, I guess you're not as progressive as I thought. Well, no matter, dear heart. We'll work it out once we get into this case of yours. Please sit down, and I'll fill you in on what I've come up with so far."

Come up with so far? McBride didn't like the sound of that. He could feel the investigation slipping out of his control. He was a man who could strike fear in his supervisors with only a few words, and now a middle-aged woman was taking over. He tried to recover lost ground.

"Just a moment, chief inspector . . ."

"Please, Hugh, let's use our Christian names. Mine's Harriet. I'm not one to pull rank."

McBride wasn't sure who outranked whom but he wasn't about to press the point. Things weren't going according to plan. His team now consisted of a large pushy female and a formerly smart cop turned reporter, whose brain appeared to be addled by Harriet's attractive daughter.

McBride sat hesitantly while Harriet motioned Sean and Miranda to join them on the couch. She was about to speak when a box on the desk buzzed. It was a conference-call speaker phone. Harriet clicked the switch. "Yes."

"Overseas call, chief inspector," the operator said. "It's Sir Arthur from London."

Harriet smiled. "Would you be so kind as to give my dear husband a transoceanic kiss for me, and tell him I'm in conference? I'll call him later."

There was a pause. "Ah . . . yes, of course."

"Thank you so much." She clicked off the speaker and smiled charmingly at McBride. "My husband is in the middle of a new novel. He probably wanted to chew around a few plot ideas with me."

Sean's gaze left Miranda. "Is your husband Sir Arthur Smythe-Houghton, the mystery writer?"

"One and the same."

"Gee, I've read all his books. He's terrific."

Gee? Terrific? Jesus, McBride thought. O'Keefe not only is addlebrained over the daughter, he's flipped over the father, too.

"Now," Harriet said, "how can I be of service to you, Hugh, dear?"

McBride glanced at Sean who had turned his attention back to Miranda. He looked back at Harriet Smythe-Houghton, who was giving him her most feminine smile.

I'm going to kick that limey bastard McCann's ass right over his ears if I ever see him again, McBride thought as he gripped the arms of his chair and tried to smile.

15

Upper East Side

Hugh McBride sat at his kitchen table, toying absentmindedly with his empty coffee cup. He hadn't said a word in over twenty minutes and he had neglected his regular morning exercise routine. His wife, Rose, watched him as she poured herself a second cup of coffee.

"What's wrong, Hugh?" she asked finally.

"Do you think I'm a male chauvinist?"

"Yes."

"Do you think I would resent working with a woman?"

"Yes. I don't think you really believe that women aren't as capable as men. But you've worked for too many years only with men. What's Harriet like?"

"Big, as tall as I am. English. A chief inspector no less."

"Attractive?"

"Jealous?"

"Of course, but curious, too."

Rose McBride was Hugh's sounding board. She was one of the few people in the world he could talk to about his emotions and fears without feeling awkward. They had been married, very happily, for twenty-seven years. They were both extremely loyal and devoted to one another and to their four children, all of whom were in college. They were very different, but their differences complemented their marriage and drew them closer together. Hugh and their two sons were serious and rather withdrawn. All were very athletic, but they excelled in individual sports like tennis, swimming, and track. None were team players.

Rose was friendly, outgoing, and creative. She had a good sense of humor and enjoyed being with people. Her two daughters were very much like her.

"She might be a broadening experience for you, Hugh. Is she smart?"

"Very, and very buttoned up in her own erratic way. She had the prime minister on the phone, called her by her first name. She convinced her that if the Irish get those diamonds to Ireland it would mean big trouble for England. She spent most of the time we were there on the phone. I think she has every department in Scotland Yard on this except the mounted patrol."

"Do you like her?"

"I think so. It's hard not to. God knows I've tried."

"I'm sure you did, Hugh," his wife said with a smile.

"That reporter, O'Keefe, is going to be a dead loss."

"I thought you decided that he would be perfect."

"He was, but Chief Inspector Smythe-Houghton's daughter has turned him into a boob."

Rose was about to say something when the doorbell rang.

"Who in the hell can that be at seven in the morning? Why didn't the doorman ring?"

Rose went to the door and opened it. Harriet Smythe-Houghton stood there with a gigantic bouquet of roses.

"Roses for you, Rose." She handed them to the attractive smaller woman. "I'm sure Hugh has described me fully. I'm Harriet, the other woman in his life."

"Well, as long as you keep bringing beautiful flowers like this you can have him."

Both women laughed, liking each other immediately.

Harriet glided into the room. "Hugh, dear heart, hate to barge in on you at such an early hour, but I've set up a few appointments for us today, and we're already a little behind schedule."

Appointments? "I don't recall asking you to set up any appointments," McBride growled.

"I'll fill you in on the way. I have a limo waiting." She glanced at her watch then opened the door for him.

McBride held his temper in check and managed to answer calmly.

"I think I'll call O'Keefe and see if he wants to come."

"Oh, he and Miranda were up at the crack of dawn. They've gone to the Catskill Mountains."

"What?" McBride exploded. "O'Keefe is supposed to be helping me."

"He is, dear heart. Inspector Conrad called after you left. I took the information. It seemed a shame to call you at home. You've been so busy, I thought you could use the rest."

"Madam," McBride said tightly, "I'm perfectly capable of determining when I need rest. Good Lord, next you'll try to control my bowel movements."

Harriet was slightly taken aback by his anger. "You're quite right, Hugh. It was presumptuous of me, but do hurry. We have a busy day ahead."

This woman is going to drive me back to cigarettes, McBride thought as he grabbed his coat and stormed out the door toward the elevators at the far end of the hall.

"Oh my, I get the feeling that I have been a bit overbearing."

"A bit," Rose said. "Do you mind some advice, Harriet?"

"I'd welcome it."

"Take him on woman to man and things will work out

fine. If he decides he's going to take you on man to man, you'll both lose."

"You're a very observant woman, Rose."

"I live with a very complex person. A very good person, but not the easiest person to understand. Don't jump to any conclusions about him."

"I'm usually good at figuring out what makes people tick. I've certainly failed with your husband, and I'm very embarrassed about that."

"Hugh's strong point is figuring out things, not people. He's also very good about getting people to work with him, not under him, not over him, but with him. If the two of you get your act together, as they say nowadays, you should work well together."

"I think I'd better eat some humble pie."

"But don't overdo it. That would be just as bad."

Harriet nodded, waved and left.

Rose smiled and closed the door. This should be a very interesting situation.

Catskill Mountains

Miranda's body was tired from lack of sleep, but her mind was wide awake and clear. She, Sean, and her mother had stayed up late talking after Hugh McBride had left. Her mother was on and off the phone constantly so most of the talk had been with Sean.

She liked him. He was smart, and he seemed to care about people. He had a sense of humor, but there was loneliness there, too. She knew the feeling.

Sean rubbed the stubble on his face. He should have shaved. He was trying to think of something to say. He always felt at a loss for words when he was around a woman he really liked and didn't know very well.

"Your mother is a very special woman," he finally said.

Miranda nodded. "Very. She and my father are two of the greatest people I know, strange as that may sound."

"Not so strange. It's rather nice actually."

They drove for the next few miles in silence. Miranda studied Sean's profile as he concentrated on the road, wondering how he would respond to her next question.

"Sean, would you like to go out to dinner tonight when we get back? There's a pretty good Italian restaurant in my neighborhood."

There was an awkward pause.

"You aren't hung up about a woman asking you out, are you?"

Sean said no, but his expression said yes.

Miranda laughed softly. "I think you and McBride have a lot in common."

Sean grunted and continued to stare at the road.

"Would you feel better if you asked me to dinner?"

"Yes."

"Okay."

"Would you like to go out to dinner tonight?"

"Sorry, I can't. I already have a date."

Sean did a double take, then started to laugh. "Okay, I deserved that."

Miranda's face turned serious. "Look, Sean, if I like a man, and he happens to be a little shy, I don't see the point in waiting for him to ask."

"I'm not shy. Awkward maybe, but not shy."

"Your divorce really hurt you a lot, didn't it?"

"That was a hundred years ago."

"Have you been with many women since the breakup?"

"That's a little personal," Sean said uncomfortably.

"Of course, but I'm personally interested in you."

"Okay, Miranda Smythe-Houghton, I'll tell you what I can about myself. I have a hard time sorting out the physical, emotional, and mental parts of a relationship.

I get them all mixed up and can't seem to put it together very well. I went for the physical only once and got burned."

"I did the same, but I got over it."

"Oh?"

"He was married. It happened. It ended."

"Oh," Sean said quietly.

"It disturbs you that I had an affair with a married man?"

"Yes."

"Why?"

"No logical reason, I guess. Just an emotional reaction. I'm a knee-jerk reactionary that way."

Miranda leaned over and kissed him softly on the cheek. "Let's just take it one step at a time and see what happens."

She smelled good. Sean wanted to say something, but didn't know what. The exit sign they wanted loomed up ahead. He turned off the road silently.

"It should be on the left . . . there it is." She pointed to an old limestone building with a small sign reading Sheriff's Office.

Sheriff John Devin got up as Sean and Miranda entered. He was a large stooped man in his late sixties. Besides being sheriff, he had an active apple orchard and feed store.

"Can I help you folks?" he asked. "Say, aren't you the fella in the newspaper picture?"

Sean nodded, but without the anger that usually followed that particular question. "That's right. We're here to follow up on your call to Inspector Conrad in New York."

"But you're not the police."

"I know, but we're working with the FBI on this. You can call Agent McBride at the New York Bureau if you want verification."

"No. I'll take your word for it. Besides, I'm a little embarrassed about this, and talking to another law-enforcement person would make me feel pretty dumb."

"You were smart enough to put two and two together and figure out that you've been suckered, and you have the guts to admit it. If some of our public officials would do that once in a while we'd all be a lot better off."

"That's very kind of you, Mister—?"

"O'Keefe. And this is Miranda Smythe-Houghton."

The sheriff tipped his hat politely to Miranda.

"You want to tell us what happened, sheriff?" Sean asked.

"Well, there's not much to tell, really. These fellas were up in the woods driving trucks around in some sort of maneuver. They were mostly all black, so I got suspicious . . . not because they were black . . . well, maybe . . . but it was just unusual. Anyway, there were these white guys . . . one of them had a beard . . one was a kinda pimply-faced kid . . . a mousy little *guy* . . . and a guy that looked like a young Tyrone Power except his hair wasn't slicked down like that. Real black hair and eyebrows . . . nice-lookin' young man. Anyway he tells me they're making a movie. They had some cameras and stuff, and I believed them. They even took some pictures of me getting in and out of my car. I guess I was kinda stagestruck, like a kid."

"Don't feel bad, sheriff. You should see blasé New Yorkers when a camera's on the street." Sean said.

"Anyway, I saw the TV report on that diamond robbery, and I read about what those trucks did, and it just seemed too much of a coincidence." He looked down at his well-worn shoes. "I thought about not telling anyone, but there were a lot of people killed, and there has to be an accounting for that."

Sean nodded somberly. The sheriff had expressed it

well. Beyond the money . . . there had to be an accounting for those dead people.

"Could you show us the area they used? We'd like to take a look around and get some pictures."

"Sure, it's only about ten miles away. I'll take you over there in my car."

Tire marks marred the remote beauty of the place. Miranda immediately started taking pictures. The sheriff and Sean both watched with fascination as she bent down on one knee to take a shot, putting her well-rounded posterior in the air.

"She sure is well put together, ain't she?"

"She certainly is," Sean agreed.

They spent about an hour checking the area while Miranda took pictures. They looked through the debris that the terrorists had left behind, but Sean decided that the FBI was better equipped to check it out thoroughly. They were the real experts on that sort of thing. He was ready to pack it in when he noticed something catch the reflection of the sun near a pile of rocks. His eyes widened as he went toward it, then narrowed in disappointment as he picked it up.

"What's this stuff, sheriff?"

Devin looked at the crystalline formation Sean had in his hand. He smiled. "Thought you had your hands on a diamond, huh?"

"It crossed my mind for a second."

"Hard rock candy crystals. Nothing but crystal sugar. They make it around here to sell to the tourists' kids."

Sean tossed it back on the ground.

"You think those guys up here were the ones that pulled off that thing in New York?"

"Looks like it's a good possibility."

Miranda straightened up and stretched causing the thin gauze shirt she wore to accentuate her breasts. Both the sheriff and Sean noticed and both blushed when Miranda smiled at them.

"Did you gentlemen find anything interesting?" she asked in a teasing way.

"Other than you, nothing. This should be gone over by the experts."

Miranda suddenly realized that she was very hungry. She hadn't eaten since lunch yesterday. "Sheriff, is there a nice restaurant around here where we could get something to eat?"

"There's one of those big fancy Jewish hotels a few miles away. The food's good."

"Hungry?" Sean asked.

"Starved," Miranda answered.

They got directions to the nearby resort and drove off. Sheriff Devin watched the car disappear down the dirt road. Nice young couple. Probably end up shacking up. That little lady had a body and a half. He felt the cloth in his work pants tighten in the crotch. He looked down to see the first erection he had had in months. "Well, hello there, stranger." He got carefully into his car. "I think I'll just smuggle you back to town and see if Lana at the diner can put you to good use."

16

Upper East Side

Mary Osborne was a proud woman. She wouldn't scrounge the garbage outside the A&P for bits and pieces. She wouldn't borrow money from strangers she knew she would never be able to repay. She wouldn't go on welfare. She wouldn't take food stamps. She'd steal before she would do any of that . . . and steal she did. Nothing grand, a can of stew here, a pair of shoes there, a small bunch of violets to brighten her small drab apartment on the first floor of a decaying building in the east Eighties. But she wouldn't be there much longer. The Irish Resettlement Society had paid for her ticket to Ireland, given her some comfort money, and bought a nice house for her in the free part of Ireland.

For years, Mary Osborne had worked for the state of New York and had managed to put away a little for a savings account and a little for the Irish Relief Fund. Now inflation had gobbled up her pension. What she had was hardly enough to keep body and soul together. She had used up her savings years ago just trying to maintain her dignity. The state could care less. She was just a name on their computerized retirement list. But the Irish, the Irish, God love them, came through. They took care of their own.

She would never have known about the special fund for retired ladies of good character if she hadn't met that nice young man at the Bingo game. He had made all the arrangements, filled out all the papers. She didn't have to do a thing. Such a nice young man that Pat Mahoney. Not like the young men his age in New York. Dirty young men who would urinate in the hall, drink beer on the front stoop, and smoke strange terrible-smelling cigarettes. But he was from the old country and he believed in God and the Virgin Mary, and he looked like Tyrone Power.

She'd finally be rid of the smelly apartment with a sink in the kitchen that doubled as a tub. No more cockroaches. No more screaming, fighting neighbors. She was going to live in a nice little house near the River Shannon. She'd bake fresh cakes for the local children, and she'd be able to share a real turkey dinner with her neighbors at Christmas. She would be able to hold her head up proudly.

Mary Osborne looked around her tiny kitchen at her few paltry possessions: grocery store dishes that she had borrowed, holy pictures, a picture of John and Robert Kennedy, a refrigerator that made disgusting gurgling noises at night, a tarnished tea service, a penny jar, and a cigar box filled with her unreported income from baby-sitting in the big buildings that had sprung up along York Avenue. That was her Bingo money, guarded by her lucky pieces so nothing would happen to it. Not much to show for a hard and lonely life.

She picked up the color picture of her house. It was small, but beautiful with a lovely little garden. She put the picture on top of her airline ticket from Aer Lingus and a manila envelope with her comfort money.

She went into the tiny bedroom, lifted the mattress with some difficulty, placed the three special items on top of her "go visitin' " dress and dropped the mattress back in position.

She took a pack of matches from the top of her dresser near the pictures of some of the children she baby-sat for. She lit a new candle. The flickering candle cast dancing shadows across the picture of the Virgin over her head.

Her seventy-year-old knees cracked as she bent and placed them on the rugless hard linoleum floor. Her small arthritic hands covered her tired lined face and tears trickled between her ringless fingers.

"God bless you, Pat Mahoney . . . God bless you."

New York City

During the limo ride to the post office, McBride and Harriet put their cards on the table.

"Let's get one thing straight from the start, chief inspector. This is my case, and I'll be running the bloody show. That doesn't mean I'll be sitting on you, but I damn well want to know things up front. I hate surprises."

"All right, Hugh, since we're letting our hair down let's get to the heart of the matter. We've both been used to running our own show in the past. We're on your home ground now, so we'll play by your rules."

McBride tried to hide the satisfied look on his face, but didn't do a very good job of it.

"But . . ."

The satisfied look disappeared from McBride's face.

"But . . ." Harriet continued, "I have my own ways of doing things, and I'm too old to change methods now."

"And what is your way?" McBride asked cautiously.

"I can't stand to have someone looking over my shoulder all the time. I think we both have our strong points. Mine is people, figuring them out, drawing them out and making use of something they say or don't say. What's yours?"

McBride had never considered his strong points before. He always thought of himself as an across-the-boards investigator. He thought for a moment. Then took another moment before answering.

"Putting things together, events, actions, reactions—that type of thing."

As the limo pulled up to the post office building on Thirty-fourth Street Harriet had a satisfied smile on her face.

"Our strong points make us a strong team. We might even break this thing with a little luck."

"And what about Sean O'Keefe? Do you know why I picked him, and why he'll be good for the team, as you call it?"

Harriet smiled kindly. "We both know why you picked Sean. Certainly because of his ability and his unique position as a firsthand observer of the takeover, but he has something that neither of us has, Hugh."

"And what's that?"

"Youth. We may both look younger than we are, but that doesn't change the hands on the clock. If I'm not mistaken, Sean has both of our strong points plus youth. That's hard for us to beat."

"It was a mistake to send Sean to the Catskills, Harriet. From what you told me when we left my apartment, the Catskills thing is a good lead, but that area should be covered by experts not amateurs. Sean has good street smarts, and he should use that here in the city."

Harriet nodded in agreement. "You're right. I jumped the gun on that one."

"And while we're talking about Sean, do you think you could have your daughter give him the cold shoulder for a while until we get this thing solved? I want his mind on this case, not Miranda."

Harriet shook her head. "Can't help you there, Hugh. Miranda is her own person, always has been. She likes O'Keefe, and he seems to like her. There's not a thing I can do about that and wouldn't even if I could."

They walked up the long steps to the post office entrance. People from the area were enjoying the warm morning sun on the steps. McBride wished he could join them. He was tired. Maybe just getting old, he thought.

Their business at the post office was routine and McBride hoped it wouldn't turn out to be a dead end. They needed a make on the postal trucks used in the heist and he hoped to get some names of missing postal employees. He had a strong hunch that some of the black foot soldiers were postal workers, and if they were lucky they'd get a make on the black leader who had gotten away.

The Long Island trip might also prove valuable. Conrad had called Harriet late last night with news that the armored trucks had been traced to a firm in Garden City. If they were twice lucky that day they might be able to get some more information about the elusive Michael Duggan.

Upstate

Michael Duggan got off the bus at the small country store that doubled as a bus station. It was on the edge of town. When he had been here as a boy the station was in the center of town, but now it was closer to the new thruway.

The old woman in the store called him a cab, and soon he was headed toward the main part of town. He rode by streets he had known as a kid. They looked about the same. Nice homes, nice people.

The taxi passed the new high school, the city square,

the library, and stopped at the town's only hotel. It was a pleasant-looking brick building across the street from the one movie theater.

He paid the driver, checked in, and went directly to his room on the fourth floor. He turned on the TV set and lay down on the bed. His eyes drooped, closed, and soon he was asleep. The first truly restful sleep he had had in months.

Lower East Side

Sean clumsily shredded a carrot while Miranda busied herself preparing the Italian dinner they had decided to have in her loft apartment. It was a huge airy room divided into sections. The bedroom area had a skylight. The only enclosed rooms were the bathroom and Miranda's darkroom.

From the outside the building looked like the other bleak warehouses in the district. Inside, the tenants, mostly artists, advertising executives and TV producers, had converted the lofts into gorgeous apartments. The only bonafide business was on the floor below Miranda. It was a *yarmulkah* factory that refused to move when the new owners purchased the building.

"How's your appetite?"

"I'm starved," Sean said, and meant it.

Two cut fingers and an hour later they sat down to a small candlelit dinner of pasta, sauce, and salad.

"I hope you enjoy the salad. I spilled blood to make it."

Miranda made a kissing sound with her lips. "Poor baby."

Sean smiled and picked nervously at his salad. Miranda watched him thoughtfully.

"Penny."

He looked up and smiled. "What?"

"Penny for your thoughts."

"Just a bunch of mixed emotions."

They ate in silence while the stereo played string quartet music.

When they had finished, Miranda cleared off the plates and brought coffee from the kitchen. Sean took a sip and looked around the tastefully furnished room filled with antiques, framed numbered lithographs, and many of the pictures that Miranda had taken. The shelves were filled with books that looked as if they'd been read. The whole place had a comfortable lived-in look.

"I feel at home here," Sean said quietly.

Miranda put her hand on his softly. "What's the problem, Sean?"

"You."

She looked hurt and withdrew her hand. Sean, embarrassed, took her hand in his and kissed it gently. "I have a bad habit with you of saying nothing or saying something badly."

"Is it because you think we might be headed for some type of permanent relationship, and you're not ready to handle something like that?"

"No, that's exactly what I do want, but the timing is all off."

"What do you mean?"

Sean got up and walked around the table, pulling her gently to her feet. He drew her closer, with one arm, tilted her head, and kissed her with all the passion that had been building in him since he first saw her. She returned the passion of his kiss. They both felt dazed when they parted.

"I've been wanting to do that ever since I first saw you."

She put her head on his chest and held him closely

with her arms. He stroked her hair gently. She looked up and he kissed her again, less passionately, as if his mind had slipped off somewhere else. Miranda sensed his mood. She drew away, walked over to the couch, and sat down moodily.

Sean began to pace the floor silently, then finally came over and sat next to her. His face had the same expression she had captured in her photo during the takeover. She remembered she had called the picture *Man in Emotional Pain*.

She gently drew his body next to her, cradling his head in her lap, and softly soothed his face with her slender fingers.

"Mixed emotions, you said?"

He nodded sadly. "Miranda, I made myself a promise that I was going to get those creeps who took the street and killed all those people, but I can't get you out of my head. When I'm trying to piece together facts about them, I'm thinking of you. When I'm with you, I'm thinking about them. It's like trying to go in two different directions at once."

"It sounds like you're about to give me the 'A man's got to do what a man's got to do' line."

"It's not that simple, Miranda. I wish it were. I have two medals that say I'm a hero. One from the Marine Corps. One from the New York City Police Department. But I'm no hero. I was at the right spot and I reacted. It's as simple as that."

"But the street takeover is past history, and you reacted bravely. Why not just let the whole thing drop?"

"I can't. People that I knew and cared about were killed, and if those creeps had their way both I and the rest of the hostages would also be dead. You know why we were to be blown up? A diversionary tactic to give them more time to get away. That stinks."

"I agree, but . . ."

"One guy got away. He was the one that called all the shots. Right now he has more diamonds than any man in the world. If he gets the diamonds into the IRA's hands you can kiss merry old England good-bye."

Miranda was silent for a moment. "And you're the only one who can catch this man?"

"Maybe. With McBride and your mother . . . maybe we can."

"The reward had nothing to do with it?"

Sean frowned. "Not really. I won't throw it away if I get it, but it doesn't change the way I feel."

"How do you feel about helping an English police officer against the Irish?"

Sean tried to smile but failed miserably. "Does it go against my roots? Hell, yes. It's funny, though, for some reason I don't think of either you or your mother as English, even though you both certainly sound very British."

Miranda laughed. "Well, I'm Americanized, and my mother's an international. She's done so much traveling that she doesn't belong to any one country anymore."

Sean smiled at her attempt to lighten the conversation but he was unable to let the subject drop. It had almost become an obsession.

"There has to be an accounting for what Duggan did. I'm tired of thugs coming over here to make their bones and press coverage, even if they happen to be Irish. I have a lot more respect for the Irish slugging it out with the British."

Sean got up suddenly. "Miranda, I've got to leave. I'm just getting angry and that's going to make things worse. I just have to be by myself and get my head straight about this whole thing."

Miranda followed him to the door of the elevator. She

took his face in her hands and kissed him gently. "Do what you feel is right, Sean."

He returned her kiss. The elevator came. They kissed again.

"Right now I feel very noble, but tomorrow I may hate your guts, Sean O'Keefe."

"I'm not too crazy about myself right now either," Sean said as the doors closed.

Miranda walked back to the table and snuffed out the candles. She picked up one of the plates, looked at it for a moment, then threw it against the wall.

"Well, Miranda, did that make you feel any better?" she asked herself.

"Hell, no." She flopped down on the couch, wishing she could cry.

Sean's mood matched the bleakness of the area as he walked toward Delancey Street in search of a cab. A group of surly young men were standing on the corner. As he approached, one of them started to move toward him as the others watched.

"Hey, man, howsabout a couple of bucks for me and my friends?"

"Get lost, creep."

"Hey, man, that's no way to talk." The others began to move in closer. Sean saw them coming and grabbed the closest man around the neck. "Did you ever hear a man's neck break," he yelled at the group. "If you don't disappear this dude is done."

"Do as he says," screamed the man who was in considerable pain from the pressure Sean was applying.

The men swore, but left. Sean saw an empty cab coming along Delancey. He pushed the would-be mugger and sent him crashing into a garbage can. He jumped into the street and hailed the cab, which squealed to a stop. He could see the driver appraising the situation as he got into the cab. The driver put the meter down and pulled away. "That's a bad neighborhood to be walking around at night, mister."

"It matches my mood," Sean said. "Eighty-seventh and First, please."

17

Waldorf-Astoria

Hugh McBride poured the remainder of the split of wine into Harriet's glass. His spirits had risen noticeably. He was quite pleased with the progress they were making.

"You don't mind me paying for the meal, Hugh?"

"Not in the least, my dear. With four children in college every penny I can save is a blessing." He took a slow sip of wine. "I'm a male chauvinist only to a point."

"You're also in a much better mood."

"Much. I can see some light starting to filter in at the end of the tunnel."

"Well, I'm glad you're seeing light, because I'm no further ahead at all."

"I think you did an outstanding job at the post office. I was getting no place with that pompous ass until you started that spiel about how superior the American postal system was compared to the English . . . by the way, is that true?"

Harriet shrugged. "How would I know? I do most of my communicating on the phone, you know that."

McBride smiled. "I've noticed. Anyway it paid off. We got the names of four missing black postal workers. We've accounted for three—two dead and one at Bellevue. My hunch is that this Fred Stone is the only one besides Duggan to escape."

Harriet nodded. "From his background check, I'd say

he was the head black. Good organizer, high intelligence, a born leader, and according to some of his co-workers he was into some shady sideline operations."

"Hired help. Probably very rich if he's loose, but still an employee. If we catch him he might be helpful in getting a lead on Duggan."

Their dinner arrived. Steak for McBride, rare. Lobster for Harriet. The waiter also delivered a manila envelope to Harriet.

"This was delivered to the desk, the clerk had instructions that all messages were to be delivered to you here."

Harriet reached into her purse and slipped some currency discreetly into the waiter's hand. He smiled, nodded, and left before looking at the denomination on the bill. McBride saw the British consul general's name on the envelope.

"You do have clout, Harriet."

She smiled, opened the envelope, smiled again and pulled out a glossy eight-by-ten which she handed to McBride. "Michael Duggan," she said.

Hugh took the photo and looked at the man carefully.

"So that's Michael Duggan."

"Bit of a hunk, as they'd say in my country."

"Mmmm, he's a nice-looking guy . . . looks like someone . . ."

"The actor Tyrone Power. Any woman my age could tell you that."

"You're right." He put the picture back in the envelope. "We'll have copies of this run off for my men and the police."

McBride cut into his steak and murmured approvingly. "Let's table the shoptalk during dinner. I'd like to know more about you. How did a member of the British aristocracy come to join Scotland Yard?"

"I think you have a rather old-fashioned notion of British society," Harriet said. "This isn't the eighteenth century. But, to answer your question seriously, I guess I always wanted to do something with my life. The role of society lady simply didn't suit me. I always was a bit of a rebel, and the excitement of police work caught me. My mother didn't approve, but my father, who's a general, encouraged me. He's rather a special man and I owe a lot to him."

"Did your background help or hurt your advancement?" Hugh asked.

"It didn't hurt, but I came up through the ranks and made every branch along the way except mounted patrol . . . they couldn't find a horse for me. I don't sit a horse very well anyway."

"Sounds like a pretty well rounded career. Any regrets?"

"None. Oh, I have a knife wound in my side from a panderer, a bone chip in my ankle when a smuggler tried to run me down with his car, and I got a black eye once from a dope pusher. I could have lived without those. How about you, any regrets?"

"Once in a while, when I see what some of my friends are making as lawyers in private practice. Maybe I could have done more for my family. I worry about getting the kids through college with retirement right around the corner. But then I think, if I'd been a lawyer, I probably would have been bored stiff."

Dessert and coffee arrived and the small talk ended.

"Since we didn't get out to Long Island today, how about making the trip tomorrow morning?" Harriet asked as she finished her chocolate mousse.

"Sounds good to me. I'll be interested in seeing how they pulled that off. Conrad filled me in on the details. Apparently they didn't even know that the damn trucks were missing. It sounds like there was someone on the inside."

"Seems probable," Harriet said. "By the way, I had a

call from Miranda earlier. Sean has decided to cool their relationship until this thing is resolved. I knew you'd be glad to hear that."

"Oh?" McBride said questioningly.

"Miranda thinks that if their feelings are genuine, a few weeks of separation and reflection won't make any difference."

"A few weeks? You think we'll have Duggan under wraps by then?"

"If we don't, Hugh, we've got big trouble, and by we I mean England."

McBride escorted Harriet to the lobby where she slipped the desk clerk a fiver for delivering the envelope to the restaurant.

"Well, Hugh, my dear, I'll leave you here. I want to call my husband before I turn in."

"About eight in the morning okay for you?"

"Fine."

Harriet departed for the elevators. The desk clerk smiled. "A lady of great dignity," he said.

"She is indeed," McBride replied.

A Waldorf-Astoria suite

"Smythe-Houghton here."

"And Smythe-Houghton here," Harriet answered cheerfully.

"Harriet, my love. How wonderful to hear your voice."

Harriet smiled because she knew that he meant it. "Did I wake you? I would have thought that you would have been up and about for hours."

"I was having a magnificent erotic dream about you, and I didn't want to wake up. It was much more exciting than working on this latest novel."

"That's very flattering."

"It was meant to be. How is your investigation going?"

"Well, I had it made very clear to me by Hugh McBride that this was not my personal investigation, and that I was not to come on like the Light Brigade."

"He could be right, you know," her husband said cautiously.

"He was, and I admitted it."

"He sounds like a very straightforward gentleman."

"He is, and I appreciate it. Very few men have the character to stand up to me, and I know that if I'm given an inch, I'll go for a mile."

"At least," her husband chuckled. "What's this chap McBride like, a cigar-chewing red-faced Irishman?"

Harriet put her fingers to her temples as she talked into the voice box. "You're stereotyping. No, he has quite a nice face. Black hair, gray on the sideburns. Deepset brooding eyes. Lean and muscular, was probably a good athlete in school. Doesn't smoke or drink. Very seldom swears, especially in front of me."

"Might make an interesting character in my book. What's he like inside?"

"Complex. Religious, but not a fanatic. Good family man, but more devoted to his job than anything else. Afraid of failure, but not afraid to put his neck out. Very good at putting facts together. Weak on understanding what makes people tick. Probably doesn't know himself very well. He doesn't seem to like figuring people out. Seems to just take them as they come."

"A bureaucrat?"

"Not really, too independent for that."

"Honest?"

"Almost to a fault."

"Sounds like the two of you should get along well. Are you any closer to catching that Duggan fellow?"

"We have bits and pieces. We know what he looks like. And I just received a psychological profile from the prison he was in. McCann should be calling me later with the results of his computer check on Duggan."

"What was he in prison for?"

"Murder."

"Charming."

"Actually charming is a good word to describe him. From all the data I have on him so far, it appears he could charm the birds right out of the trees."

"How's McBride doing?"

"He has agents running all over the country checking out Irish-Americans. My God, there are more Irish in this country than you can shake a stick at. They must be the most homogenous people in the world. They're at all levels of society from the top to the bottom. And we've discovered that there is a very strong and active pro-Ireland network here. Needless to say they are very anti-British. Lots of heavy activity in Boston, New York, New Orleans, Miami, Washington, Baltimore, and Canada. McBride's people have turned up weapons and very militant groups."

"Does he think the militants are hiding this Duggan fellow?"

"Yes, but I have a feeling that Duggan won't follow the normal channels of escape. He's a loner."

"How did he get out of prison?"

"From what I can gather, off the record of course, he talked his way out."

"He sounds more interesting all the time. By the way, whom did he murder?"

"His mother."

Harriet could hear the intake of air on the other end of the phone. "I don't have all the details yet." Harriet added.

"Premeditated?"

"Accidental, to some extent."

"Can I be any help to you on this end?"

She laughed heartily. "I think the Yard has all the bases covered, and Sergeant Simmons has duplicates of everything I have."

"How's Miranda?"

"Fine. Lovely as always. Lonely, I think, but she seems quite taken with that TV chap O'Keefe."

"And his intentions," Sir Arthur asked sternly.

"Always the protective father."

"Of course."

"Well, I think the young man's completely bowled over by her."

"Physical or serious?"

"Both, I suspect. He's a nice-looking young man. He has a cynical sense of humor, but basically he's quite stable except for an occasional burst of temper. I think he's seen a lot of hurt in his time and tries to conceal the fact that anything touches him. A man with a wall around him."

"We all have walls. It's just natural self-protection."

"But a wall with no openings can be suffocating."

"True. Well, my love, keep me posted."

"I will. Have a good day."

"And you have a good night."

Harriet clicked off the speaker and walked into her bathroom. She took a quick shower, toweled her body, and walked to the bedroom. She paused to examine her nude body in the large dresser mirror. Not bad for a fifty-three-year-old woman, she thought. She could still give some of the youngsters a run for their money if she were so inclined. Her delicate features and good facial bone structure had come from her mother, but her height had come from her father. Long, big-boned, and muscular. Her breasts had dropped slightly, but were still firm and well shaped by any standards. Her skin had a healthy glow, highlighted by a soft golden tan seen only on women who know how to tan carefully and properly.

All in all, Harriet thought, not a bad total package for a slightly battered middle-aged woman. Good skin tone, good muscle, a flat stomach, plenty of meat on her bones, but no fat. She sighed contentedly, pulled on a candy-striped nightshirt, and crawled into bed with her notes on Duggan.

The phone woke her up an hour later. It was McCann. She made some quick notes, asked a few questions, and hung up. She checked her watch. It was too late to call McBride; she'd give him the information first thing in the morning. She left a wake-up call for seven the next morning and fell asleep to visions of a gigantic uncompleted puzzle of Michael Duggan's face.

East Side

Sean O'Keefe sat in a hammock on his terrace with Dog on his lap. He watched with some intrigue as two lesbians made love in the apartment across the courtyard. It was strange how front-building people always seemed to pull their blinds down while back-building people let it all hang out. Sean soon got bored and irritated. He set the alarm for six and went to bed.

A few blocks away

Mary Osborne had packed her bag early and gone to bed. She would be taking a short trip, but would be back just in time for next week's Wednesday night Bingo game. It would be her last before she left for Ireland.

Uptown

Fred Stone was awakened by the sound of someone picking at the front door. He looked next to him at the woman who was still asleep.

The noise at the front door stopped, then started again. He got up and quietly took out a pistol from the nightstand. He made his way carefully to the living room, but tripped over something before he was able to reach the front door.

He could hear footsteps running down the hall and the fire door to the stairs slam shut. Stone hurriedly undid the locks, flung open the door and stepped into the hall with his gun poised. He ran to the stairway door and opened it, just in time to hear hurried footsteps below and the slamming of another door.

Stone returned to his girl friend's apartment. Cops didn't scratch and run. They kicked down the door. Probably some crud trying to bust in and score. Not uncommon in the projects.

Upstate

Michael Duggan was still asleep, but it was no longer peaceful. He tossed and turned with his personal nightmares until a voice in his mind calmed him, "There, there, Mickey . . . Gram's here . . . not to worry, lad . . . not to worry."

18

East Side

Sean awoke to the insistent jangling of the alarm clock. He had had a bad night. He had dreamed about Miranda, but whenever he took a step toward her she seemed to float out of his reach. He couldn't get her out of his mind. He had wanted to make love to her last night, but he had felt very awkward. He was always somewhat ill at ease with women in a sexual sense in spite of his flip manner and casual confidence. Perhaps it was his strict Catholic upbringing, or his habit of putting women on a pedestal. When he really cared about someone, he found it very difficult to be loose. He still couldn't shake some primitive notion that nice women weren't sexual.

He and his wife had had, in the first few years, a really wild sexual relationship. But after only a few months of marriage, Sean had realized that he didn't like his wife very much, so sex with her was easy.

Miranda was different. He genuinely cared about her, and that scared the hell out of him. She was all woman. Would she be too demanding? Would she expect too much?

Well, this kind of worrying wouldn't get him anywhere. It certainly wouldn't help him find Duggan. He decided to forget about Miranda until the case was closed. At least, he would try.

An hour later he returned Dog to the apartment after her morning run and took the subway down to Bellevue Hospital. He had an appointment to see one of the deafened black terrorists in the prison section of the hospital. He left after only half an hour in poor spirits. He had had to write all his questions and the man refused to answer any of them. A dead end.

His next stop was a luxury building on West Fifty-seventh Street—the apartment of Pat O'Malley, a loan shark and racketeer. The apartment was large and expensively furnished with lots of chrome and glass. The effect was stark and cold, an atmosphere that suited O'Malley. He greeted Sean in an expensive silk suit that didn't do much for his burly figure.

"I don't like you, O'Keefe, so let's get that out up front," he said.

"We're starting off equal, O'Malley. I think you're a fucking parasite, but personal opinions aside, I need your help."

"What's it worth to you?" O'Malley asked.

"You've got it wrong. What's it worth to you?"

"What do you mean?"

"The mayor's on another big cleanup binge. How do you think he'd react if he knew a couple of his appointees were into you for a bundle?" Sean asked.

"Who says?"

"I have my sources. You want names and numbers?"

O'Malley nervously picked his nose as he thought. "So what?" he finally answered.

"I drop a dime and there will be a dozen reporters who would love to pick it up," Sean replied.

O'Malley figured the percentages in his head and finally nodded. "What do you want?"

"I hear you sold Katz's ass to the IRA?"

"Who told you that?"

"I know Katz was into you. You don't let people off the hook, so someone paid you. My guess is the Irish."

"The price was right. Strictly business. They covered his obligation. No more, no less. Look, O'Keefe, if you're trying to tie me in with the IRA, forget it."

"Tell me about the Irish. Was one of them a Michael Duggan?"

"Yeah."

"Where is he now?"

"How the fuck would I know?"

"Take it from the top, Pat."

O'Malley lit up a Cuban cigar and deliberately blew smoke in Sean's direction. "This guy Duggan and his goons hear I've got a couple of Jew boys on the leash in the district. They need a guy with the knowledge. I give them a name, and they pay his freight. Period."

"Plus a little extra."

"Of course. I ain't a charity."

"How were they going to get the diamonds out of the country?"

"Slingshots. How the hell would I know?"

"Because I know you, Patti. You never let go. You wanted a piece of the action."

"It crossed my mind, and I might have had something going with that goon O'Leary or Logan, but that guy Duggan dropped a rock on it. I don't think he trusted me."

"He sounds smarter all the time."

"It doesn't matter anyway 'cause those two got wasted."

"Any ideas how Duggan planned to get away?"

"Ideas will cost you cash."

"Forget it. If you knew anything you'd have made a pitch by now."

Sean left. Another zero. Next stop Harlem.

The Indigo was where all the high rollers went with their ladies. Pimps, pushers, and hustlers, the cream of the black underworld.

Midge Campbell owned the Indigo. A onetime city civil servant turned prosperous by keeping her eyes and ears open and her mouth shut. It was said that she knew how to buy politicians and civil servants better than anyone in the city. The Indigo was just a well-paying front for the big-time action that went on in Midge's luxurious apartment on the second floor. When a kid on the street saw a white face going into the Indigo he knew that another honkie had been bought.

Sean had known Midge since they were in high school together. He had always been fond of her for a variety of reasons. She was never one of his snitches when he was on the force, but she would volunteer information from time to time. And if anyone in the city knew what was going down, Midge did.

"Sean O'Keefe, you turkey, come over here, and lay one on me."

Sean walked to the end of the glowing plastic bar and grabbed the heavyset woman around the waist and planted a big kiss on her lips. A couple of black porters and the bartender frowned at the exchange, but nobody called Midge on her turf.

"What are you doing up here?"

"I'm after your bod, mama."

"Fool, you had it back in high school. Thought that would be enough to hold you."

Sean laughed. He had indeed had her in an empty classroom during lunchtime recess. It was one of the most uninhibited things he had ever done, and probably the most fun. And she was right. It was enough to last him for a long time to come. He had smiled out of context for a week even though his whole body had been sore.

Sean took her hand gently. "And I haven't had better since."

Midge smiled a broad toothy smile. "Right on old lady Stein's desk, too."

They both laughed.

"Is this social or business, Sean?"

"Little bit of both. I'm free agenting on the Diamond Street takeover."

"A lot of the blood went down on that one."

"Do you think they were set up?"

"Nope. It was just the way the cards fell that day."

"You sound pretty sure."

"I am. The initial deal went down right here at the booth over there."

"I don't suppose you'll tell me about it?"

"I'll tell you 'cause it's over and they're all dead or in the slam."

"One of the brothers is still loose. A guy named Stone."

Midge smiled. "So the Stone rolled. Well, I'll delete his name from the transcript, your honor."

"Fair enough."

"About six months ago, maybe more, this white dude comes waltzing in here and yells . . . is there a nigger in here who wants a dishonest day's work! I figured the guy was crazy or had the balls of King Kong, maybe both. Anyway, before the brothers could take him apart Sto—" She caught herself in mid-syllable. "Let's say Mister X takes this ballsy blue eyes to that booth."

Sean took a copy of a picture that had been delivered to his apartment. "Is this the guy?"

Midge put on a pair of twenty-four-carat gold-framed glasses and looked. "That's him. Nice-looking dude."

Sean put the picture back in his pocket and Midge continued.

"Anyway, they talked for a while and then the white

guy left. I learned what the score was later. It sounded pretty heavy."

"It was. I was there."

"Was that you in the newspaper?"

"Yes."

"Was that dead guy you were carrying a friend?"

"I liked him well enough."

"I'm sorry, Sean."

"Me too, Midge."

"You after the white guy?"

"That's right."

"Personal?"

"Right again, plus I'd like to get a piece of the reward. Can you tell me anything about him?"

"There were two of them in here a couple of times. The other was a mean-looking dude."

"The mean-looking one is dead."

"Good. He was a bad number. The other guy, the one in the picture, seemed pretty nice. No jive. Upfront money from the start for everyone, and from what I hear, lawyer money, too. You couldn't ask for it straighter."

"Anything more about the guy in the picture?"

"He was Irish . . . not the American kind . . . the Irish kind. I think he was the main man. I heard the diamonds were going to be used as collateral for weapons. Maybe even a bomb."

"Any ideas where this guy is now?"

"Probably back in Ireland, if he's smart."

"I don't suppose you'd drop a dime on Fred Stone."

"Nope."

"If anything comes up that you think I should know, will you give me a call?"

"Sure."

Sean gave Midge a kiss and started to leave. Midge put

her hand on his arm. "Sean, can I ask you something that I've always been curious about?"

"Sure."

"Was I the first one you ever balled?"

Sean's face reddened slightly. "Yes, and as they say, the first is the best . . . I haven't topped it yet."

Midge smiled. "I'm glad I started you off on the right foot."

Sean waved and left.

Midge picked up a phone from under the bar and dialed. She checked to see if anyone was listening.

"Hello, Lonnie. Midge. When you see Fred . . . no, don't tell me where he is 'cause I don't want to know. Just tell him that Sean O'Keefe, the TV guy who was on the street, was here and they've connected Fred. No . . . he wasn't that interested in Fred . . . he's after the Irish dude. Tell Fred to keep a low profile. Okay. And be careful, your old man has been looking for you. Take care of yourself, miss."

Midge hung up. She thought about Sean and that day in the classroom. She had been his first, but she didn't tell him that he was her first, too. Maybe not the best, but the first, and that made him special. She was glad that he had not been killed because she knew that they had planned to kill all the hostages as a diversion.

Sean spent the rest of the afternoon following up bits and pieces, and at ten o'clock that evening as he lay on the hammock on his terrace with Dog he realized that was all he had. Bits and pieces. For all he knew, any of them knew, Michael Duggan could be back in Ireland, or in some Middle Eastern country dealing for guns and ammunition, maybe even an atomic bomb.

Dog yawned and started to fall asleep on Sean's chest. The windows across the back court were starting to come alive with scenes of erotica, but Sean was too tired for voyeurism, too tired to even think of Miranda, too tired to think of Michael Duggan or the missing diamonds, too tired to think. Soon he and Dog were both asleep.

Upstate

The cool night air was alive with laughter in the small town's square near the library. A large movie screen was set up on the bandstand and the townspeople were watching a comedy about big-city life. They laughed at all the right lines, but they had no empathy at all with the characters on the screen. For these upstate New Yorkers, New York City was as foreign as any European capital.

The town made its livelihood from a large paper mill, some small manufacturing, and a large insurance company. It was a nice place to live. Nice homes. Friendly people. Clean air, picturesque lakes, and rugged mountains.

It hadn't changed much since Duggan had lived there in the early fifties. The downtown area had changed because most of the businesses had moved to the shopping centers north of the town, but the homes were the same. Even the poorest dwellings had a certain dignity and pride to them.

Gram had sent eight-year-old Michael to visit a cousin when the troubles had started at home. The growing tensions between Catholics and Protestants was only one problem; Michael's mother, well on her way to becoming the village whore, was an even greater one.

His cousin had married a Presbyterian, but Michael was taken to mass regularly and enrolled in the parochial school. The happiest two years of his life were spent here.

The Schermerhorns had been a warm and tightknit

family. They lived in a big white house near the park at the far end of town. They had three children, all boys, and they were like brothers to Michael. But the family was gone now. Mr. and Mrs. Schermerhorn had moved to Florida. Curt, the oldest son, and Michael's hero, had been killed in Korea. John, who was Michael's age, was somewhere in California. Young Peter was with some government agency in Washington. All were gone now, but the good memories remained.

The movie ended and Duggan walked to his hotel across the square. Some sort of reunion was taking place in the lobby. The name tags read Class of '63. One of the name tags stood out more than the rest, not only because of the chest it was on but because of the name, Rachel Rosen. The name sparked pleasant memories in Duggan's mind. A beautiful young girl who had turned into a fantastic-looking woman. She had lived next door to the Schermerhorns, and all the boys had a crush on her, including Duggan.

She glanced his way and Duggan turned quickly. He did not want to be recognized, but another part of him wanted to be remembered.

He made his way into the bar, sat at the far end and ordered a local draft beer. There were name tags all around him, at the bar, at the piano, at the surrounding tables. Duggan felt out of place, but that was far from a new feeling. He had felt that way most of his life, except the two years here as a child, and the time he spent at Gram's house. He had certainly felt out of place in the English army, and at an English college. His short acting career had been interesting, but not very rewarding emotionally or financially. He had liked working on the docks where you could see the result of your labor, but it was a job that only led to an early grave. It wasn't until he found the IRA that he felt he belonged. They appreciated him. They depended on him, but he was beginning to have regrets about what he was doing. Nagging feelings that he was just making matters worse for everyone.

"Mike? Mike Duggan?"

Duggan looked up quickly to see the carefully and tastefully madeup face of Rachel Rosen smiling at him.

"It's you, isn't it, Mike?"

She had really become a beauty, Duggan thought to himself.

"I certainly wish my name was Michael Duggan, but unfortunately it's Fred Kramer," he lied, regretting the words too late.

"Oh." She pouted slightly, "that is disappointing. There was something about your eyes."

"I assure you the disappointment is mine," Duggan said meaning it.

Rachel Rosen hoped that the conversation would continue, but Michael got up and dropped a couple of dollars on the bar for his unfinished beer.

"Well, good night," he said.

She nodded and sat down in his chair. Duggan ignored her inviting eyes and left the bar. Sadly, he decided that he had to leave the peace and quiet of the small town and return to New York. He had come too far to be stopped now. His mission was not complete. Too much depended on his getting the diamonds to Ireland. It seemed he was always on the move. Well, it wouldn't be too much longer now.

19

East Side

At eight o'clock, a chauffeured limo pulled up to McBride's building. He approached the car and the driver quickly got out and opened the back door with one hand while tipping his hat with the other.

McBride lowered his head and peered into the back to see Harriet, in a suede pants suit, sipping orange juice from a tall cut-crystal glass.

"Good morning, Hugh."

McBride grunted his good morning as he got in and sat down. He reached for the door handle, but the driver slammed the door shut, and he had to withdraw his hand quickly to avoid getting hit.

Harriet continued to sip her orange juice as she pointed to two metal containers on a small pullout table. "The one on the right has chilled juice and fresh strawberries. The one on the left is hot, so be careful. It's eggs, bacon, hot buttered scones, and a pot of coffee."

McBride gave a little sigh of exasperation. "Harriet, you said you'd rent a car, but . . ."

Harriet gave him her most innocent look. "But it is rented, dear heart."

The driver started the engine and the limo moved down the street.

"You eat. McCann called me last night and I want to fill you in on Duggan's background. It's fascinating.

"According to McCann's sources, Duggan's a very smart young man. A planner. College-educated and an ex-actor. A good athlete. And a murderer."

"Did you get any more details about the murder?" McBride asked. "He killed his mother, right?"

Harriet nodded and paused for a moment to consult her notes. "Apparently, it happened in a bar. He was having a drink, which was unusual because he's not a drinker. Anyway, this old barfly tried to pick him for a few shillings, and . . ."

"And it's dear old mom," McBride interrupted.

"Right. She didn't recognize him, but he recognized her and hit her right in the face with a beer mug. I'd say it was a reflex action that had been building over the years. According to McCann, he hadn't seen his mother in years. She took off when he was five. She was a real bitch. Used to beat him up and force him to watch while men made love to her."

"Nice lady," McBride commented.

"Anyway, after she left, her mother, Duggan's grandmother, brought him up. Strict Catholic upbringing, but basically a very loving relationship. Somehow along the way he got involved with the IRA, possibly looking for masculine approval, a father figure, or something like that. The better he did, the more praise he got. From what McCann heard, he was very good at coming up with outlandish ideas and making them work."

"But he didn't serve a full sentence for the murder, did he?" McBride asked.

"Not exactly. He gave himself up after the murder, served some of his sentence and then . . . left. From what the warden told McCann, he worked in the library there. Read just about everything and jokingly told one of the guards that if they didn't get any new books in he was leaving. They didn't, so he left. Actually, I think he was doing his own form of penance and when he figured it was enough, he took off."

"Fascinating. What about his education?" McBride asked.

"Well, he was educated in an English college. Exceptional student from all reports. One of his professors said he had an insatiable curiosity about everything. And he was an actor in Dublin for several years. A very good one too, according to reviewers and peers."

"Does McCann have someone checking out the grandmother now?" McBride asked.

"Yes. There's something else, too. Duggan spent some time in the United States as a child in a small town in upstate New York."

"That's important, Harriet. I want to get my people on that immediately. I'm sure you've been thoughtful enough to provide a phone for me." McBride grinned.

"Right here," Harriet said, indicating a panel in front of them.

She waited patiently while he gave instructions to his staff. When he'd hung up, she said, "I'm afraid I also have some unpleasant news for you from England. Against my wishes, the home office has been checking out both you and Sean."

"What!" McBride yelled, nearly spilling his juice on his seersucker suit.

"I knew that you'd be less than pleased, but I thought you'd rather hear this sort of thing from me first."

McBride put his empty juice glass back into the container and slammed the lid shut. "What the hell are they trying to pull, Harriet?"

"Don't take it personally, Hugh."

"How the hell should I take it?"

"Like the professional that I hope you are. Both you

and Sean are Irish-Americans. You'd do exactly the same thing if the situation were reversed."

"You're right, Harriet. I would have done the same damn thing, and did. It's no secret that Duggan had help from some law-enforcement people who were Irish. I think this pertains to my operation as well as the New York City police. We're checking out our people, and Conrad has his shooflys checking out some Irish cops."

"Shooflys?" Harriet asked.

"Police Internal Affairs. And I guess I can't get too angry at your people either, because now that we're letting our hair down, I had you checked out, too."

Harriet loooked at him inquiringly.

"After I got over the initial shock that you were a woman, I called McCann to get a fix on you. He said that you were one of the best in the Yard."

"That was very kind of McCann. We have had our differences from time to time."

"I presume that Sean and I passed inspection, or you wouldn't be telling me this."

"You did. They still haven't decided about Sean. He was on the street. He could have been part of it."

"Bull. He wants to get Duggan so bad it's almost an obsession with him."

"I agree with you, but just to be on the safe side, let me get clearance first."

McBride opened the hot container. His appetite was gone so he only poured himself some black coffee in a small china cup.

"What are your feelings about what is going on in Ireland, Hugh?"

"Professional interest or curiosity?"

"Maybe a little of both."

"I think the English should get the hell out of Northern Ireland. Most Irish-Americans probably feel the same way."

"So do most English, even on the higher levels. It's costing us a fortune which we can't afford. Ireland could become our Vietnam."

McBride refilled his cup. "And this whole thing is starting to mushroom. We're not the only players in the game. When diamonds are at stake in large quantities, there's always the off chance they might try to flood the market for some reason. That means the Israelis, South Africans, and even the Chinese and Russians are starting to nose around."

"They could never flood the market with what they have. DeBeers would cut that off in the bud," Harriet said.

"Of course, but there are some very nervous countries out there. The faster we wrap this up, the better for everyone."

"I'm more interested in the people here. You're Irish Catholic. Tell me about yourself. Do you think you're typical?"

"Probably. I'm not much of a joiner so that may make me atypical in some regard. There are a lot of Irish organizations here, in Boston, Washington, and New Orleans. They're the largest and most powerful, but there are others growing all over the United States."

"All because of the situation in Ireland?"

"Partially, but I'd say they were mostly interested in national issues based on the perception, real or imagined, that there is a growing anti-Catholic wave on the horizon. Most of the groups that I know of are primarily interested in the abortion issue, aid to parochial schools, declining morality, and the creation of an organization like B'nai B'rith Anti-defamation League."

"Do you think there is an anti-Catholic mood growing in the country?"

"It's always been there. Whether or not it's growing is debatable. But I must admit that even I am getting a little tired of the movies and TV shows that poke fun at Catholics. There was a local columnist who said it better than I. If I can remember the words . . . how come if you say anything against women, you're a sexist. Say anything against blacks and you're a racist. Say anything against Jews and you are an anti-Semite, but say anything against Christians, especially Catholics, and it's free speech."

"As you say, side issues. What about the others, the more militant pro-Ireland groups?"

"From what we've gathered so far, there were splinter groups in both Boston and New York who had knowledge of the takeover. Duggan, O'Leary, and Logan were known to these groups. This is all just bits and pieces from informants. We're keeping them under surveillance in case Duggan tries to use them to get out of the country. And of course all travel is being monitored, although for all we know Duggan may well be out already."

"Somehow I don't think so," Harriet said. "Our people are on full alert just in case. From what I know about Duggan, he's a loner. I don't think he will use the Irish here in America to get away. Logan would, but not Duggan."

"You may be right, Harriet. I hope so. I really want to catch that bastard." McBride sighed. "Anyway, I hope this trip will provide some more information about him. Everything we can learn will bring us a little closer to figuring him out and trying to second-guess his plans."

Harriet settled herself more comfortably and poured them both a cup of coffee. "Do try to eat your breakfast, Hugh; it's very good."

He laughed. "Harriet, you're incredible. One of a kind. And I'm glad we're working together on this, although I never thought I'd hear myself admit that."

She laughed. "I guess you just know a good thing when you see it." She smiled modestly.

Harlem

Fred Stone lit a cigarette and handed it to Lonnie, who was lying next to him. "What's up, baby? You have something eating at you."

"It's Rufus. He's going to make trouble. I can just feel it."

"Look, baby, that dude is nothing but a little hustler, and we all know it. He's not going to mess with me because he's scared shitless. So what's he going to do?"

Lonnie took a long drag from the cigarette and passed it to Fred. "He's been hanging around the club bad-mouthin' you and making threats."

"And that's all he's going to do. He's all mouth. Look, in three days you'll have a passport and shots and I've already taken care of mine. It looks like the real thing. Five days from now we'll be sunnin' and funnin' in the Brazilian sun. We'll be living like the jet set."

"You don't know Rufus like I do, Fred. He can get mean when he thinks he's losing something that belongs to him. And he thinks I belong to him."

Stone took a puff of the cigarette and put it out in the ashtray next to the bed. "You just forget about that turkey. He's nothing to worry about."

Lonnie put her head on her man's chest, but the worried look remained. Stone frowned when he saw that she was still upset. Normally he would just look Rufus up and come down on the side of his head, but he had to keep a low profile. He hadn't been out of the project since he bought his travel papers. The confinement was beginning to get to him. He wondered how Duggan was making out. He hoped Duggan made it to Ireland. He liked him. A straight dealer, no cute tricks.

20

East Side

Big Betty stood on the corner of Madison and Sixty-seventh Street and swung her purse back and forth. She was late for an engagement and couldn't get a cab. She was about to apply one of her tricks of the trade, chest out to a full thirty-nine, stomach in, butt out. It never failed to get a cab. She assumed the position with a deep intake of breath which she quickly exhaled at the sound of the pistol shot.

Midway down the block stood a small man with bifocal glasses. He wore an ill-fitting police uniform and was leading a mangy dog on a rope leash. In his other hand he held a police revolver which he fired into the air for the second time.

"That bitch is going to get what's coming to her this time. I told her I would sic the law on her. I told her," he yelled.

The busy early-morning traffic sped by and foot traffic disappeared around corners and into nearby buildings. Big Betty wiggled to the next street and the subway entrance.

"She wouldn't let up on me, but now I've got her." The man threw his head back and cackled at some joke known only to him. "I'm going to blow your ass off, bitch!"

As the little man fired the third shot a police cruiser

slowly eased up behind him. Two officers got out of the cruiser with guns in hand. A black officer put his gun back in his holster and signaled to his partner to do the same.

"McCarthy, you simple bastard, what the hell do you think you're doing?" the black cop yelled.

The man turned around with a smile of recognition. "Hey, Simmons, I'm going to get her ass this time for sure."

"Sure you are. Come here, my man, I want to talk to you."

"She didn't send you looking for me, did she?"

"You know better than that, Mac. We're all on to her tricks. You know that. Now put that thing in the holster and come over here. We need your help on a big bust that's coming up."

The little man's eyes danced. "You're not bird turdin' me, are you?"

"Hey, my man, have I ever done a number on you?"

The man thought for a minute. "No, not that I can remember, but my memory ain't what it used to be."

"Holster the gun, Mac. You're scaring people. They don't know that you're an undercover agent."

The little man put his finger to his lips. "Shhhh, you want to blow my cover?" He holstered the gun and started to walk slowly to the patrol car dragging the bedraggled dog behind him. Simmons's partner, a rookie, looked at the black officer questioningly. "Undercover cop?"

"He thinks he is. Crazy as a bedbug, but harmless."

"Harmless?"

"If we get the gun away from him. He's been doing this, 'I'll get you you bitch' routine for years now. Everyone in the neighborhood knows him."

"Who's the woman he's yelling about?"

"His imaginary mistress. She's a real bitch. Plays

around a lot," Simmons said with a half smile on his face.

As the man neared the car both officers stared at the uniform. It was a real uniform and instinctively their hands touched their guns.

"Give me your weapon, Mac."

"Why? It's mine."

"You know the department rules. You have to turn over your weapon to another officer after a shoot."

"Jesus, you're right. I forgot. Here's my piece." The little man handed it to the black officer butt first. Both cops looked at the gun. The real thing.

"Who gave you the gear, Mac?"

"God."

"Uh-huh. Where did God give it to you?"

"In the alley behind that clothing store off Sixty-fifth. You going to take me to the station so I can make my report to the lieutenant?"

"Nonstop delivery."

"He got mad at me the last time 'cause McGillicuddy peed on the floor."

"I think he'll forgive you when he hears your report."

"Yeah?" The little man climbed into the back seat and the rookie got in next to him. McCarthy put the mangy dog on the rookie's lap. "Here, you hold the mutt. He stinks and has fleas and worms."

The rookie grimaced. Simmons stifled a laugh and called in to tell the dispatcher to get a car to the alley behind the Blade Boutique on Sixty-fifth and cover it until the detectives got there. They were on their way in with a very important witness.

On the word *important* McCarthy threw his head back and cackled.

Long Island

The limo was given clearance by the guard at the front gate of the Atlantic Security Company. McBride had regained his appetite and finished his breakfast and the rest of Harriet's.

"It seems hard to believe that an armored car company could lose six cars and not even know about it."

Harriet nodded in agreement. "Although I've run into stranger things."

They got out of the limo and entered the front door of the administration building.

Stella Zonker sat in the small reception area and filed her nails. She had been working for the company for nearly four years, ever since she graduated from high school. It wasn't a good job, but it was the best she could get. She didn't know how to type, take dictation, or even add a simple column of figures without putting little dots next to the numbers. But she answered the phone in a low, sexy voice, and that was qualification enough to keep her job as a combination switchboard operator and receptionist.

She was pretty in a cheap way. She always went braless because she got a kick out of catching the reactions of the drivers and executives. She knew it turned them on, and that was fun. But she never messed around in the office. She saved that for after hours with men like that Irish guy she's been dating.

The front door opened and McBride and Harriet walked in. Stella eyed Harriet's outfit with a certain amount of envy.

"I'm Agent McBride, and this is Chief Inspector Smythe-Houghton from Scotland Yard. We would like to see Mister Seely, please."

Stella offered her sexiest blink, but got no reaction from McBride. "Do you have an appointment?"

"I have something even better," McBride said pleasantly with a trace of sarcasm in his voice. "I have a search warrant."

Stella looked at them blankly for a moment, then picked up the phone and called the executive vice-president. She pushed a button on her desk and a door swung open to a hall.

"You may go in. Mister Seely's office is the fourth on the right," she said in her most officious tone.

Ed Seely's office was more lavishly furnished than the reception area. It was one of his fringe benefits. Seely was a meticulous man who liked everything in its proper place. If his coffee cup was moved on his desk, he'd know it. The six missing armored cars were a major catastrophe in his well-ordered life.

"We'd like to talk to you about your stolen trucks," McBride said very matter-of-factly.

"Are they all right?" Seely asked with deep concern, as if he were inquiring about the health of six friends.

"They're doing very well, Mister Seely," Harriet said pleasantly, "but we are a bit curious how you could misplace six new armored cars."

"They weren't misplaced. They were stolen," Seely snapped.

"Why didn't you report them as stolen?" McBride asked reasonably.

"We didn't know they were stolen."

"Isn't that a little unusual for a security company like yours, Mister Seely?" McBride asked sarcastically.

"Now wait just a damned minute," Seely yelled.

"Gentlemen," Harriet said, "we're all after the same thing, and shouting will get us nothing but sore throats. Mister Seely, would you tell us anything and everything you know from the beginning, please."

Seely looked at her as if she had just rescued him from the inquisitor's rack.

"Thank you Miss— Mrs.— Ms—?"

"Chief inspector will suffice for the time being, Mister Seely," Harriet said with a tinge of authority in her voice.

"Yes, chief inspector. Well, we all know that our trucks were involved in the incident on Forty-seventh Street in Manhattan. The newspapers certainly have made that fact well known to the whole world."

"I would say you are correct so far," Harriet interjected.

"Anyway," Seely continued, "two days before the diamond thing, six men showed up here with an official-looking piece of paper saying they had to return the armored cars to the manufacturers, and they were here to take them back. I told them that I had received no notification, but later I discovered that indeed we had received a registered letter from Montreal, and that it had been directed to the wrong person."

"Do you still have that letter?" Harriet asked.

"Yes."

"We would like it along with the envelope. You should, however, make a copy for your files," McBride said.

"The letter was from a senior vice-president of the manufacturing firm, a Mister Spellman."

"Did you verify the letter?" McBride asked.

"I did, sir. I placed a call to Mister Spellman in Montreal. He told me that there were malfunctions in the exhaust and that carbon monoxide could escape into the interior where the guards sat. He told me that the six men were to drive the armored cars to a subsidiary of theirs in New Jersey. They would replace the defective parts and return them to us within a week."

"Did you have any conversations with anyone else regarding the trucks prior to the arrival of the drivers?" Harriet asked.

"Yes, a Mister Haynes."

"Did you confirm this with him?"

"I initially asked to speak to him, but he was out of town."

"Who told you that?" McBride asked quickly.

"Stella. She places all the long-distance calls for us."

"Is Stella the *zaftig* young thing in your reception room?" Harriet asked.

Seely paused, working on the word *zaftig*. He finally figured it out and smiled. "Yes, that's Stella."

"Have you contacted Canada since you found what really happened to your trucks?" McBride asked.

Seely blushed. "I contacted Mister Haynes. They sent no letter. They have no Mister Spellman and no subsidiary in New Jersey."

"Would you have Stella come in here, please?" Harriet asked.

Seely looked at the FBI man as if to ask permission.

"Do as the chief inspector asks," McBride said.

Seely picked up the phone and dialed a single number. "Stella, have Grace relieve you at the desk and come in here."

There was an uncomfortable silence as they waited for the receptionist. Finally there was a knock on the door and Stella came in. Harriet smiled at the girl, who looked nervously from face to face.

"Sit down, my dear. We would like to ask you a few questions."

"I did something wrong, didn't I?"

"Perhaps. What do you know about the diamond robbery and the terrorists that took over that street in New York City?"

Stella looked blankly at Harriet and McBride. "What robbery?"

"You didn't see anything on TV, hear anything on the

radio or see anything in the newspapers about the robbery and the armored trucks that were used?"

"No." Stella shook her head. "I think the news is icky, too depressing." She looked innocently at Harriet. "They used armored trucks? We have armored trucks here."

McBride gave a low groan.

"Yes, I know, Stella. That's why we're here. They used Atlantic's armored trucks."

"No shit." Her face reddened slightly. "Sorry, that just slipped out, kinda."

"That's all right. I'm sure we've all heard the word before." Harriet took a picture from her large purse. "Stella, have you ever seen the man in this picture before?"

Stella glanced at the picture and smiled. "Sure, he's a guy I dated a few times. He's a friend of Mister Seely."

McBride and Harriet stared at Seely, who looked shocked and bewildered. He jumped up from his desk and looked at the picture.

"I never saw this person before in my life."

The stares returned to Stella.

"But he's a fraternity brother of yours . . . that's what he told me," Stella said nervously.

"We didn't have fraternities where I went to college," Seely said defensively.

"How long did you date this man, Stella?" Harriet asked.

"About two weeks."

"What was his name?" McBride asked.

"Patrick Walsh."

"Stella, what the hell does this man have to do with our armored cars? What did you have to do with this?" Seely was starting to yell at the top of his voice, and Stella looked like she was getting ready to cry.

"Gentlemen, I think we're only upsetting the young

lady. Why don't you be good chaps and leave the two of us alone so we can chat."

"Chat?" McBride asked.

"Chat," Harriet reiterated with a wink at McBride.

"Mister Seely, can we go somewhere to have a cup of coffee?" McBride asked.

Seely scowled at Stella, then shrugged. "I guess we can go to the conference room. I think there's some coffee on, but right now I think I could use something a little stronger."

After the men left, Harriet smiled at Stella. "Don't worry, dear, I won't bite you."

"I really screwed up didn't I?"

"Yes, I think you did, but tell me what happened."

"Well, I met this guy in a singles bar, and we got to talking, you know. He goes, Hi, can I buy you a drink? Then I go, Sure, why not? Then he goes, Why don't we go have our own party. And I go, Sure, why not? I tell him that I work here at Atlantic, and he says do you know Fred Seely. And I say, sure."

"Did this man have an Irish accent?"

"No . . . kinda midwestern I'd say."

Harriet made a mental note that Duggan apparently had a talent for imitating different accents.

"He told you that he was an old friend of Seely's and wanted to play a trick on him, right?" Harriet asked.

"That's right." Stella relaxed a little. "But that was later on."

"What kind of a trick?"

"Well, see these guys were supposed to come in with orders to recall some of the new trucks. Then Mister Seely would call Canada, but I would place the call to Pat . . . is that really his name?"

"No."

"Figures. Anyway, what's his name would tell Seely

that it was all a put-on, and they would both get a big laugh about it."

"What happened after you placed the call?"

"The drivers came out of Mister Seely's office and left. Then Pat calls and says that Mister Seely didn't think it was funny, in fact he was pretty pissed off. It would be smart if I didn't mention anything about it."

"And you didn't?"

"No way."

"Were you sleeping with this man?"

Stella's eyes opened wide at the change in Harriet's voice and the directness of the question.

"What does that have to do with anything?" Stella asked defensively.

"Were you?" Harriet repeated, ignoring Stella's question.

Stella examined her sculptured nails.

"We balled a few times," she finally answered.

Harriet had heard about every sexually descriptive word in at least four languages during her police career, but it still rubbed her the wrong way to hear younger people refer to lovemaking in such crude and casual terms. "Good," she finally said.

"Good?" Stella asked.

"Good for me. I can't tell how it was for you. I'm mainly interested in finding out all I can about this man, and if you were having an affair . . ."

"We weren't having an affair," Stella interrupted, "we just balled a couple of times, that's all."

"Where did this take place?"

"In his car, at a motel, and once at one of those swingers clubs in the city, but we didn't get it on. He just watched me. I don't think he dug the scene too much."

"Did you?"

"Hell, yes, wouldn't you?"

"I doubt it."

"You think I'm a bimbo, don't you?"

Harriet laughed. "I'm not here to make moral judgments, Stella. I just want to find out about the man. What kind of lover was he?"

Stella shrugged. "He was okay. I've had better and worse. His mind always seemed somewhere else."

"Did you have any idea that he might have been using you sexually to get you to help him?"

"Come on, inspector, everybody uses everybody nowadays. That's the way things are."

"Is there anything about him that was unusual or different?"

"No. What are you after him for?"

"Stealing over a billion dollars' worth of diamonds, murder, stealing your armored cars, and a few other things."

"Heavy. Jesus, I'm not going to be arrested, am I?"

"I doubt it. Did you see him after the phone thing?"

"No, we were supposed to go out that night, but he called and canceled. Same excuse he used once before."

"Oh, what was that?"

"Something about taking some old lady to a Bingo game."

"That sounds a bit dubious."

"Sounded like a line of crap to me."

"Is there anything else you can tell me about him?" Harriet asked. Stella shook her head.

"If you do remember anything, or if he contacts you again, please call me immediately. You can reach me at this number," Harriet added, handing Stella a piece of paper. "Now I suppose we should rejoin the gentlemen. In the future, Stella, I'd be a little more careful about playing tricks on your boss."

"I'm not *that* dumb," Stella said indignantly. "I don't fall for the same line twice."

"Did you two have a nice chat," McBride asked when they entered the conference room.

"Are you going to arrest Stella?" Seely asked abruptly.

"I don't think so. Stella was taken in just like you were, Mister Seely."

Seely look unconvinced so Harriet added, "If we arrest her, we'll probably have to arrest you as well."

Seely looked very uncomfortable. He cleared his throat. "Yes, I guess you're right. Well, if you're finished with us, we'll go back to our work." He looked questioningly at McBride.

"You're both free to go, but we would like to question some of your other employees, with your permission, of course."

"Of course," Seely said as pleasantly as he could. "Let me know who you want to see and I'll send them in here." He turned to leave. "Stella," he said, "I'd like to see you in my office." McBride and Harriet laughed as they watched Stella follow Seely unwillingly down the hall.

"I wonder if Seely will fire her," McBride mused aloud.

"I'm sure they'll work out something to their mutual satisfaction," Harriet said with a wink.

"You have a dirty mind, Chief Inspector Smythe-Houghton."

"Just a realist, Hugh my love."

"Did you learn anything interesting?"

"Just that Duggan canceled a couple of dates with Stella to go play Bingo."

McBride's eyebrow went up as he looked at her. "That's the dumbest thing I've ever heard of."

"Maybe, maybe not," Harriet said.

An hour later, they were back in the limo heading toward the city. The rest of their interviews had been next to useless. The other Atlantic employees knew nothing about the missing trucks or Duggan.

"I wonder how Sean made out today," McBride said. "He had a couple of leads to check out."

"We can find out tomorrow. I have some business I want to take care of when we get back, so I'll drop you at your office."

"Good idea. But drop me a block away. I don't want anyone to see me getting out of this car."

"Why don't we have dinner tonight, just you and I and Rose. No shoptalk."

"Sounds good to me. I don't think Rose is jealous of us, but I do know that she is jealous of the meals I've been eating with you."

Harriet laughed. "Then it's a date. You and Rose meet me at the hotel about eight."

21

East Side

While Harriet, Hugh, and Rose McBride dined at the Rainbow Room atop Rockefeller Plaza and enjoyed the view of the city along with their leisurely meal, Mary Osborne was putting on her best dress, the one she kept neatly pressed between the mattress and the bed.

When she had finished dressing she placed her small suitcase on the bed and examined the contents. It contained her toiletries, nightdress, some religious articles, her airline tickets to Ireland, her money, and the specially wrapped can of hard rock candy crystals that Pat Mahoney had given her to take to Ireland for a friend. The least she could do to thank him for all the help he had given her.

She hadn't seen Patrick in a few weeks and wondered if he was all right, although he had told her that he probably wouldn't see her until the day she was to leave. Maybe he would show up at tonight's Bingo game or next week's. She was leaving after tonight's game for a short trip upstate, but her hosts had promised to get her back in time for next week's game. It would be her last.

Mary had packed everything she valued in the small blue suitcase which she had found out in front of one of the large apartment houses. Those people in the big buildings were so wasteful. There wasn't a thing wrong with this case except for a small scratch on the side.

She arrived at the church promptly. After setting up her boards she exchanged pleasantries with some of the women, the ones she was particularly fond of.

"Are we ready for Bingo?" The caller's voice echoed over the speaker system. A resounding "yes" echoed back from the nearly three hundred players on the upper and lower levels.

"And how are you tonight, Miss Osborne?"

Mary looked up from arranging her lucky pieces for the third time. "Good evening, Officer Gallagher. I feel real lucky tonight."

"I see you brought a suitcase to take all the winnings home."

Mary laughed girlishly. "Oh, no. I'm going away for a bit, but I'll be back fifteen minutes before next Wednesday's game. They promised."

"It wouldn't be the same without you."

Mary looked suddenly wistful. "Next week will be my last game, I'm afraid. I'll be leaving for Ireland the following Friday."

"Ireland, you say," Gallagher said with an exaggerated Irish accent.

"And I'll have my own house and everything."

"That's really terrific, Miss Osborne. You certainly deserve a break."

Mary Osborne liked Gallagher. She liked all the people at Bingo. They were special people to her. They were nice and went out of their way to be helpful.

"I will dearly miss this place, Officer Gallagher."

"And we'll miss you." Gallagher smiled, partially because he was an easygoing man who smiled a lot, and partially because Miss Osborne insisted on calling him officer even though he was one of the youngest detective sergeants in New York City.

Gallagher was always friendly with the Bingo players, but tonight he had an ulterior motive. He hadn't gotten to be the youngest detective sergeant on the force for nothing. He was a keen observer even when he was not on duty. He enjoyed watching the people at Bingo. He would study their faces, mannerisms, and the way they played. It was a way to kill time and make the evening more interesting. He had noticed two things that had become very important to him. Miss Osborne had been accompanied two or three times by a young man, and they seemed to be friends. Not unusual, maybe he was a nephew or something. But the young man had not been around lately. Again, not unusual.

The second thing Gallagher had noticed was a small gem stone that was one of Miss Osborne's lucky pieces. Again, not unusual, probably solid glass. Something that had some sentimental value, nothing more.

Bits and pieces, nothing more, until this morning when he had seen a picture of Michael Duggan and the bits and pieces fell together. Duggan was the young man who had been with Miss Osborne at the Bingo games. The small glass stone had turned up after the siege on the diamond street. Chances were pretty good that it was more than just cut glass.

"Tell me, Miss Osborne, where is that nice young man who used to bring you to the games?"

"Patrick? Oh, yes, he is a lovely young man. If it weren't for him I wouldn't be going to Ireland."

"Really?"

"He arranged for the whole thing, even a house for me. I don't even have to bring my furniture, not that I'd want to. The house is furnished by the Irish Resettlement Society."

"Hmmm, yes, fine organization," Gallagher said making a mental note of the name.

"Where is ah . . . Patrick now?"

"Oh, he's away on business, I think, but I'll be seeing him next Friday at the airport."

"Are you the only one going on this trip?"

"I think there will be others, but I'm not sure how many."

"Will you all be going on the same plane?"

"Yes, as far as I know . . . Aer Lingus, of course."

"Of course . . . certainly not on an English plane."

They both laughed.

"Well, I certainly wish you all the best, Miss Osborne."

"Oh, I'll see you next week." She paused, then asked shyly, "You don't suppose that the priest could announce my leaving on the loudspeaker, like they do when it's someone's birthday, do you?"

Gallagher winked at her. "It's as good as done."

"BINGO!"

A cherubic white-haired woman two tables away waved her card in the air. Mary rechecked her numbers as Gallagher excused himself and moved quickly to the woman with the card. He took it and cleared his throat. "Under the B . . . two . . . three . . . six . . . fourteen."

"That's a good Bingo. Are there any more upstairs? Downstairs?"

"No Bingo downstairs," answered a voice over the loudspeaker.

"One winner at twenty-five dollars," the caller said.

Gallagher motioned to the caller that he was going to the lower level. He stopped at the men's room and used one of the stalls because the urinals were built to accommodate small boys. He flushed the john, washed his hands, and then walked down the remaining stairs to the lower level game in the school lunchroom.

He glanced around at the players and then walked to the counter in front of the small kitchen area and ordered a cup of coffee.

John Gallagher had a decision to make. He was on to something big and he knew it. He could handle it himself and be a hero and maybe the youngest lieutenant detective in town, or share the glory with the department and get lost in the shuffle, or he could turn it over to the FBI who had jurisdiction in the case and get a pat on the head. Then there was the reward. A lot of money. The problem was that cops could not get the reward.

John Gallagher thought for a while and then made his decision. He wanted it all. The honor, the glory, the collar, and the reward.

He walked over to the downstairs pay phone and picked up the thumbworn telephone book. It was two years old, but he turned to the O's anyway. His finger stopped by the name Sean O'Keefe.

O'Keefe was after the terrorists and the reward. That was the scuttlebutt around the precinct. If Gallagher was right, his information might be worth something. He dialed the number and after a few minutes the operator cut in and gave him a new number. He dialed it and waited. After seven rings an answering service picked up the call. Gallagher left his name, precinct phone number, and a message for O'Keefe.

Gallagher spent the remainder of the night thinking about Duggan and the diamonds. He was so engrossed that he miscalled some Bingo winners, which brought good-natured boos from the players. His mind was still clicking off alternatives and plans of action while he was helping to clean up. It suddenly dawned on him that he had no idea where Mary Osborne was going for the week. He glanced around. Mary was already gone. He strained his eyes from the far end of the auditorium and saw her getting into a car in front of the school.

Gallagher started to run toward the door, but caught the plastic bag of garbage he was carrying on the edge of the table. The bag split and the contents fell on the floor. He dropped the bag and ran to the door. When he reached the street the car was turning right on to Park Avenue, too far away to catch the license plate or even the make of the blue car.

Gallagher muttered a curse under his breath. Now he had no idea where Mary Osborne would be until next Wednesday's Bingo game.

22

East Side

Sean O'Keefe awoke with a sinus headache that would last the entire day. He never knew for sure if it were his sinuses or nervous tension that brought on the headaches, but the one he had this morning was a beaut.

He poured himself some orange juice with one hand as he dialed his answering service. Sarah greeted him with a warm good morning.

"Any interesting messages?"

"They're stacked up like incoming planes over Kennedy."

"Scrub all bill collectors, ex-wives, lawyers, etcetera."

"That narrows it down to three. A woman named Smythe-Houghton wants you to call her."

"Miranda Smythe-Houghton?"

"Harriet Smythe-Houghton."

"Oh . . . okay. Who else?"

"Hugh McBride. He'll be at his office this morning."

"Who else?"

"Detective Gallagher at the Nineteenth Precinct. He says it's very important that he talk to you about the diamond robbery, and that it would be to both your benefits if you call him first thing this morning at the Nineteenth."

"Okay . . . he leave a number?" Sarah gave him the

number and he wrote it down on the back of a shopping bag.

Sean took Dog for a walk to clear the cobwebs from his head. He was very disappointed that Miranda had not called. When he returned to the apartment the phone was ringing, but by the time he answered the party had hung up. He glanced at his watch. Ten o'clock. He'd better get on the ball. After the zero he pulled yesterday, today had to be uphill. He dialed Gallagher's number.

"Gallagher, this is O'Keefe. You wanted to talk to me."

"Right. I think I have something hot on the diamond thing, but I want to talk to you first before I tip my hand."

"In other words you want a piece of the reward."

"Maybe, maybe not. Can you meet me here at the precinct in about half an hour's time?"

"You want to talk over rewards in the station house?"

"No, there's something I want to show you, and I want to find out if you know anything about the deep freeze the Irish cops are getting."

"What deep freeze?"

"Well, that answers one of my questions. See you in half an hour."

"I'll be there." Sean hung up the phone and called Harriet at the Waldorf. The operator told him that she had gone to see a sick friend in the hospital. Sean remembered that he had not been to see Ben Levi. He felt a little guilty about that, and mentally promised to try and get over to Roosevelt Hospital before the day was over. He picked up the phone again and dialed McBride.

"McBride here."

"It's Sean. How did you make out yesterday at the armored car company?"

"Pretty good. How about you?"

"Nothing much. I got a fix on the shy who had Katz on the string."

"Anything?"

"He made the connection for the Irish, but that's about all. Duggan wouldn't trust him with anything else, which makes Duggan a pretty good judge of character."

"Find out anything else in Harlem?"

"Not much except where the deal was made with the blacks and a little bit about what went on, but no lead to Stone."

"Do you think your contact knew where he was?"

"Yeah, I'm pretty sure, but I wasn't about to push."

"Hmmm, maybe we all better get together this afternoon and compare notes."

"Could you use another cop who may have something?"

"What's his angle?"

"Maybe the reward, maybe glory . . . maybe both."

"Bring him along, we'll check him out."

"Speaking of checking out, is there some sort of freeze with the Irish cops in town?"

"Where did you hear that?"

"From a cop."

"There is until they can be checked out. We already caught some blue helpers for the IRA, so we'll have to check out your friend, too. What's his name?"

"Detective Gallagher of the Nineteenth."

"You'll be glad to know that Scotland Yard cleared you."

"Scotland Yard did what?" Sean yelled.

"Cleared you. You were on the dubious list for a while."

"Well, screw them. Who the hell gives them the right to vote on me?"

"Don't get your bowels in an uproar, they checked me out, too. And if it makes you feel better I had you checked out even before I contacted you."

"Well, thanks a lot, McBride. You think I nearly got

my ass blown to Georgia just to work myself into your confidence?"

"No, but I still checked you out."

"Harriet is out. Do you know where she is?" Sean asked.

"She wanted to talk to Ben Levi at the hospital for some reason. Have you been to see the old man?"

"No, and I feel guilty about it. I'll go over later."

"Plan to be in my office around three. Bring the detective with you."

Sean hung up and started dressing. For the first time since the takeover, he felt some confidence that they'd get Duggan.

Harlem

At the corner of 139th Street a tall man with a skull cap and braided hair watched Lonnie Kane as she carried a bag of groceries into the project building. He was tempted to follow her, but he didn't want to mess with Stone. He had nearly been caught the other night, but it proved to him that Stone had taken up residence with Lonnie. The word on the street was that Stone was involved in the big diamond heist and that the cops and that TV reporter were looking for him.

Rufus ("the Skull") Carter wouldn't help the cops with anything even if it meant getting rid of a rival. O'Keefe wasn't a cop, though, not anymore.

He walked to a nearby pay phone. The receiver had been ripped off. He threw it angrily into the street nearly hitting a passing cab.

Rufus walked out of the booth and down the street to a small drugstore with boarded-up windows. Inside he quickly thumbed through a dog-eared phone book and then stepped into the booth and closed the door behind him.

"Sean O'Keefe there?"

There was a pause and Rufus scowled. "When's he comin' back?"

Another pause.

"Well, I got an important message for him, mama, so you make sure your pencil is sharp and you get it right."

Another pause.

"Don't jive with me, mama, I ain't got the time for it. Just get what I'm going to tell you down right."

Pause.

"Tell O'Keefe that if he and the cops are still interested in bagging Fred Stone, they can find him at Five Hundred East a Hundred and Thirty-ninth Street . . . apartment seventeen-oh-three. You got that?"

Rufus paused for a moment, then added, "The gal he's shackin' with has a secret ring, probably still uses it . . . two fast . . . two slow . . . two fast. Got that? Read it all back to me. Don't give me no lip, woman."

Rufus listened, smiled to himself, and hung up the phone. He tried to open the door to the phone booth. It wouldn't budge. He gave it a kick. It opened and he left the booth muttering to himself. "I'll teach that motherfucker to mess around with my woman."

He bumped into a wino who was coming into the drugstore to mooch some wake-up money. The wino looked at Rufus with fear in his eyes. "I ain't been messin' with your old lady, bro. I swear to God. I ain't done no messin' in months."

Rufus shoved the wino roughly out of his way, sending him crashing into an ice cream case. The wino slowly regained his footing and watched Rufus cross the street and turn the far corner.

"You better run, turkey, 'cause you got this child pissed off now." The wino started to spar with his reflection in the glass door. "Good thing you took off, 'cause you'd be messin' wit the kid, and he's just plain bad."

The wino hit the door and broke all of his knuckles.

East Side

The Nineteenth Precinct building was old, but it was home to the uniformed police and detectives who spent most of their time there. Sean climbed the well-worn wooden stairs to the detectives' section, after getting directions from the desk sergeant.

"Can I help you?" asked a large man dressed like a truck driver.

"I'm looking for Detective Gallagher."

The man nodded his head to the right. "The guy next to the window in the suit."

Sean walked over as Gallagher got up and put out his hand. "I'm John Gallagher, O'Keefe."

"Don't tell me, you recognized me from the picture in the paper."

Gallagher shook his head. "Nope, from the TV news."

"Before we get down to the nitty-gritty, what do you have to show me?"

Gallagher swung around in his rickety swivel chair. "Hey, Goldman, could a couple of Irish *goys* look at what you have in that box on your desk?"

A heavyset detective in a loud suit picked up a large box off his desk and brought it over to Gallagher. Gallagher opened it to reveal the police uniform and gun.

"The dead cop's from the gay hotel?" Sean asked.

"That's it."

"Where'd they find it?"

"One of the local crazies was playing cops and robbers when we picked him up wearing it. He found it in back of some swish boutique on Sixty-fifth."

"Did he see the guy who dumped it?"

"God gave it to him."

"Swell. Did he happen to see what God looked like?"

194

"Nope."
"Any prints?"
"None."
Sean's eye caught something sparkle in the box and he picked up a piece of crystal sugar candy.
"Hard rock candy crystal," he said in unison with Gallagher.
"Yeah," Gallagher said. "How'd you know?"
"I found some where they were having practice runs in the Catskills."
"We checked it out. They turn this stuff out by the ton up there, loose, in boxes and even fancy cans," Gallagher said. "We thought the bag of candy belonged to the cop, but I guess it was Duggan's."
"I wonder why he dumped it with the cop's uniform," Sean mused.
"Who knows? But the important thing I want to talk to you about is that I know where this guy has been, and if I'm right, I know how you can land him, at least I think I do." Gallagher turned around, then continued, "But I don't want to talk here."
"Agreed," Sean said. "But we'll want to check you out before we bring you in."
"Then there is an Irish freeze on this thing."
"From what I gather the answer is yes. They even checked me out and I nearly got blown away. We'll head down to Federal Plaza. There are people there who should hear this. I can't promise you anything on the reward. You know the rules, but I can damn well make sure you get credit. McBride is that kind of a guy."
"You working with McBride on this?"
"And a chief inspector from Scotland Yard."
"It sounds like an interesting game. Can McBride get me off duty here to work on it?"
"You'll have to ask him. He's the one with the clout."

Upstate

Michael Duggan was up early. He ate breakfast in the dining room, then took a taxi to the post office, and arrived just as it was opening.

"Good morning, sir. May I help you?"

"Yes, I'd like to send this package to the Basse-Bretagne region of France."

The postal employee took the package and weighed it. "Not too heavy, shouldn't run you a lot. Do you want to insure it?"

Duggan shook his head. "No, I don't think so. It's just candy. If it gets lost, it gets lost."

"It shouldn't if the address is right. And it seems well packed."

It was well packed. Duggan had checked and double-checked it. It was a long shot that was to be used as a backup, but much too risky to chance with the whole haul. Fred Stone had come up with the idea. Diamonds were frequently shipped by mail, uninsured, so attention would not be drawn to them. Chances were it would reach its destination without any problems. It was too risky to send it from New York because all packages were probably being checked. But an uninsured package from an upstate town this long after the heist . . . the most that would probably happen would be sloppy handling.

One quarter of Duggan's diamonds were gone, or would soon be. The remaining three quarters were in the hands of three old women who would soon be delivering them in person at the Shannon Airport in a week and a couple of days. A much sounder plan, Duggan thought complacently. A plan for which he could take full credit.

After he left the post office he took another cab to the cemetery on the edge of town. The man at the main gate gave the driver instructions and they parked in front of a row of small gravestones. Duggan got out and searched through the stones until he came to one inscribed "Curt Schermerhorn—killed in Korea."

Duggan stared quietly at the grave. He bent over and picked up some leaves that had fallen near the headstone. When they were kids they used to play in the cemetery. He wondered what Curt would think about what he had done, what the other Schermerhorns would think. In a way he had violated their country. Would they forgive him if they knew his reasons? They were good people, but nothing in their lives had prepared them to understand the complexities of political terrorism. He wished he could explain his reasons—why death was sometimes necessary—but he knew such a wish was futile and dangerous to his own survival. He was committed to carry out what he had started. He must not dwell on the destruction he left behind.

The cab driver blew his horn. "I hate to hurry you, mister, but if you want to get back to the hotel and check out and still make the plane at the airport, you'd better hurry."

Duggan nodded, said a silent prayer over his friend's grave, crossed himself and got into the cab.

He picked up his bags at the desk and checked out. Twenty minutes later he was at the airport. He went directly to the men's room and into the nearest stall. Fifteen minutes later he emerged wearing a blond wig and mustache. He stopped at the mirror and attached two blond eyebrows that he had glued while inside the stall. Finally, he looked at himself in the mirror and added a pair of horned-rimmed glasses. Satisfied with the result, he walked out of the men's room and went to check in.

Ten minutes later Michael Duggan was airborne. One

hour and a half later he was crossing the Triboro Bridge into Manhattan. Two hours later he was checking into a small transient hotel on East Eighty-sixth Street.

The last leg of his journey back to Ireland had begun.

23

Downtown

To call Hugh McBride's office at 26 Federal Plaza spartan was an understatement. There was one desk with a chair behind it and three chairs in front of it. A leather desk blotter and family picture were the only items on the bare desk. The windows were also bare. Wall-to-wall carpeting, supplied by the building, was the only real luxury in the room.

"Good Lord, Hugh," Harriet exclaimed, "this is the most sterile room I've ever been in!"

"We only moved here recently from Sixty-ninth Street."

"What did your office look like there?" Sean asked.

"The same. Different picture."

Harriet started to speak, but McBride interrupted her. "No, Harriet, you and Rose are not going to decorate my office. I've been fighting that battle with Rose for years. I like my office this way. There's nothing to distract my attention while I'm thinking, and nothing to distract anyone I'm talking to. And right now I'd like to hear what Detective Gallagher has to say and why he wants to be a part of this operation."

Gallagher started to speak, but McBride interrupted him. "And don't tell me what you think I want to hear. Speak your piece straight out."

Gallagher paused a moment as if to rearrange his

thoughts. "Okay. Right now I'm the youngest detective sergeant in New York City. I got there by being smart, lucky, good at my job, and using every bit of political clout I could gather. I would like to be the youngest lieutenant and eventually police commissioner. That means getting the breaks and playing them. What I have is important enough to get me into the game."

"What about the reward?" McBride asked casually.

"I'd love to get a piece of it, but I can't figure out how . . . yet."

"Undoubtedly, you've heard that the Irish-American police are under rather close scrutiny at the moment. How do we know what your loyalties really are?" Harriet asked.

"Look, lady, when push comes to shove you'll find that most Irish are cops first and Irish second. During the Civil War there were Irish revolts against the draft. Irish cops broke them up. Maybe their hearts weren't in it, but they did their job. That holds true today, and it goes for the black cops, the Jews, and the Hispanics, too. Sure, you'll find bad numbers and bigots, but that's the exception not the rule."

McBride felt a flash of annoyance at Harriet's interference. "Harriet, I believe that Gallagher's precedent about the Irish was well taken. In fact, a non-Irish friend of mine made the same point during the siege."

"What you're politely saying is to butt out, isn't it, Hugh?"

"It is, Harriet."

Harriet laughed. "You don't beat around the bush."

"I think that if you hear what Gallagher has you'll both agree that he's on to something," Sean said. "He's seen Duggan and he knows how he's going to get the diamonds out and when."

McBride turned to Gallagher excitedly. "Start talking. There'll be no more interruptions."

"Duggan and his couriers will be leaving next Friday on the Aer Lingus flight for Shannon, Ireland. I know one of the carriers, but not the rest. The one I know is out of touch right now, but I'm sure she will be back next Wednesday for the Bingo game."

"Bingo game," McBride repeated. "That's the dumbest thing I ever . . ." He could hear those words echo back in his ear. The same words he had said when Harriet had told him that Duggan had broken a date with Stella to take some old lady to a Bingo game.

"Sounds familiar," Harriet murmured, a slight smile on her face.

"It certainly does. I think Gallagher just qualified for the team." McBride leaned back in his chair. "Take it from the top, son, and don't leave anything out."

Gallagher smiled happily. He could almost see his name being typed on the promotion list.

Upstate

Field Agent Jim Conlon also had visions of promotion as he pushed down on the accelerator of one of the Albany field office's Fords. He had shaved fifteen minutes off the usual hour's drive to the small town Duggan had left hours before.

The Bureau knew that Duggan had been in this town as a boy and had ordered Conlon to do a background check, but Conlon had the feeling that Duggan might be holed up somewhere in the area. A long shot, but sometimes long shots paid off. This one almost did.

He drove immediately to the police station in the middle of town. Nothing. Just for the hell of it he checked the hotel. Pay dirt.

The hotel led him to the cab company, which led him to the cemetery and then the airport. There the trail ended. Nobody who was on duty when the one departure left could identify Duggan as one of the passengers, but then they were looking at a black-haired man without a mustache and glasses.

Conlon was disappointed, but he had answered one important question. Michael Duggan was still in the country.

24

Downtown

By midafternoon McBride had agents checking out the entire passenger list on the Aer Lingus Friday flight. Calls were coming in from offices as far away as Memphis. All but seven passengers had been contacted and were under surveillance.

The seven who were unaccounted for were all in the New York metropolitan area. Miss Mary Osborne, Manhattan; Miss Angela Coughlin, Staten Island; Miss Jane O'Toole, Queens; Mr. and Mrs. Fred Goldberg, Montclair, New Jersey. And finally Father Kevin Flynn of Saint Thomas's Church in Scarsdale. There would be no further search for Father Flynn because there was no Father Flynn. There wasn't even a Saint Thomas's Church in Scarsdale.

"I think it's fair to assume that Father Flynn is Duggan," McBride said.

"And we already have our suspicions about Mary Osborne, thanks to Detective Gallagher," Harriet added.

"And I'm worried about her," Gallagher said. "I don't think she knows what's going on."

"You're probably right. Duggan, the actor, is probably doing a number on her and any others that are involved," Sean said.

"It makes sense. I'd say our best probables are the O'Toole woman and the one on Staten Island."

"What about the Goldbergs?" Sean asked.

"We'll check them out, too, but I think Duggan has himself a group of grannies he's using to mule the diamonds for him."

"It fits what we have on him. He was devoted to his own grandmother, probably one of the few people in the world he really trusts," Harriet said.

Sean got up from his chair and stretched. "Hugh, can I use your phone to call my answering service? Maybe I've got some interesting messages."

"I want to keep my line open. Use the one in the next office."

As Sean left the room, Harriet and McBride began giving Gallagher a rundown of Duggan's background. The phone startled them all.

McBride picked it up before the second ring.

"McBride . . ."

Harriet and Gallagher watched him impatiently. He finally hung up and smiled.

"Duggan is still around."

"Where?" Harried asked excitedly.

"One of our men got a fix on him upstate where he used to live. He tracked Duggan to the airport, and a flight back here left about the same time. Nobody was able to make him, though."

"Probably put on a little makeup and played actor again," Harriet said.

The door burst open as McBride was about to speak. Sean ran into the room. "When it rains it pours! A snitch just dropped a dime on Stone, address, apartment number . . . even the secret knock to get the door open."

"Well," Harriet said, "which comes first? Check the incoming flight from upstate, the missing passengers from the list, or go after Mister Stone?"

"All three at once," McBride said emphatically. "We can't afford to slip up on anything. I'll keep men staked out at the homes of the three women and the Goldbergs and send some more agents to check out that incoming flight from upstate." He filled Sean in quickly on the recent call.

"Do we get to go after Stone?" Sean asked excitedly.

"It's your tip, Sean. I'll call Conrad. We'll need some good street cops on this one."

Harriet's face reddened slightly at she spoke. "I hate to say this, but it might not be wise to have any Irish officers involved."

McBride, Sean, and Gallagher looked at her silently. She could tell that they were annoyed by her remark, and she truly regretted having to say it even if it had to be said.

"Well, this Irish cop couldn't give a damn about going," Gallagher said. "I'm going to spend my time trying to get a fix on Mary Osborne."

"I wasn't including you in that remark, John," Harriet said quietly.

Gallagher smiled, but it wasn't his usual warm outgoing smile. "I know that chief inspector, and I understand it. I just think I could be of more use following up an area I'm familiar with. I just have bad vibes, as they say. I've seen too many old women hurt in this city. Mugged, raped, killed. I just want to follow through." He smiled again. This time it was more natural. "Besides, I promised my wife and son I'd take them to a movie, and this is the last night of the only movie around here that I could take them to without blushing."

Gallagher left. Sean promised to pick him up at the station house first thing in the morning and fill him in.

"Seeing I've already endeared myself to one and all, I'd like to offer another suggestion. That we have the preliminary strategy meeting at my suite instead of any police facility."

Both McBride and Sean were silent. Finally McBride

spoke. "Only if you agree to feed all personnel and make damn sure Scotland Yard gets the bill."

"Fair enough."

Waldorf-Astoria

Arnold Danforth had spent most of his adult life at the Waldorf. He liked being a desk clerk. He knew most of the regulars by sight and name. Royalty, jet setters, superstars, business leaders, he had seen them all. He was always polite and efficient and never got flustered when celebrities approached his realm behind the black marble counter.

Sir Arthur and Harriet Smythe-Houghton were among his favorite regulars. They were a bit eccentric, but one expected that from the British. The Smythe-Houghtons always occupied the same suite when they came together or singly to the city, which was usually once or twice a year. And because they were so well liked by Danforth, and all the staff, the chief inspector and her famous author-husband were always given their special suite. It had been their honeymoon suite. Danforth had had a bit of trouble once convincing a wealthy Arab to abandon the suite. Fortunately the Arab was an avid fan of Sir Arthur's and graciously moved to smaller quarters.

Danforth had autographed copies of all Sir Arthur's books and they were among his most cherished possessions. And whenever Harriet Smythe-Houghton checked out she always shook his hand and slipped a bit of currency into it. It wasn't necessary, though. Danforth liked their style. Old money. Good stock, Nice people.

They did have their little quirks. Harriet liked to have a speaker conference phone, and she often entertained some very strange people. Sir Arthur liked to sing bawdy songs in the bar occasionally, but he had a pleasing voice and was well received by his fellow drinkers.

Danforth was examining a hangnail on his right index finger when he heard a voice in the lobby. He looked up in amazement. Before him stood a tall black man who was the gaudiest looking pimp he had ever seen. Danforth's lips drew together as if he had just sucked a lemon.

"Hey, my man, where's the Smythe-Houghton pad?"

"Are you expected, sir?" Danforth said coolly.

The man was about to answer when another man approached the desk and Danforth did another double take. The second man was a scruffy-bearded, shabbily dressed wino of Italian extraction. Danforth's stomach churned. Whatever was the world coming to when people like this could walk casually into the Waldorf lobby.

"Rizzo, my man," the black pimp yelled.

"McPhearson, you black bastard. They've got you on this gig, too?"

The two men slapped hands. "Who the hell did you expect them to get, Donny Osmond? We're going up past the great divide. How come they grabbed a guinea like you?"

" 'Cause I'm not Irish. I have to baby-sit the suits."

"Wooooeee, they're going to love you."

"McBride's riding herd on this. He's not a bad guy."

They both turned to Danforth. "My good man, would you be so kind as to announce that Sergeants Rizzo and McPhearson are here for the meet?"

Twenty men and a little old black lady checked in with Danforth and went upstairs to the Smythe-Houghton suite. There was Inspector Conrad, McBride, O'Keefe, six FBI agents in suits and eleven street cops in various disguises.

Harriet Smythe-Houghton was holding court and she

loved it. The street cops were having a ball eating canapés in the Waldorf, and the FBI agents thought the whole thing was very strange, but were very polite.

This would probably go down in history as the only joint NYPD-FBI operation ever planned in the Waldorf-Astoria, and Harriet was sure she could find some way to insert the story in the memoirs that she and Sir Arthur were writing.

Conrad and McBride used a large blackboard to block out the action. Sean filled everyone in on the little that he knew including the special ring. A housing cop described the layout of the building. There were no escape routes from the apartment except for the windows and it was a seventeen-floor drop.

The briefing lasted one hour. At 8:15 everyone checked his weapon and moved out to the Waldorf garage where the cars were waiting. They were met at the precinct boundary by three patrol cars that would block off the perimeter.

The five cars carrying the FBI and police detectives parked in the project parking lot at 8:45. A housing authority cop stayed with the cars.

The little old black lady walked slowly to the lobby. Two youths got out of the elevator. They didn't live in the project, but had been stalking in hopes of a quick score. They spotted the little old lady and smiled as they approached her.

"Hey, mama, let me carry that heavy pocketbook for you."

"Yeah, we'll take some stuff out and make it lighter for you," the other youth giggled.

"Get the fuck out of here, you suckers. If I wasn't on a stakeout, I'd kick your little asses. Now get lost, punks."

The two youths stared at her in amazement for one second, then ran out the front door, nearly knocking over a wino who appeared to be talking to his paper bag. They cursed him and ran toward the street. A patrol car near the corner started to move toward the boys. The wino—Rizzo—let out a piercing whistle and waved the car off.

The old lady and a housing cop held the elevator doors open. Rizzo, McPhearson, and six cops entered the lobby and split into two groups. One group headed for the left stairwell. The old lady listened to a small receiving device that looked like a hearing aid. Then she spoke into her purse, confirming their positions. Within minutes, the FBI agents, three cops, O'Keefe, and Harriet entered the lobby and got into the elevator. Two of the cops stayed with the old lady, who was really a young black cop named Netty Monroe. The elevator headed for seventeen.

Fred Stone sat in the small Harlem project apartment and looked at his small pile of diamonds. It still amazed him that such a small pile was worth ten million dollars, but he had to take the Jew's word that diamonds were rated in quality not quantity.

He looked at his watch. Lonnie should be back soon with the tickets to Brazil.

The two passports next to the diamonds looked alike, but his was a forgery because he didn't want to take a chance of coming out into the open. Things were still hot. Lonnie's passport was real. Nobody was looking for her. Everyone was looking for him and Duggan.

Ten million dollars, only one half of one percent of the total take, but more than enough to set him up in high style for the rest of his life.

The doorbell rang, two fast . . . two slow . . . two fast. He went to the door and opened it. Instead of his big-chested lady, he was greeted by three guns, all pointed at him.

"FBI. Don't move."

Stone backed up with his hands over his head as the government agents quickly entered the room followed by the biggest white woman he had ever seen in his life.

25

Waldorf-Astoria

Fred Stone was questioned throughout most of the night. They learned lots of interesting background information about the siege, and they recovered ten million dollars' worth of diamonds. In regard to Michael Duggan, they learned absolutely nothing of value.

Either Stone wasn't talking or he really knew nothing about Duggan's plans. Harriet felt it was probably a little of both.

Stone and Duggan seemed so different, yet there was a bond of loyalty on Stone's part. Was it loyalty for Duggan the actor, or Duggan the man? If she had more time, Harriet would like to have pursued the matter further, but there were more important things to attend to now, like talking to her husband.

"Hello, my love. I miss you."

Harriet kicked off her shoes and put her feet on the desk as she spoke into the phone. Her whole body ached, especially her feet.

"And I, you. How goes the hunt for the wandering Irishman?"

"Moving in leaps and bounds. We captured one of his hirelings with ten million in diamonds."

"A tidy little nest egg. Who came up with that breakthrough?"

"Some informant called Sean. From what we can

gather, it was a jealous boyfriend. I wouldn't want to be in his shoes if this man Stone ever gets out of jail."

"So young Mister O'Keefe seems to have his mind on business and not our daughter."

"It would appear that way." Harriet got up and stretched. She had spent most of the night listening to Stone's interrogation. "Fred Simmons called me at the FBI," she added. "He filled me in on his trip to see Duggan's grandmother. Absolutely charming woman. If Duggan has half the gift of gab she has, it's no wonder he talked his way out of prison. It seems his grandmother used to take him to Bingo games when he was a child, and he was a master at it. Could play more than a dozen cards without putting anything on the numbers. He was apparently extremely bright as a little nipper. Well liked by all the older people, and he seemed to like them, too. This ties in to what we have going. It appears that Duggan has recruited some gullible old Irish women over here to carry the diamonds back to Ireland. Seems he promised them homes in Ireland or something like that. It may have been a bona fide promise. His grandmother said he had titles to some houses."

"Hmmm, a man of his word," Sir Arthur said.

"That seems to be what the fellow we captured felt about him, too. Simmons also mentioned that Duggan had a nervous breakdown after he was involved in a department store bombing. Apparently there was some sort of awful mix-up and a lot of innocent people were killed. Duggan hadn't intended that to happen and he felt responsible. His grandmother nursed him back to health since he had a morbid fear of being committed. And, of course, he couldn't go to a hospital even if he wanted to since he was still on the wanted list from the prison break."

"What's the grandmother like?" Sir Arthur asked.

"Well, she reminded Simmons of an older version of me. She's as tall, although her features aren't as good, according to Simmons, tactful chap that he is. She's a tough lady, very proud and very honest. She apparently wasn't surprised about Duggan's involvement in this, although she obviously didn't approve. But he's her grandson and she's crazy about him. I'd like to meet her. Get a good look at her, maybe ask a few questions. I'll have to see if the home secretary can expedite some form of travel. There's an idea forming in my mind . . ." Her voice trailed off, as if she were lost in her own thoughts.

Sir Arthur waited patiently for a moment, then added, "I've heard rumors from some of my contacts that there has been increased Irish activity in some of the Arab countries, especially those that harbor terrorists."

Harriet sighed. "There's something brewing with those diamonds. If Duggan gets away we're in for big problems."

"More than likely. Well, you have ten million accounted for and that's a start. How are they going to handle the reward?"

"Ten million is just a drop in the bucket, and payoff money at that. It's good that you mentioned the reward because I wanted to talk to you about it. If all the diamonds are recovered the ten percent reward will mean a lot of money, but when I talked to Mister Ben Levi at the hospital . . ."

"Who?" Sir Arthur interrupted.

"Ben Levi. He's one of the leaders of the Diamond Council. We cooked up the most marvelous scheme for the handling of the reward."

"Why do I have the strange feeling that you volunteered us for something?" Sir Arthur asked.

"Committed, actually. We will be the trustees for the investment and dispersal of the reward."

"Don't tell me how you wrangled that, let me guess. First you told him about our family connections with Kimberley Mines and my holdings in DeBeers."

"I did happen to mention the fact, yes."

"And then to put the frosting on the cake, you told him that your father was in attendance at the cleaving of the Cullinan in 1907."

"Impeccable logic, my dear."

"And I'm sure you hit every high point."

"Of course." Her voice took on a storytelling quality. "Asscher, the master diamond cutter, held his heavy cleaver over the one and a quarter million Cullinan, the largest gem ever found. Three thousand one hundred and six carats . . . one and one half pounds . . . four inches high and two across. Asscher had studied this magnificent gem for two months in preparation for the moment. He knew every grain by heart. Then the blade struck and the blade broke. So he struck it again, splitting it neatly into three stones as he planned."

"And your father fainted dead away, and had to be revived by a doctor and two nurses," Sir Arthur added.

"One nurse, and I left that part out."

"I wish I had tuppence for every time your father has told that story. We'd have a controlling share in the Kimberley by now instead of a fraction."

"Well, it convinced Ben Levi that I knew a little more than a window-shopper at Tiffany's."

"How do you want to handle the trust?" Sir Arthur asked.

"Well, I told Ben Levi that I thought the best way to handle it would be ten percent in GIA flawless diamonds."

"Sounds interesting. Did he agree?"

"After some amiable haggling. It wouldn't affect the cash flow and could be taken from inventory without tax hassles for the street association and the dealers."

"And how shall we handle this fortune that's probably ten times our net worth?"

"The same way we handle our own diamonds. We give them to our Swiss bank in Zurich, and they use the diamonds as collateral, paying the trust the going interest with yearly reappraisals of the diamonds," Harriet said.

"It's as good a way as any, I guess."

"Ben Levi thought it was a capital idea. You know, he wasn't even aware that the Swiss would do that."

"Well, the Americans are fairly provincial when it comes to salting away assets for a rainy day, probably because they haven't had as many as Europeans. I think Ben Levi might have been pulling your leg, though."

"Possibly. Well, I better get some sleep. I have to be up with the birds."

"I wish you love and pleasant dreams."

"I'm too exhausted for dreams, I'm afraid, but I'll settle for the love."

Harriet hung up, made her way to the bedroom and collapsed on the bed, where she fell asleep fully clothed.

East Side

Sean and Gallagher spent most of the morning asking people if they knew where Mary Osborne had gone. Nobody knew and nobody seemed to really care. The neighbors were mostly young and had problems of their own. The super was completely indifferent. The neighborhood stores couldn't tell one old person from the next. Finally, they gave up and returned to Sean's apartment.

Sean brought two cups of coffee out to the terrace and set them on a table. Dog was sitting happily in Gallagher's lap getting her ears scratched.

"Somehow I thought you'd be living in something a little more luxurious than this," Gallagher said.

"What's wrong with this place? It's a good building and

the apartment is five hundred a month," Sean said indignantly.

"It's a mess."

"It's home."

"To each his own," Gallagher said with a shrug.

"I've been avoiding saying this, but do you think we should check out the morgue?" Sean asked quietly.

"That thought has occurred to me, too, but I keep pushing it out of my mind. I've seen too many old folks there. Sometimes nobody even comes to claim them."

"You'll never make it to commissioner, Gallagher. You worry about people too much."

Gallagher just grunted and stared off into space. Sean was about to say something else when the phone rang. He left the terrace and went to the kitchen and picked it up.

"We've scored," McBride said immediately.

"You've got Duggan?"

"Not yet, but we're getting hot." Sean could hear screaming and crying in the background.

"What the hell is that?"

"A very angry Miss Angela Coughlin. She's a bit of a secret lush and has been on the town. She's very unhappy with Michael Duggan, or Kevin Sullivan as he called himself. And guess what we found in a can of candy she was supposed to take to Ireland?"

"Hard rock candy crystals and diamonds."

"That's it. I want you to get over here. Harriet is on her way." McBride gave Sean directions and hung up.

"Hey, Gallagher, pay dirt!"

Gallagher came in from the terrace carrying Dog. "Duggan?"

"Almost as good. They got the old lady in Staten Island, and some of the diamonds. McBride wants us to meet him there."

Gallagher shook his head. "There's not much I can

do. I think I'll take a trip to the morgue." There was sadness in his voice.

The two men left and got a cab. Sean dropped Gallagher off at the morgue and continued on to the Staten Island Ferry. He hoped for Gallagher's sake that the trip to the morgue yielded nothing.

26

Staten Island

Harriet arrived ten minutes after Sean. She surveyed the house before she entered. It was in a bad state of disrepair. The old building had been divided into numerous small apartments. Two men in the suits were standing at the door. From the number of cars she judged that more agents were in the apartment. She mounted the creaking stairs and walked to the last door at the end of the hall. It was open so she walked in. The apartment smelled like a cheap bar.

A heavily made up woman in her late sixties sat on a threadbare couch, tears streaming down her face, streaking it with the various colors of her makeup.

"Jesus, bloody Christ, now who the hell is this?" the woman shouted as her bloodshot eyes squinted at Harriet.

"This is Chief Inspector Smythe-Houghton from Scotland Yard," McBride said.

"A bloody limey. I'm not talking to any English broad."

"Oh, dear, that is a shame. I was about to suggest that you be my guest at the Waldorf-Astoria until we get this thing straightened out."

Angela's frown turned to an enchanting little girl smile. "Forgive me my dear, I've had a bit of a turn today, and I'm not quite myself. Sit down, please."

"Looks like Duggan isn't the only actor," Sean mumbled under his breath.

McBride spilled the contents of the can he was holding on the cluttered coffee table. "Here's what we found, Harriet."

"Covered by the same rock candy crystals that we found with the cop's uniform, and in the Catskills," Sean added.

"Hmmmm, nice idea. Have a sweet gentlewoman like Miss Coughlin take them into Ireland. Who would suspect such a lovely woman of concealing diamonds?"

McBride's eyebrows went up, and Sean made a wry face.

Angela patted her hair, which looked like an unwrapped Brillo pad. "I admit that it was a shock to my sensibilities. Of course, I was completely taken in."

"So was Duggan," Sean said. "A Mother McCree she ain't."

"I beg your pardon, young man." She started to cry again. "I've lost everything. My trip to Ireland, my nice new house . . . everything."

"Perhaps not," Harriet said. "You might be eligible for part of the reward."

"Reward?" The tears stopped and the smile returned. "Is there a reward?"

"If you help us there is a possibility," Harriet said.

"Oh, I'd be more than happy to help the law. How much is the reward?"

"Well, you'd have to be of some value in catching the man who gave you the diamonds."

Angela's voice developed a slight whine. "But I told these men everything that I know about the Bingo game and the plane tickets and everything."

"What do you think Michael Duggan . . . ?"
"Who?"
"The man who . . ."

"He called himself Sullivan."

"Whatever. What do you think the young man would do if he knew you turned the diamonds over to the police?"

"He'd be mad as hell."

"And that's why Mister O'Keefe here is going to make sure that he knows."

"What!" Sean exclaimed.

"You'll get me killed," Angela wailed.

"What are you up to, Harriet?" McBride asked.

"Don't worry, Miss Coughlin, about revenge. He doesn't have the time for that." She turned to Sean and McBride. "If he knew that we have these diamonds, he might panic and try to get the others back. Some of the diamonds are better than none."

"But how will he know that we don't have them all?" Sean asked.

"Because of the story that you'll give your friends in the media. We'll put the story on TV and into the papers."

"Couldn't that be dangerous for the other two women?"

"It could, Hugh. We don't know where they are. All we can do is hope Duggan doesn't know either." Harriet turned to Angela. "Miss Coughlin, has Duggan or Sullivan, as he calls himself, tried to contact you lately?"

"No, I haven't heard a peep from him in weeks."

"I'll have my men continue to stake out the women's apartment buildings. They're already keeping a watch out for the women. I'll have them tighten the security to include Duggan. They all have his picture."

"I'll take Miss Coughlin to my suite. I won't be needing it for a few days because I'm flying to Ireland, and she can be my guest."

"Ireland?" McBride and Sean repeated in unison.

"I want to talk to Duggan's grandmother face-to-face.

The home secretary has sent an RAF jet for me. It should be here tonight."

"Are you going to fly it yourself?" Sean asked with a chuckle.

"Of course not. It's a Harrier and I've never flown a jet that takes off straight up. I'm only cleared for the more conventional jets."

"I guess that answers my foolish question."

Harriet turned to Angela Coughlin. "Miss Coughlin, you may charge food to my room, but no liquor. Is that understood?"

Angela's eyes dropped and she looked ashamed. "I only take a nip now and then, when it gets very lonely. I only hurt myself, not anybody else."

Harriet, McBride, and Sean felt very awkward as the woman rose on shaky feet and made her way to her bedroom with a certain amount of dignity. "If you'll excuse me I'll powder my nose and pack a few things."

Once Miss Coughlin had closed the door behind her, Harriet turned to Sean. "Here are some of the things you should tell the news people. Things that will get Duggan to react."

East Side

Duggan, still disguised in the blond wig and mustache, left his transient hotel on East Eighty-sixth Street well after dark. He blended easily into the young single crowd who roamed the East Side bars looking for companionship or sex. And sex was exactly what Duggan was looking for.

He had lived a relatively celibate life since the operation began over a year ago. There had been a few diversions: a would-be actress in Dublin, a telephone operator in Boston, and that kinky broad from the Atlantic Security Company who'd taken him to a swingers club. But all that had been business and ultimately unsatisfying. He'd chosen to avoid women deliberately. The operation was more important and he couldn't afford any mistakes. Too many people were depending on him.

Now that it was all coming together nicely he felt he had earned a night off. Everything had gone according to plan so far. It had been easy to convince the Belfast Council to finance an operation in America to raise money for the cause. That had been well over a year ago, and it had been very successful. There were literally thousands of Irish-Americans willing to donate. And he'd even drawn up a list of hundreds of others actually ready to fight with them. As a realist, though, Duggan had known that many of those promises were no more than barroom bravado. But the money had just poured in. And with the money came Logan. Logan was the muscle to make sure that all the money went to the cause. The council liked and respected Logan even if he was a thug. He had been an active member of the IRA for years. Duggan, on the other hand, was a relative newcomer. Smart, but maybe too smart, so Logan was sent to keep an eye on things. Fortunately, Logan was not very smart, and Duggan was able to stash away extra money, not for himself necessarily but just as a hedge against unexpected emergencies.

It was during the money drives that Duggan was quite accidently introduced to diamonds. One of his biggest contributors was a wealthy southerner named Calhoun. Calhoun had many interests. He owned newspapers, radio and television stations, real estate, and a small company that bought and sold investment diamonds. He had given Duggan two small diamonds for the cause. Each was valued at about five thousand dollars, Calhoun's purchase price. Duggan found someone on Forty-seventh Street who was glad to pay twenty thousand for them. Hard cash. He had told Calhoun about it and the southerner had roared with laughter. "Of course you got twenty, you turkey. That guy will probably make himself another twenty off them. When you've got diamonds, good buddy, you don't turn them into cash. It works the other way around. The cash you got will bring you thirty guns if you're lucky. The diamonds would have gotten you a truckload and probably the ammunition to go with it."

Duggan began to realize that Calhoun was right. If he had diamonds to negotiate for weapons he would do much better. If he had a lot of diamonds he could arm almost every Irish Catholic in Northern Ireland twice over. And where could he get large quantities of diamonds? A diamond shop. Diamond shops! And Forty-seventh Street was wall-to-wall diamond shops. But how could he hit them all? Take over the whole street!

It was a wild idea, but with some planning it could be done. The key elements would be surprise and fear. Taking the street would be the easy part. Holding the street would be harder. Picking the right stones would be harder still. Getting away would be next to impossible.

He had sold the idea to the council with Logan's enthusiastic support. Logan liked the idea of being able to train the troops that would take over the street. He was less than delighted when the troops turned out to be black, but he and Stone had done a good job and, surprisingly, in their own ways, had respected one another.

Everything had gone smoothly. The recruitment and training of the blacks. The hours spent exploring every inch of Forty-seventh Street until everyone could describe it blindfolded. The theft of the mail vans and armored trucks. Hiding the trucks, ammunition, weapons, and personnel before the attack. That had been solved by O'Leary, who had a friend who owned a warehouse in the Bronx. The whole operation was run from there. Gathering information about police operations. Again, no problem. A few drinks in a bar and they'd got all the information they wanted plus a few recruits to boot. That's one reason Duggan decided not to use Irish-Americans in the siege. They talked too much and too freely. The blacks were more prone to keep a low profile.

Duggan thought about the people who had been killed in the operation. It was impossible to dismiss them as necessary casualties. Logan could have done that, but he could not. Secretly Duggan agreed with what O'Keefe had said that night on the street—it wasn't right that someone should have to die for another man's cause. But it had been going on for years, and there wasn't anything that either of them could do about it.

Duggan had liked O'Keefe and was glad that he had not been killed. In fact, he was glad that most of the hostages got out alive. It was Logan's plan to kill the hostages with an explosion just before the break, and Stone had agreed that as a diversionary measure it might increase their chances. Duggan had gone along with the plan, but he didn't like it. He was sure that no matter how noble his motives were he would burn in hell for what he was doing, but then he would probably burn in hell anyway for killing his own mother, even though he hadn't meant to.

He felt a sudden urge to go to confession, but disregarded the thought as a rash impulse. He hadn't been to church in years. It would be a bit hypocritical to go now.

He would be back in Ireland soon and he was glad. He felt very uncomfortable in America, especially New York. The pace was too fast. Most of the people his age were into some form of drugs; the women acted like men, and the men acted like women. It confused and frightened him. Everyone in this city was locked into his own private world, doing his own thing. Well, Michael Duggan's thing was getting the English out of Ireland, and where others had failed, he would succeed.

The others were dead or captured, but he was free and he had the diamonds and the means to get them out. The others would have never made it. They had planned to get out as fast as they could via the Irish-American underground. A mistake, he had told them, but they wouldn't listen. Lay low until things calm down. Don't use the militant Irish organizations, they'll be the first to be questioned.

By the time he reached First Avenue it was nearly eleven o'clock. It took him another twenty minutes to reach the Sixties, where most of the better singles bars were. Many of them had lines. Duggan picked the place that had the smallest line and queued up.

He thought of the woman's apartment where he had spent the night after the escape. He wondered if she might be in the bar and what she would be like. He could still remember that bed with its hot pink silk sheets. The piles of diamonds had looked pink when he spread them on the bed. It was the first time he'd had a chance to really examine them.

Only his pile and O'Leary's remained. Logan's was gone and so was Katz's, but that still left well over a billion dollars in diamonds. If Stone was alive and free that would mean another ten million was out. But Duggan had the lion's share.

After studying the diamonds for a while he had realized that he couldn't judge their individual worth so he categorized them into four neat piles according to size. The color and clarity should have been uniform if Katz had done his job properly.

He had retrieved the four tall metal containers of Catskill Hard Rock Mountain Candy from his suitcase and emptied their contents into a paper bag. The candy was nothing more than crystallized sugar, but to the untutored eye it did resemble diamonds. He filled the containers with the diamonds, covered them with several layers of the candy, then boxed the containers and gift wrapped three of them in colorful wrapping paper and a bow. The perfect gift, he thought wryly, for a nice little old lady to carry overseas. He set one box aside, wrapped that one in brown paper, and returned all four to his suitcase. He had stuffed the remaining candy into a bag in the cop's uniform, and dropped that into an alley the following morning.

As he waited on line he realized that he wasn't far from the spot where he had dumped the uniform. He wondered idly if it were still there. He'd delivered the three wrapped packages to his couriers. The fourth package had been taken care of. Now there was nothing left to do but kill time until next Friday, when he would appear to the rest of the world as another Catholic priest boarding an Aer Lingus flight to Ireland. The women wouldn't recognize him, but he'd be able to keep an eye on them and make sure they delivered the packages to Coleman and Ryan at the airport. It was a good plan and he was proud of it.

Now there was nothing to do but kill time. And what better way than with a woman. He checked the progress of the line impatiently and cursed its slow progress under his breath. A woman behind him must have heard because she eyed him speculatively for a moment, then spoke.

"It's really getting bad when you have to wait in line to get laid."

Duggan turned around in surprise. The woman was short, fairly young, and dressed in a tight pants suit. She was slightly overweight, and obviously braless. She had prematurely graying hair, which, for some reason, turned him on.

"Yes, it's a real problem," Duggan agreed, not knowing what else to say.

"Why don't we skip all the preliminary bullshit and just go to my place and get it on?"

Duggan was momentarily at a loss for words. He wasn't used to aggressive women. But she looked like she would be an active bed partner and that was all he was interested in. He had to release some of the tension that had been building up.

"It will have to be your place or my hotel room."

The woman shrugged. "Where's your hotel?"

"Over on Sixth Avenue," he lied.

"I'm just three blocks away."

"Why waste any time?"

"My feeling exactly."

Michael Duggan was not quite prepared for the evening ahead. As they got out of the elevator on the eighteenth floor of her luxury building she stopped momentarily and took off her shoes and jacket.

"Start stripping," she said in a commanding tone.

Duggan looked around and his face reddened. "Here? Somebody is liable to come out and see us."

"That's right. It's a real turnon."

Duggan shrugged, still feeling very awkward. Her apartment was at the end of the hall. By the time they reached the door they were both naked. The woman fished a key out of her jacket and opened the door.

"Give me your clothes." He did so obediently but with a questioning look on his face. The woman tossed the clothes into the apartment, clicked the latch so the door could be opened without a key, then closed it. "Here and now," she said breathlessly.

The idea excited Duggan, but he paused to look around the hall quickly. The woman sensed his hesitation and grabbed his erect penis, quickly inserting it into her vagina. She wrapped her arms and legs around him, grinding her body frantically against his. Her nipples were hard against his chest as he grabbed her buttocks with his hands and lifted her up and down in tempo with her frantic thrusts. Their mouths met briefly. Then she pulled hers away and let out a string of dirty words that would normally have shocked Duggan, but now only added to his excitement.

At the end of the hall the elevator door suddenly opened and Duggan heard several voices. The woman's eyes flew open with excitement. She reached back to release the door and she and Duggan fell onto the carpeted foyer. The voices got nearer and Duggan just managed to kick the door shut with his foot before they both exploded in unison.

They lay on the floor for a few minutes, trying to regain their strength. Finally the woman took his limp penis in her hands. "Not bad for openers," she said as she started to massage him with her fingers.

27

East Side

It was close to three o'clock in the morning when Duggan got up from the bed. The night had been spent in sexual combat. It had been a battle for dominance, a marathon of endurance which he had finally won. Physically it had been challenging and rewarding, but emotionally it was empty. And that's how he felt as he stared out the window at the city below. Empty.

Things hadn't always been like that. There had been happy times in upstate New York. Times in Ireland when he and Gram would go to the Bingo games, and she would look on proudly as he spread out his cards and kept track of all the numbers without putting down a single marker.

But as he grew older he realized there were very few people who could really be trusted. The older people were more reliable. Maybe because they were brought up differently, maybe because they didn't have much to lose. They had had their day on the center of the stage. They didn't have to prove anything to anyone. But people his age and younger were desperately trying to be noticed. He was no different. He thrived on recognition. The IRA had given him that recognition, but he didn't trust them any more than they trusted him. They had wanted him to use established channels to get the diamonds out, but his way was better. He had found people he could trust.

Duggan walked to the large mirror on the wall in front of the king-sized bed. He examined the scratches on his chest and back. Uncomfortable, but not deep. He moved to the side and stared at the reflection of the woman lying naked on the bed asleep. She seemed less appealing now.

He retrieved his clothes, which were still in the hall near the front door. He dressed in the living room and then went into the kitchen. He turned on the kettle and put some instant coffee into a cup. The kettle whistle shrilled and he turned if off quickly. Not quickly enough however. The woman stood in the doorway, completely naked.

"Not staying for an encore?" She took a pack of cigarettes from the counter and lit one. She extended the pack to Duggan, but he shook his head. She coughed as she took the first drag. "That's why you finally won. You don't smoke."

He looked at her. "What did I win?" There was sadness in his voice. He left the apartment without even having his coffee. He had to get away. He had to be alone.

He walked along Fifth Avenue. It was just getting light and he was tempted to go for a stroll in the park, but from what he had heard and read that might not be such a good idea. The last thing he needed was to be a mugging victim when he was so close to success. Instead he walked toward Eighty-sixth Street and his hotel. As he passed a small newsstand a *Daily News* truck was just delivering the last edition. Duggan glanced casually at the newspapers that the dealer was stacking in front of his little glass enclosed stand. He was about to proceed on his way when the front-page picture stopped him in his tracks. It was a picture of a smiling Angela Coughlin holding a handful of diamonds. The headline was in bold black type:

BREAKTHRU IN DIAMOND HEIST!

Duggan grabbed a copy and quickly turned the pages. There was a picture of himself, Stone in handcuffs, and a picture of a smiling Sean O'Keefe. He closed the paper and started to walk away.

"Hey, sport, I'm not a charitable organization."

He turned to see a scowling newsdealer. He reached into his pocket. He had no change so he handed the man a dollar and didn't wait for the change.

"Hey, thanks, sport," the man shouted as Duggan hurried away.

Inside the hotel he read every word and examined every picture. The center spread contained a series of pictures taken at the siege as well as more pictures of Angela Coughlin.

Duggan studied his own photo and then looked in the mirror. His new disguise would suffice for the time being. He looked at the pictures of O'Keefe and Angela and cursed them out loud. He should have killed O'Keefe.

The chain had been broken, and by now the FBI was probably on to his whole plan. One quarter of the diamonds were gone forever. The FBI had them, and there was no way to get them back, but the others?

Duggan quickly reread the parts of the story that interested him.

> *Stone would not cooperate in giving the police any information about the elusive Michael Duggan . . .*

And he wouldn't, thought Duggan. Stone would keep his mouth shut because he and Duggan had made a side arrangement to cover legal expenses if Stone was caught.

> *Police and FBI agents are still searching for Aer Lingus passengers Mary Osborne, Sarah O'Toole and Fred and Mary Goldberg, who all may be Duggan's unknowing accomplices in smuggling the diamonds out of the United States.*

They didn't have Mary Osborne or Sarah O'Toole? Why? Where were they?

> *It is feared that Duggan may have killed them or is holding them captive.*

A trap to get him to react? Probably. But he would have to find out.

> *Anyone having knowledge of the whereabouts of the Osborne and O'Toole women or the Goldbergs is urged to contact . . .*

Had they searched the women's apartments? That took warrants and time. Or were they just keeping the places under surveillance? Were the diamonds still in their apartments? Duggan had to find out even if he were caught. He could not fail now that he was so close.

He pulled his suitcase out from under the bed and opened it. Besides his clothes there was a small makeup kit, duplicate keys to the women's apartments, gained from wax impressions made when he had opened their apartment doors for them, and a 9-mm PPK with the numbers filed off.

He had purchased the German pistol in New York, where weapons were more readily available than in either Ireland or England. He put the gun, which was already loaded, into the pocket of a light raincoat. He left his room and took a cab to Queens, stopping the driver five blocks from his destination. He walked the remaining distance on foot. There was just one thing on his mind. Retrieving the diamonds.

Queens

The two agents in front of Sarah O'Toole's building were tired and irritable. It had been a long watch. The apartment had been searched. No Miss O'Toole. No diamonds. They had to sit and watch for a woman they only had a vague description of, or Duggan, who would be a damn fool if he tried to get near the building.

The agent at the wheel nudged his partner as a man approached the building. The man was staggering. He stopped at the entrance, unzipped his fly, and urinated near some shrubs. The agents watched with mild amusement. "Boy, does he have a snootful," one commented.

The man then took a key from his pocket and unsteadily opened the door and went inside. The agents relaxed their vigil.

Duggan got off at the top floor where Miss O'Toole lived. He walked quickly down the freshly painted hall to her door. He put his ear to it. No sound. He knocked lightly, and called her name. No answer.

He took the duplicate key from his pocket, opened the door and quickly closed it behind him. Nobody in the living room. A quick search of the other rooms; nobody. No diamonds. But Duggan's keen eye for detail told him that the apartment had been professionally searched.

He was about to leave when he remembered something she had once told him. She would sometimes cat sit for a few days for the lady who had the apartment below her. She would take her valuables and her small portable TV set and move in with the cats until the other woman got back. There was no TV set in the apartment.

Duggan hurried down the stairs to the apartment below. He put his ear to the door. He could hear the TV. He knocked. No answer. He called her name. No answer.

He took a small tool from his pocket and quietly opened the old lock. He saw her sitting in a chair in front of the set which lit up the darkened living room. Two fluffy Persian cats jumped off her lap as Duggan called her name, but the woman did not move.

Her eyes were wide open. She had been dead for hours. Duggan kneeled down next to her and took her stiff cold hand in his. There were tears on his face as he gently closed her eyes and kissed her on the forehead. Old people too often die alone, he thought sadly.

Near her was a shopping bag with some of her valuables, including the colorfully wrapped can with the diamonds. Duggan tore it open and emptied the contents into his pocket. He was about to leave when he stopped. Someone should know that she was dead. Somebody should take care of her. He went over to the TV and turned the sound up as far as it would go, then left.

Twenty minutes later as the agents expectantly awaited their relief, the drunk came out the front door. Both agents turned their attention to the entrance. The agent nearest the street put his hand on the door handle.

"This is the last time you'll ever lock me out of my own house, bitch," the drunk screamed at the front of the building. "I'll get you for this. I'll get you!"

The agent relaxed his grip on the door, and the two men watched the drunk stagger off down the street cursing at the top of his voice. The agents sank into their seats and glanced at their watches. Their relief should be arriving soon, but it was the police answering a complaint about a loud TV who arrived first.

East Side

Duggan entered his hotel room and immediately went to the bathroom and vomited. He had been stifling this reaction ever since he saw the body of Sarah O'Toole.

The sight of the dead woman unnerved Duggan. His hands were shaking, and he was soaked with perspiration. He had to get control of himself. He still had to get into Mary Osborne's apartment. He would have to chance the same approach. He hoped he would not find her in the same condition.

28

East Side

When Duggan arrived at Mary Osborne's street his heart sank into his stomach. The whole street was cordoned off with police barricades. In front of the building were several police cars. People in the neighboring buildings were leaning out of their windows watching the police and FBI agents coming and going out of the building. Duggan stood behind the barricades with a small group of people. He had to find out what was going on. He approached one of the policemen standing guard near his squad car.

"What's going on, officer?"

"Nothing for you to worry about, mister. Just move along, please. There's nothing to see."

Nothing to worry about? Nothing to see? Duggan knew he had a lot to worry about.

McBride was talking to his men in Mary Osborne's living room when Sean and Gallagher arrived. They had both received the news about Sarah O'Toole, and they entered the apartment apprehensively. McBride saw them and came over. "Don't worry. There's nobody here. No diamonds either. Wherever she is she took them with her . . . I hope."

"We're a little late to help that woman in Queens," Gallagher said sarcastically.

"That wasn't Duggan's doing. She had been dead for a day at least. He was there last night, though, or at least we think it was him. He pretended to be a drunk coming home, but nobody in the building fits the description."

"So this brings us back to Mary Osborne as our main lead," Sean said.

"That's it."

"If she is all right, she'll be at Wednesday's Bingo game," Gallagher added. "She told me she'd be there. She might even have the diamonds on her."

"It's a strong possibility," McBride said.

"If we can't find Mary Osborne, and Duggan is having the same problem . . . would he think of looking for her at the Bingo game?" Sean asked pensively.

"Chances are he'd check out the women's habits carefully. It's a possibility," McBride agreed.

"It's the only possibility we have," Sean said.

"Can you help us set up the operation with the people at the church, John?" McBride asked Gallagher.

"That could be tougher than getting Duggan. I don't think they will go for the idea."

"Because of the Irish thing?" Sean asked.

"Possibly, plus the fact that if the shit hit the fan, we'd place people in danger."

"Will you give it a try?" McBride asked again.

Gallagher shrugged his big shoulders. "I'll try, but I'm not promising anything."

"Harriet should be back tonight, God and the RAF willing. Her input can be important, but go ahead and try and get things rolling."

Gallagher and O'Keefe left. McBride stayed for a few more minutes and gave instructions to the agents in the apartment. The apartment depressed him. It was so tiny and shabby. Finally he left for home.

East Side

Late Sunday afternoon, Detective Frank FitzPatrick was finishing up a report on a shootout at a singles bar when the phone rang. He picked it up and cradled the receiver with his shoulder as he typed. "FitzPatrick . . ."

His normal pallor became even whiter as he recognized the voice at the other end. He glanced around to see if anyone was listening. "What the hell are you doing calling me? Don't you know every cop is looking for you . . . yeah . . . yeah . . . that's right. We're all on ice, thanks to you."

He paused and scowled at the phone while continuing to glance around without moving his head. "No . . . from what I hear they came up empty." He paused and listened again. "There's something planned at some church or school or something . . . No, I'm not in on it . . . sounds like something big 'cause they've rounded up cops from all over . . . Jews, Italians, blacks, Hispanics . . . no, no . . . that's all I can tell you. Don't ever call me again. I don't know you."

FitzPatrick hung up the phone and glanced around one more time. Everyone around him was busy. So much the better.

He finished his report about twenty minutes later and was just about to go out for lunch when his lieutenant stopped by his desk. "Hey, Frank, can you come into the office for a second. I've got something for you."

Frank followed his superior to the office and closed the door behind them. There were three men already in the office. One of them was dressed in a suit, the other two were ranking uniformed officers. The man in the suit clicked on a tape recorder. "What the hell are you doing calling me? Don't you know every cop is looking for you?" A different voice answered. "I'm well aware of that. Is it true that all Irish cops are being frozen out? Yeah . . . yeah . . ."

One of the uniformed policemen clicked off the tape recorder. The men all looked at FitzPatrick who buried his head in his hands as he envisioned a spotless career going down the drain.

Ireland

Harriet had carefully watched every movement and gesture that Duggan's grandmother, Mary Kavanaugh, had made. The older woman did indeed resemble Harriet, especially her height.

Harriet had listened to each and every word carefully, and certain phrases struck her as possibly meaningful.

"Michael is a very lonely person. I guess I'm about the only person he really trusts."

"Lonely?"

"Yes, I remember when he was sick. He just fell apart. He felt he had failed and he couldn't accept that. I had to keep reassuring him that everything was all right. Everything is all right, Mickey . . . Gram's here. I had to keep saying that over and over for weeks."

Everything's all right, Mickey . . . Gram's here. That stuck in Harriet's mind.

The old woman had accompanied Harriet to her car. The woman limped and had to walk with a cane.

"How did you hurt your leg?" Harriet had asked curiously.

"A land mine a couple years ago. I guess I was lucky. Two children were killed."

"Does Michael know you walk with a cane now?"

"Oh, yes. He got it for me, paid all the medical bills, too. Michael's really such a kind lad, but then a lot of good people have done a lot of horrible things here in Ireland."

Harriet remembered those words as she flew toward New York. Ireland was like this case in many respects. There would be no winners, only losers.

29

St. Ignatius's Rectory

Sean and Gallagher had arrived at Father Grogan's office shortly before ten o'clock in the morning. They didn't leave until nearly three o'clock, when the children from the attached parochial school were leaving for the day.

Both Gallagher and Sean knew they had their work cut out for them the minute they walked in. Sitting in the office was the head of the Bingo committee, a New York City police sergeant whose nose was out of joint because he had been frozen out of the Duggan operation and was now being asked to help, Sister Rose, the principal of the school, and Father Grogan's assistant, a tough young Jesuit named O'Regan.

Ground rules were finally laid out after much arguing. The one thing the priest demanded was a promise of total security for the people in the Bingo game.

Sean had told him that there would probably be more police and FBI agents at the game than players.

Sean had wanted to place a lot of cops at Mary Osborne's table, but the head of the Bingo committee nixed that. Many of the players had their regular seats and would give hell to anyone caught sitting in them. It was finally decided where the police could and could not sit.

Gallagher and Sean had left the meeting wearily. "I

told you that you just don't argue with the Jesuits and walk away with all the marbles," Gallagher said.

Sean nodded in agreement. As they walked toward the front door they accidentally bumped into a stooped old man who was coming from the rectory library that was open to the public.

"Sorry, old-timer. I didn't see you."

"That's all right, young fella," the old man said with a slight bronchial wheeze. "I'm too old to be in a big hurry for anything."

Sean held the door open for the old man, and Gallagher stood aside so the man could go out first.

"Thank you, gentlemen. Have a nice day."

"You, too," Gallagher replied.

The old man walked to the corner, then stopped and turned around to see Gallagher and Sean get into a cab. He smiled. Sean O'Keefe had looked him right in the eye and hadn't even recognized him. Duggan continued to walk down the street as slowly as an old man would. Taking the chance to come to the rectory had paid off. He found out firsthand that the police would more than likely be waiting for him Wednesday night, but the rectory library had shown him how he could get in and out without detection. He would discover how feasible his plan was later tonight. If it was operable, he would have only two days to prepare. A definite challenge, considering that it took months and dozens of people to pull off the Forty-seventh Street takeover. The whole success of this would be up to him. He liked that. If everything went well this evening, he could move on to the second part of his plan. The diversion.

Waldorf-Astoria

Harriet looked at the bills that Angela Coughlin had been running up while she was away.

"How much has your guest been costing you, Harriet?" Sean asked.

"Not all that much."

McBride laughed. "I'm glad you're paying for it and not me."

"Where is she?" Sean asked.

"She wanted to go shopping for a few things. An agent went with her."

"Did Sean fill you in on what's happened so far?"

"Yes. On the way in from the airport. Sounds interesting."

"If Mary Osborne shows up," Gallagher said.

"You still worried about her, John?" Harriet asked.

"Yes. I wish I knew where she was."

"Hopefully a lot of our questions will be answered Wednesday night. We all have a lot of work ahead of us."

Harriet ordered lunch and they settled in for an uninterrupted planning session.

East Side

There were few cars and even fewer pedestrians on Park Avenue at midnight. A doorman on the corner of Eighty-sixth watched a jogger in a bulky sweatsuit run from one center island to another, breaking his pace only at the cross streets to avoid traffic.

He would have continued to watch since there wasn't much else to see on this warm quiet night, but one of the tenants pulled up in a cab and he went to help take some suitcases from the trunk.

When the jogger reached the southern end of the island between Eighty-fourth and Eighty-third streets he ran in place, glancing from side to side. He stood next to the grating that led to the underground train tunnels beneath Park Avenue. He suddenly stopped, as if to tie his shoelace. Actually, he pulled out a lock cutter that was strapped to his leg, and he quickly clipped the lock on the grating. He glanced up carefully, but his movements were concealed by the waist-high wrought-iron fence that surrounded the island.

Duggan then lifted the grating and climbed down the steel ladder, carefully closing the grating behind him. He glanced at his watch. Fifteen seconds in all.

At the bottom of the ladder he pulled up his sweatshirt. All the tools that he would need were strapped to his body. He was glad sweatsuits were the current fashion. No one had given him a second glance.

He pulled the taped flashlight from his chest, along with a crowbar and some metal clippers. He winced slightly, thankful that he wasn't as hairy as someone like Logan.

He shined his light along the east wall of the tunnel. There was enough room to walk. He crossed the tracks carefully and walked slowly northward.

According to the book he had read in the rectory library, a relic printed in 1917 which carefully traced the history of the church, a side tunnel existed that connected the main tunnel to the church. He could visualize it from the rough drawings the church had submitted when they sued the railroad for placing escape exits on church property, which in turn caused smoke to fill the lower St. Lawrence Chapel every time a train went by. It was one of the few cases the railroads ever lost, and privately they had blamed the judges, who happened to be Irish Catholics, and the clout of Irish Tammany Hall politicians. As one Jesuit law professor said, "You don't blow smoke in God's face in an Irish-dominated New York City church and get away with it."

Duggan found the entrance to the side tunnel easily. He followed it until he reached a heavy wooden door sealed with one big lock. One big old lock that fell off with one sharp blow.

That was the easy part. Opening the rotted wooden door took him four hours. When he had finished he was covered with grime and perspiration. But it was open. Twenty minutes later he was pushing open another door that led to the subbasement under the lower chapel. Fifteen minutes later he was in the lower chapel which now held stacks of school books and furniture. To the side were confessionals that hadn't been used in many years.

Duggan checked out one of the confessionals. It suited his purpose. Then the boys' bathroom. Then upstairs to the school auditorium where Mary Osborne would sit. He visualized the Wednesday night scene and mentally noted where the regulars sat. He knew where he would sit. Close enough. It would work.

Duggan returned to the St. Lawrence Chapel and threw the tools he would no longer need in one of the empty desks. He looked at his watch, then retraced the path he would follow. Slowly. He would have a hostage and that would slow things down. At the entrance to the heavy tunnel door he placed the crowbar and the flashlight. They would be safe until he needed them. He closed the door.

He continued north along the railroad tunnel. He knew from his research that there were entrances at both ends of every island the full length of Park Avenue. He bypassed the Eighty-sixth Street entrance. Too much heavy crosstown traffic. He proceeded to Eighty-seventh Street and climbed the ladder on the south side. He gripped the ladder with his legs, snipped the lock, then pushed up the grate and crawled out.

The cutters were no longer necessary so he dropped them back down through the grating. There wouldn't be any checking of the locks unless there was trouble with a train in the tunnel, and that was unlikely.

Duggan glanced at his watch. He'd have time to spare.

He walked slowly to the subway entrance in Gimbel's East and looked at his watch again. Plenty of time.

Waldorf-Astoria

It was close to four in the morning when Inspector Conrad, Commissioner Hamlin, and the various FBI agents and police brass left. McBride, Harriet, Sean, and Gallagher sat slumped in their chairs. They were all exhausted.

"Well, from what Conrad told us, the shoofly's tape of Duggan talking to that detective clinches it. He knows about the trap," Sean said.

"And for all we know Mary Osborne may not show up, and if she does she may not even have the diamonds." Gallagher yawned. "This could be one big jerk off." He glanced at Harriet and blushed. "Sorry, chief inspector. I forgot you were here."

"I've heard worse, John, and for God's sake stop calling me chief inspector. We have no rank here. All our fannies are on the line."

Gallagher smiled tiredly. "Okay, Harriet."

"Gallagher could be right," McBride said. "Duggan would have to be nuts to try and get to Mary Osborne."

"Nuts, he's not," Harriet said. "A little on the edge maybe, but not over the line. He won't try unless he thinks he can pull it off, but he's smart enough to do it. He also has the guts to do it."

"So we go ahead as scheduled?" Sean asked.

"We don't have any other choice. If he does show I have a little something for him that might just catch him off guard," Harriet replied.

"What's that?" McBride asked.

"Duggan's grandmother."

"You've got her here?"

"No, but the next best thing. Me," Harried said enjoying their confusion.

"I got lost somewhere," Gallagher admitted.

"Don't feel alone," Sean said.

McBride's eyebrows went up. "Okay, Harriet, what's this all about?"

"Duggan isn't the only thespian. I've treaded the boards myself, and I'm not bad, Hugh, so lower that eyebrow. I studied Duggan's grandmother and I can pull it off." She got up from the desk and walked in a slow halting fashion, pretending to lean on a cane. "There, there, Mickey . . . not to worry . . . Gram's here . . . Gram's here."

The three men stared at Harriet. Her gestures and mannerisms were that of an older woman. Her voice was entirely different from her usual refined British accent. It was coarse, raspy. A pleasant voice, but totally alien to what they had been used to hearing these last few days.

"Not bad," Sean said. "But does it sound enough like the grandmother to fool Duggan?"

"And so what if it does?" Gallagher added.

"Duggan is a desperate young man in many ways. He wants to prove he can pull this thing off. He has to pull it off. And even if he won't admit it to himself, he is ruthless enough to take everyone and anything with him if trapped. The sight of dear old Gram might just put him off kilter enough to take him."

McBride shook his head. "It sounds off the wall to me, Harriet, but it's worth a shot."

"But will you look like the grandmother?" Sean asked.

"I'll know that in the morning," Harriet said.

They spent another half hour discussing logistics like the location of the relay station. All officers and agents inside were to carry miniaturized communications devices that were hooked into the central radio unit, which in turn could transmit to all the police units surrounding the area. Units would be placed in the Metropolitan Museum garage and private garages circling the church and school. Well out of sight, but capable of quick dispatch.

They were just about to call it a night when Angela Coughlin entered from Harriet's bedroom. Everyone including Harriet did a double take. Her hair and makeup were flawless and she wore a smart silk lounging suit. "I thought I'd wait up until you folks got all your business done." She handed them a bottle of ten-year-old Scotch.

"I thought you could all use a good-luck drink." She looked wistfully at the bottle. "I won't join you, though. I've taken a bit of a fancy to that Perry water."

"You mean Perrier?" Harriet asked.

"Whatever," Angela answered.

Harret went to the small refrigerator unit and set chilled glasses on the bar counter. Four Scotches. One Perrier.

Sean raised his glass. "Here's to the lovely lady who made this occasion possible. May she thrive and prosper."

Angela smiled modestly.

"Hear! Hear!" Harriet said.

Angela raised both eyebrows and gave her haughtiest look. "Harriet, my dear, must you always be so British?"

Harriet smiled whimsically. "Stuff it where the sun don't shine, Angie."

30

10th Avenue

Duggan had had very little sleep since he'd seen Angela Coughlin's picture in the paper. He was surprised that he was not more tired. His head was still clear, and his body still responded quickly. He could rest once he was out of town, if all went as planned later tonight.

A year of preparation. Six months cultivating the friendship and trust of the old women. He wasn't about to see that all go down the drain. He had to succeed. And he would if Gino had what he wanted. For money Gino had anything. It was short notice, but Gino had assured him that he would have everything first thing in the morning.

Duggan walked into the warehouse on Tenth Avenue and headed to the glass-enclosed office at the far end. Two beefy Italians stopped him before he reached the door. They didn't say a word, just professionally frisked him. One man stayed outside on guard. The other went into the office with Duggan.

Duggan had studied the entrails of New York's criminal society while setting up the takeover. Gino Pinelli was the man who could get anything for a price. Gino had supplied the M-16s used by the blacks.

"So you're still loose. Thought you'd be out of the country by now."

"In my own time," Duggan answered.

"I hear there's a big piece of change on your head."

"Too big for you, Gino. Reach for it, and my people will kill every wop in the city to get you."

Gino's jowly face went from smile to scowl. "You've got a bad mouth, Irishman."

"Yeah, I know. Do you have what I ordered?"

"Do you have the payment?"

Duggan dropped a three-carat diamond on the fat man's desk.

Gino picked up the diamond in his pudgy fingers and examined it under the light. "I ain't givin' you no change."

"Consider it a tip."

Gino placed a passport, some official-looking papers and an airline ticket on his desk. "One British diplomatic passport and all the necessary papers. You'll have to take care of the picture, but you know how to do that as well as I do. And one ticket to France via Washington."

"And . . ." Duggan said.

"And that thing is in the special shopping bag you ordered."

Gino smiled as he watched Duggan walk over to the shopping bag in the corner. He waited with amused anticipation for Duggan's reaction when he lifted the bag which weighed over fifty pounds. To Gino's disappointment Duggan lifted it with one hand and carried it easily back to the desk.

The burly bodyguard shook his head. "Shit, that damn thing nearly ruptured me."

"That's because you're a fat overweight slob," Duggan said casually.

The bodyguard looked at him menacingly, but decided against any physical action after seeing a demonstration of Duggan's strength.

"You know how to work that thing?" Gino asked.

"Logan taught me how to use munitions in Ireland. If everything is there I won't have any trouble."

"Logan was my kind of man," Gino said. "Not a pretty-boy operator like you, Duggan."

Duggan picked up the passport, papers, and ticket and put them in his jacket. Then he picked up the shopping bag and walked to the door. He opened it, then turned around.

"Logan's dead, Gino. I'm not."

Gino shrugged and Duggan walked out the door. Gino watched him until he was out on the street, then examined the diamond again.

"I wonder what he wanted that thing for," the bodyguard said.

"Who gives a shit? We got about twenty times what it was worth. Where'd you get it?"

"A couple of spic revolutionaries bought it from us a couple of months ago."

"You bought it back?" Gino growled.

"Are you kidding?"

They both laughed. Gino dropped the diamond into his vest pocket and left the warehouse to take his mother to early-morning mass.

5th Avenue

René Michel, renowned beauty consultant to the rich and famous of two continents, looked at Harriet's face then rolled his eyes dramatically to the ceiling of his mirrored salon.

"Ye gawds, Harriet. How can you do this?"

"Hush, dear heart. Just do your best."

"If you breathe a word of this to a living soul, I'll kill myself. And for gawd's sake, please use the side entrance."

Waldorf-Astoria

Harriet was playing hostess at the catered lunch she'd ordered for all the police and federal agents at the final briefing. She answered a knock at the door and smiled at Sean's confused expression. "Come on in, Sean. There's still plenty of food left."

"Harriet?"

"Of course."

He laughed. "God, this job has really aged you."

She glanced at her own reflection in the mirror as they entered the main room. "I must admit that I'm delighted with the transformation."

"You make me want to start singing Mother McCree. Do you think it will fool Duggan?"

"If my acting is up to par with René Michel's makeup, Duggan will think it's dear old Gram. If not, I'm in big trouble."

Hugh McBride tapped a spoon on a glass. "All right, everyone, it's time to get back to work."

The men and women who were to be the Bingo workers and players gathered in front of McBride and the many maps and drawings that were taped to the wall. Once he had the attention of the twenty police officers and agents he continued.

"Detective Gallagher has instructed you on how to act. To the regulars you are all from a parish in Staten Island and are merely at the game to observe. Let the workers there do all the work. I'll be calling the numbers with the help of Bingo chairman Detective Donovan. I will be in contact by radio with the counting room so the officer on the radio can contact backup units who are covering the area. You have all studied the maps and drawings of the school. You people at the front desk let me know by the prearranged signal the minute Mary Osborne arrives."

"If she arrives," Sean muttered under his breath.

"And," McBride continued, "if you see anyone who might be Duggan, give the high sign to one of our people near the door. You people on the lower level keep your ears on that loudspeaker. If there's trouble, you'll hear it from me. I'll be on the microphone. Block off those lower stairs. Harriet, as soon as you arrive go in the east door and right into the counting room. Nobody is to get edgy or trigger-happy. All commands will come from me. Is that clear?"

Everyone nodded in agreement.

"Are there any questions?"

A short bald police officer in the back raised his hand. McBride nodded to him.

"If I win at Bingo do I get to keep the money?"

Everyone laughed including McBride. "That's between you and your conscience, officer."

The briefing ended on an up note, but everyone would have been very nervous if they knew what Duggan had planned for the evening.

St. Ignatius's Church

Three hours before the doors of the adjoining school were to open for the Bingo game, Duggan walked up the steps to the church disguised as an old man; the same disguise that had proved successful with Sean and Gallagher.

He gritted his teeth as the heavy shopping bag pulled at his arm causing it to ache from fingers to shoulder joint. He had felt the same pain at Gino's, but it was imperative that he walk naturally, carrying the bag in one hand. He had done that convincingly this morning.

It was important he do even better tonight. The specially constructed interior of the bag was steel mesh to support its heavy weight. The remaining top of the bag was filled with books purchased at a nearby bookstore.

There was nobody in the front entrance. Duggan moved to a side door and went down the stairs to the St. Lawrence Chapel. It was deserted except for some people near the front sorting books, but they were too far away to see him slip into the unused confessional on the side and close the curtain. He would have more than three hours to wait.

Duggan rubbed his aching arm. He would spend this time covering every detail in his mind. Both the locks on the entrances to the train tunnel were still broken. He had retraced his steps into the subbasement early this morning and this time he had left the door to the tunnel open. He had placed two flashlights near the entrance to the lower Bingo floor. He felt the left pocket of his jacket. The pistol was there. He patted the right pocket, but very lightly. Once emptied of its contents it was large enough to hold the can of diamonds.

He started to retrace the course of action he would take to keep his mind more alert.

Into the tunnel. What happened there would depend on the prior events. Prior events were key. Everything else would be easy. Exit the railroad tunnel at East Eighty-seventh. Take an express subway from East Eighty-sixth Street. Pick up suitcase in Grand Central Station locker with clothes, disguises, papers, and the can of diamonds from Sarah O'Toole. Take a taxi to Penn Station. Sleep on the Metroliner to Washington. Sleep was important. Check into the Mayflower Hotel to change clothes and meet contact for passport picture to be taken. Board plane in Washington for France with diplomatic passport.

Duggan felt the handle of the shopping bag. The

diversion. He felt another sudden urge to confess. His right hand was shaking. He steadied it with his left. Probably just a delayed reaction from the stress of carrying the heavy bag. He began to perspire even though it was quite cool. He glanced at the illuminated dial on his watch, then started a step-by-step visualization of how he would enter the Bingo game.

31

St. Ignatius's school auditorium

John Gallagher paced nervously between the rows of tables on the upper level. The tables were nearly filled and the game would be starting soon. Mary Osborne still had not shown up. She had never been this late. Gallagher began to worry and his face showed it. He had another worry, too. Sean had reported to McBride from the radio room that Harriet Smythe-Houghton had not arrived yet either. He glanced at the people at Mary's table as he passed; three of them were cops. The others were regulars, plus a few newcomers. His eyes stopped at the chair across from Mary's usual spot. The old man sitting in it smiled and waved. Gallagher couldn't place his face, then remembered it was the old man he had seen at the rectory.

"Hello, there." He glanced at the shopping bag of books next to the old man. "Hope you signed out for all those books," he kidded. "If you didn't, Sister Scholastica will chew you ears off."

The old man laughed, coughed slightly, and shook his head. "Oh, they aren't rectory books. I bought these."

"I haven't seen you at the game before, have I?" Gallagher asked.

"No, this is my first time here. I just moved to the parish."

Gallagher glanced at his watch. The game would be starting in five minutes. He wanted to go up front to check in with McBride when the old man spoke again. "Where's the other young man who was with you at the rectory?"

"Oh, he's around somewhere." Gallagher glanced at the boards laid out in front of the old man. "Hey, you forgot to get marking pieces for your boards."

"Oh, I never use them."

East Side/West Side

Both Harriet and Mary Osborne were having problems getting to the Bingo game. Traffic problems.

Mary wasn't in that big a hurry. She sat comfortably in the front seat next to Dawn Wilkinson, who was at the wheel of the blue Chrysler. The Wilkinsons were such a lovely family. She had been the main baby-sitter for their three children before they moved to the suburbs, and they had kept in touch. When they found out that she was leaving the country they had invited her to their home in Tarrytown. It had been a wonderful week of laughing children and oafish dogs who always wanted their ears scratched.

"Mary, I'm so sorry about this, especially after I promised I would get you to your game on time, but this traffic is impossible," Dawn Wilkinson said apologetically.

"Not to worry, dear. The week with your family was worth all the Bingo games in the world."

There was a break, and Dawn took advantage of it by quickly turning a corner and heading crosstown toward the East Side.

Harriet Smythe-Houghton had a more personal involvement with her traffic problem on the East Side. Her cab had sideswiped another cab, and the drivers were on the street verbally assaulting each other.

"You stupid jerk. Who the hell taught you to drive like a baboon?" Al Karvacus screamed.

"Why you . . . you're the one who hit me," Hector Garcia sputtered.

Harriet looked at her watch. She had started late, and it was getting later. She got out of the cab and checked the damage to both cabs. It was minimal.

"Gentlemen, could you settle this later please, I . . ."

"Hold your water, lady. I'll get you there as soon as I take care of this *shmuck*."

"*Shmuck*," Garcia screamed.

The two drivers continued to curse one another. Harriet sighed, and climbed into the front seat of the cab. Both drivers were struck momentarily speechless as the cab sped up Madison Avenue.

"Did you see that?" Karvacus yelled. "That old broad stole my cab!"

"And she's driving on the wrong side of the street to boot," Garcia added. "Come on, we'll use my cab and get her."

The two men jumped into the front seat of Garcia's cab. As the cab took off Garcia put down the meter.

"Jesus, you're going to charge me?"

"Shit, sorry, force of habit . . . don't give me a tip."

St. Ignatius's school auditorium

Gallagher poked his head through the door to the counting room. The radio operator and Sean both stood up at the sound of the doorknob turning.

"Don't get jumpy. It's just me. No Mary Osborne or Duggan. It looks like a dud operation."

"No Harriet either," Sean said. "What's happening inside?"

"McBride's busy calling. He's doing a good job."

"Anyone even vaguely suspicious at Mary Osborne's table?" Sean asked.

"No. Mostly old folks, except for the cops. You remember that old guy we bumped into coming out of the rectory?"

"Vaguely," Sean said.

"He's at the table. Nice old guy. He's one of those no marker players . . . damned if I know how they can keep track of the numbers. He said to say hello."

"So say hello back," Sean said in a slightly bored voice.

"Gallagher . . . Gallagher," yelled a voice from the hall. "She's here."

"Shit . . ." Gallagher slammed the door and left.

Something clicked in Sean's mind. Something Harriet had said about Duggan. He tried to remember what the old man looked like. He couldn't, but he did remember what Harriet had said . . . Duggan used to play Bingo with his grandmother and he never marked his boards. Sean jumped up and headed for the door.

Mary Osborne was hurrying to her chair with her cards in one hand and her blue suitcase in the other as Gallagher hurried into the auditorium.

Mary was seated and arranging her cards when Gallagher reached her. He was slightly out of breath. "Mary, do you have something in that bag that you are supposed to deliver when you get to Ireland?" he panted.

Mary looked up in suprise at the worried face that was hovering above her. "Why, yes, Officer Gallagher I . . ." She never finished the sentence. The whole table shook as something heavy landed on it.

As he ran into the auditorium Sean saw the old man standing on the table. Gallagher was staring with his mouth open at something in a shopping bag.

There were books all over the table. The old man was holding something in the air. The three police officers at the table were reaching for their guns.

Detective John Gallagher knew damn well what he was looking at, and it scared the hell out of him. It was a Claymore mine. He had seen firsthand what they could do to a whole damn column of troops in Vietnam.

Duggan's voice reached the last row of the auditorium clearly.

"This is a Claymore mine. This is a detonator. Any hostile move and I will kill or maim everyone in this room."

Gallagher knew how deadly those steel balls could be if there was an explosion.

"It's the real thing, McBride," Gallagher yelled.

Sean reached the table, but froze in his tracks along with the police and agents who were now all on their feet.

"Give me the package, Mary."

She recognized the voice, but not the face. The threatening tone frightened her but she obeyed calmly, opening her suitcase and bringing the wrapped can of diamonds out from the bottom of the bag.

Duggan spotted Sean O'Keefe and smiled. "We meet again, O'Keefe. Come forward, please."

McBride sat motionless behind the number-selection machine. Where the hell was Harriet? he thought. He watched Sean walk forward and stand behind Mary Osborne and next to Gallagher. He also noticed one of his men reaching for his ankle holster. McBride quickly put the mike near his mouth. "This is McBride . . . no officer or agent is to try and stop this man."

Duggan bowed to the stage. "Thank you, McBride. I read about the role you played in figuring out the plans of my siege on Forty-seventh Street. My compliments, but you lose again."

Duggan turned back to O'Keefe. "My favorite hostage."

"Get stuffed, Duggan," Sean said.

Duggan's face flushed and his hand tightened on the detonator.

"Take it easy, Sean. Don't set him off," McBride yelled into the microphone. There was a moan from the Bingo players at McBride's unintentional pun.

Duggan laughed. He was feeling jubilant at the power he again held. "O'Keefe, unwrap that can, open it, and hand it to me."

Sean followed the terse instructions begrudgingly. Duggan emptied the contents into his bulky righthand pocket. This done he tossed the empty can on the floor, then brought a gun from the other pocket. "All right, O'Keefe, you're it again." Duggan jumped off the table and waved O'Keefe toward the door to the downstairs Bingo room. He turned and spoke to his audience, again in carefully modulated tones. "We'll be leaving the same way I got in. If anyone tries to stop us or come after us I'll detonate this mine. Is that understood?"

"Understood," McBride said into the microphone.

"Tell your people downstairs not to interfere."

"Downstairs."

"Downstairs, here," a voice replied on the intercom speaker.

"Duggan and a hostage are leaving. Don't stop them. There's a bomb of some sort up here that could blow us all over the place."

"Understood."

Duggan marched Sean out the door at gunpoint and down the stairs to the lower Bingo floor. Nobody moved. The Claymore mine held everyone's attention, especially John Gallagher's, who was standing right in front of it.

A voice came over the upstairs loudspeaker. "They've gone into the lower chapel."

"Don't follow," McBride said firmly into the mike.

Duggan ordered Sean to pick up the flashlights at the entrance to the lower chapel, and took one from Sean.

"How did you get in, Duggan?" Sean asked.

"I've been here for hours," Duggan said with a tinge of pride in his voice. "Move to the front of the chapel, O'Keefe."

"You won't get away with this. The whole block's surrounded by cops."

"Not to worry, O'Keefe. I took that into consideration. I took everything into consideration. I got into the lower Bingo room and then hid in the little boys' room in one of the stalls. Then I just walked upstairs and sat down. I even had phony Bingo cards made up so I wouldn't have to go to the desk. Everyone thought I had come in the front."

There was a nervous quality to Duggan's voice that worried Sean.

They retraced the route Duggan had taken earlier. Duggan had Sean close the heavy door behind them. He also had Sean check the tracks to make sure no trains were coming.

They walked single file uptown. Sean in front. Duggan behind.

Sean was about to turn around when he heard Duggan trip, curse and fall. There was a dull muffled sound. The tunnel vibrated and soot fell from the ceiling.

Sean spun around and his light fell on Duggan, who was on the ground staring wide-eyed at the detonator in his hand.

"You rotten son of a bitch . . . you set that thing off . . . all those people!" Rage took over as Sean dove for Duggan. Duggan fired three times in quick succession. Sean felt three bullets hit his chest with deadly accuracy. Everything dissolved to black just as he hit the tracks.

32

Madison Avenue and 84th Street

Harriet jammed down on the brake but it was too late. The police car speeding along Eighty-fourth Street to block traffic at Madison Avenue smashed into the back of the cab as Harriet was about to turn the corner. It was just as well because Harriet would not have been able to stop in time to avoid hitting the three police cars that were blocking the street.

Two more police cars coming east swerved to avoid the cab and sped to Eighty-third where they turned to block the oncoming traffic. The only car that got through was the cab being driven by Hector Garcia, which screeched to a halt behind Harriet's cab.

Harriet was shaken but not hurt. She got out of the cab and started to walk around the front when the cop from the patrol car that hit her jumped out and pushed her behind the cab.

"This is uncalled for, officer. I'm Chief Inspector Smythe-Houghton . . ."

"You'll be chopped liver, lady, if that bomb in the street goes off."

"What bomb in . . . ?"

Harriet never finished her sentence. The bomb in the center of the street went off sending steel balls in a circular sweep. Windows in the Regis High School across the street shattered as did windows in some of the nearby apartment buildings. The squad cars at either end of the street lost all their windows and the sides of the cars looked like they were peppered with shotgun pellets.

St. Ignatius's school auditorium

Detective Gallagher and everyone on the main floor was pressed against the near walls of the auditorium when the glass doors at the front of the room shattered harmlessly.

Gallagher's hands were shaking and he felt like throwing up. He had been standing staring at the bomb when he suddenly picked it up and ran with it to the street. It was more instinct than anything else, but a certain amount of quick logic, too. Duggan was out of sight. How would he know?

Below Park Avenue

Sean O'Keefe was having a hard time breathing and his chest hurt like hell, but he was alive. Harriet had insisted that everyone connected with the operation wear the bulletproof vests, which she purchased and handed out at the last briefing.

Sean had debated about wearing it, but did not want to hurt Harriet's feelings. As he staggered to his feet he realized that he owed his life to her generosity.

He was too weak to pursue Duggan. He reached into his pocket and took out the miniature walkie-talkie that tied in to the radio room. Then he remembered the explosion. Everyone would be dead or hurt. He started to throw the radio on the track when he remembered that the radio was in the counting room and the counting room was off the hall from the auditorium. "Feldman

... Feldman ... can you hear me? Feldman come in. Feldman can you hear me?" There was no answer.

Radio room

Officer Sid Feldman gave a sigh of relief as he headed back to the radio room. He had managed to call the backup to block off the street and relay a call for the bomb squad and ambulance. He had wanted to stick with the radio, but McBride had ordered him into the auditorium and away from the window. As he looked at the glass scattered all over the small room he was glad that he had obeyed orders. The radio was still on. He should be hearing from Gallagher, who was leading a contingent of men into the lower level, but it was Sean O'Keefe's voice he heard. "Feldman, you son of a bitch, where are you?"

"O'Keefe, is that you? Where are you? Are you all right?"

Sean answered with a question of his own. "How bad was it ... how many bought it ... Gallagher ... McBride?"

"Everybody is okay. Gallagher grabbed that thing and chucked it in the street."

"Jesus ... can you relay to McBride and Gallagher?"

"I can get McBride. He can relay to Gallagher."

"Tell them I'm in the railroad tunnel under Park. Duggan is headed north, will probably surface along the line. Tell McBride ..."

"I hear you, Sean ..." Feldman turned to see McBride in the door.

"Are you all right?" McBride asked Sean.

"I took three shots in the chest, but Harriet's vest saved my ass."

"I'll send a team after Gallagher. How do we get to the tunnel?"

Sean gave brief instructions then said, "Oh, shit . . . here comes a train. I've got to get back to the side tunnel."

McBride left the radio room and returned to the auditorium. He sent a second group to catch up to Gallagher and relay Sean's instructions. Then he returned to the radio room. "Feldman, get on the horn and alert every car in the area . . . if they see an old man in a light blue jacket . . . grab him . . . and be careful."

McBride ran into the street. He quickly surveyed the damage. The squad cars on each end of the street were useless. Their tires were all flat. He caught a glimpse of Harriet on the corner of Madison arguing with two men in civilian clothes and two uniformed officers.

Hector Garcia and Al Karvacus, the cab drivers, were both yelling and pointing at Harriet, who was beginning to lose her temper. The two policemen were trying to calm them all down.

McBride ran up the street and yelled to Harriet, "Duggan is loose . . . he got away in the train tunnel under Park."

The two policemen and the cabbies turned to look at the priest running toward them. Harriet moved away and got into Garcia's cab and started the engine. Before the police or cabbies knew what was happening the cab was on the sidewalk of Eighty-fourth Street heading east toward Park Avenue. The cab stopped and McBride jumped into the front seat.

Garcia and Karvacus watched in amazement as the cab was stopped by the police at the far end of the street, then waved on as the contingent of blue uniforms started to run on foot across Park and along the center island.

"What the hell is going on in this city?" Karvacus howled. "Old ladies stealing cabs . . . priests stealing cabs . . . bombs going off . . . and cops letting them do it!"

Garcia started to yell at the two policemen. That was a mistake. Both cabbies were taken into custody for disturbing the peace. Charges were later dropped.

Park Avenue

Nearby police units had blocked off northbound traffic at Eightieth Street. Other units blocked off southbound traffic at Ninetieth Street. Foot patrolmen rushed to the crosstown streets to stop traffic. The first car that was stopped at Eighty-sixth was the cab with McBride and Harriet.

McBride quickly identified himself to the officers who informed him that an escape door was found open on the island at Eighty-ninth Street. Units had fanned out in both directions. McBride looked down Eighty-sixth Street at the windowless Gimbel's East building at the corner of Lexington Avenue. "Isn't there a subway at Lexington?" he asked the officer who was about to get back into his squad car.

The officer nodded his head, and Harriet immediately turned onto Eighty-sixth. McBride motioned for the police car to follow. As they screamed to a halt, McBride caught a glimpse of a light blue coat disappearing down the subway steps.

McBride and Harriet stopped and jumped out of the cab leaving it in the middle of the street. The police car did the same. Five uniformed cops followed McBride toward the entrance. McBride ordered the sergeant in charge to have his men cover all four entrances to the downtown side and to call for assistance to cover the uptown side. The cops ran for the entrances just as other units began to pour on to the street.

McBride, Harriet, and the sergeant ran down the stairs and through the exit door. The token clerk yelled after them until she saw the police uniform bringing up the rear.

McBride and Harriet looked left and right on the upper level. They looked across the tracks to the uptown side. No Michael Duggan.

A train rumbled below. "The downstairs express," yelled the sergeant. McBride took off for the stairs leading to the lower level, followed by a puffing Harriet, who envied him his physical strength, and an exhausted sergeant, who had been on desk duty too long.

They reached the lower level just as the doors to the train were closing. McBride ran to the end, looking in the cars as he went. Harriet ran toward the front as the train started to move. Then she saw him. Duggan was leaning against the door with his back to her. She screamed at the top of her voice. "Mickey . . . it's all right, Mickey . . . Gram's here . . . Gram's here!"

Michael Duggan turned, and the shocked expression on his face showed that he had not only heard but seen Harriet and that her disguise had had its impact.

McBride heard Harriet yell and realized that Duggan was on the train and on his way to possible freedom. The rear of the train moved by him. He drew a deep breath and jumped onto the back of the train, struggling for a sure grip.

Sergeant Fred Potter made it to the bottom of the subway stairs just in time to see McBride whizzing by, hanging on to the back of the train for dear life. He and Harriet stood by the edge of the platform and watched the rear red lights of the train disappear into the inky blackness of the tunnel.

Sergeant Potter turned reluctantly and eyed the stairs.

"I guess I'd better have the token booth attendant alert the transits."

He headed slowly up the stairs. Harriet sat down, and leaned her head against a pillar and closed her eyes.

33

Under the city

Hugh McBride had always hated speed. His hands never unclenched on jets. His teeth were always gritted when he had to take his kids on the roller coaster. Cab drivers who rode the accelerator always brought out his wrath. He was not a devotee of the fast chase. Even watching the chase scene in *The French Connection* had upset his stomach. So why the hell was he hanging on to the back of a speeding express train? He wished he knew.

Four cars ahead Michael Duggan sat dazed and perspiring in a seat on the far side of the car. He was rubbing his hands together and the pressure and friction had already started to peel away some skin.

There were only seven other people in the car. A wino who was sound asleep, a young Puerto Rican couple and their baby, a black nurse, and an oriental couple who sat across from Duggan and stared at him blankly.

When the doors opened at Fifty-ninth Street the nurse got off. The wino continued to sleep and the young couple tried to comfort the baby, who started to cry. Nobody got on and the doors started to close. A man dressed in black with soot all over his face pushed his way in at the last moment. He was obviously a priest, but the gun in his hand confused the old couple and they moved closer together.

"It's over, Duggan," McBride yelled.

The old man in the blue jacket stood up. He pulled a gun from his jacket. His hands were shaking.

"No," Duggan screamed as he raised the gun. Everyone except the sleeping wino moved for cover.

McBride fired three times quickly. The first shot was off target and hit Duggan in the side, tearing the fabric of the jacket and sending diamonds all over the floor. The second hit him in the chest. The third his head. It wasn't McBride's usual marksmanship, but the seven-minute ride on the back of the train had shaken his usual cool composure.

A transit patrolman in the next car heard the shots and burst into the car with his gun drawn. He aimed at McBride who quickly dropped his gun on the floor.

"McBride, FBI," he yelled as he put his hands over his head.

Transit Patrolman Anthony Tyrone looked at the body of Michael Duggan, the diamonds, and the frightened passengers. McBride sank down in a seat next to the old oriental couple, who still couldn't figure out why priests in America carried guns.

When the train pulled into Grand Central Station transit police were all over the platform. All passengers were ordered off the train. The body and the diamonds would not be touched until the train was in a secure area.

The wino, still asleep, was carried off. The young couple left as quickly as they could. The old oriental couple had to be helped. The woman had a bad foot and a noticeable limp.

The doors to the train shut, and McBride, Officer Tyrone, and six ranking transit officers assembled next to Duggan's body. The train moved off down the dark tunnel.

The oriental couple walked slowly into Grand Central Station and sat down in the front row of the high-ceilinged waiting room. The old woman slowly removed her well-worn sandal and put her wrinkled foot up on her knee with suprising agility. She carefully removed a glittering stone from between her toes. The pressure she had exerted on it the moment the three-carat stone had rolled into her sandal had cut into her flesh.

They gazed around the room cautiously and the woman quickly slipped it into the drawstring bag she was carrying. They smiled at one another happily and walked slowly back to the subway. Even under the low lights of the waiting room the stone had sparkled brilliantly.

Epilogue

England

Harriet Smythe-Houghton sat at her desk in the living room of her country home and double-checked the figures from the Zurich bank. She had no doubt that the figures were accurate, but it was her nature to double-check everything.

Sir Arthur came in searching for his spectacles, which he was constantly misplacing.

"Balancing the Duggan account?" he asked.

"Things like this can never be balanced," she said absently.

She checked the footnotes she had made on the pages. The word "Approximate" was repeated several times. When dealing with diamonds it was the only appropriate word to use.

DIAMONDS RECOVERED (APPROXIMATE)

Mail Van Drivers	9,000,000
McGraw-Hill Massacre	42,000,000
Body of Dennis Logan	1,004,000,000
Body of Sidney Katz	20,000,000
Fred Stone	10,000,000
Angela Coughlin	502,000,000
Mary Osborne's Diamonds from Body of Michael Duggan	502,000,000

O'Toole Diamonds Found in Grand Central Locker	502,000,000
	$2,591,000,000
Approximate Amount Stolen	3,095,000,000
Approximate Amount Recovered	2,591,000,000
	504,000,000 ?????

Over half a billion dollars in diamonds still unaccounted for. A miscalculation by Ben Levi and his people? A ploy for insurance money by some of the dealers? Possible. Or were the diamonds still out there somewhere? And what would they be used for? Harriet was worried. She didn't like loose ends, but neither British nor American intelligence had picked up anything so there was little she could do about it. She had wanted to pursue it, but her supervisors didn't share her concern. It was frustrating for a woman like Harriet, and she could do nothing more than hope that the diamonds hadn't reached Duggan's IRA contacts.

In the meantime, there was the trust to administrate. The diamonds recovered from Stone, Angela Coughlin, Duggan's body, and the Grand Central locker where Duggan had placed Sarah O'Toole's portion amounted to $1,516,000,000. According to her agreement with Ben Levi, the reward amounted to ten percent of that, a total of $151,600,000 worth of investment-quality stones.

The diamonds had been placed in a Zurich bank and were used as part of the bank's assets. In return, the bank paid five percent a year interest in monthly installments to a London bank's trust fund. It amounted to a tidy sum of $7,580,000 a year, or over $630,000 a month.

As executors of the trust, Harriet and Sir Arthur wrote monthly checks to various individuals and institutions. Mary Osborne and Angela Coughlin both received a share, along with the families of the twenty-four innocent people killed in the first hours of the siege. A film scholarship in the name of Stan Zimmerman, the cameraman, had been established, along with a journalism scholarship at Columbia University in honor of Cal Long, Sean's young assistant. Long's mother also received a monthly check. And a sizable onetime check had been presented to the newly formed Garcia & Karvacus Cab Company for six taxies and medallions.

Those who had a more direct involvement in the capture of Duggan received the lion's share of the reward. Four full college scholarships had been extended for McBride's children, to be used as needed. McBride was unaware of the origin of the scholarships since Harriet was sure he would have refused them. Lieutenant John Gallagher and his wife received a large monthly check. And a monthly check went to Miranda O'Keefe, so Sean's ex-wife could claim no part of it. Finally, a check went to St. Ignatius's school, part of which was earmarked for weekly Bingo. The game now claimed the largest Bingo prize in all of New York City.

But over half a billion remained missing. Where?

France

In the Basse-Bretagne region of the westernmost tip of France, four Irishmen sat in a small cottage. The cottage had been rented for them by a French sympathizer and was isolated enough to provide safe haven for top-level policy meetings, and negotiations with foreign agents.

The four men were examining a package of diamonds. Diamonds that had been sent uninsured through the mails from upstate New York. Fred Stone had been right; nobody had bothered to check packages leaving the small upstate town for France.

"Why didn't Duggan send all the diamonds this way?" Donovan asked curiously. He had joined the operation only recently.

"He didn't want to put all his eggs in one basket. At least we have something," Reagan answered.

"And there's over a half billion here," Donovan continued. "Isn't that what you've figured, Flynn?"

They all turned to the fourth Irishman, a Dublin jeweler.

"Approximately."

"Well, it now appears that the Irish problem is an English problem. If we can't convince the Protestants in the Unionist party that our cause is their cause, then we take the battlefield to England. They've had us at each other's throats for too long now," Reagan added angrily.

All nodded in agreement as Reagan absently began to scoop the diamonds back into the metal container. "If they don't get out, our only question is . . . conventional weapons or a bomb?"

Flynn put his finger to the bridge of his nose and smiled knowingly. "If we hang on to these diamonds for a year, they'll be worth a lot more. With a little patience we could have both."

New York City

Mary Osborne had decided to stay in New York now that she was a lady of means. She rang her bell as B7 was called and looked guiltily at the small diamond among her lucky pieces.

Mary Osborne had two vices. Curiosity and a craving for sweets. She had opened Duggan's gift-wrapped present and had eaten her way through the top layers of candy. And she had nearly broken a tooth on one of the diamonds. Deciding quickly that God was punishing her, she had quickly rewrapped the package, but she'd kept what she thought was just a very hard piece of candy as a reminder of her sin. Now she knew what it was, but was too embarrassed to tell anyone about it. She would have to go to mass and confession every day as penance, and to thank God for providing for her in her old age.

She smiled happily. After the game she would return to her new apartment in one of the luxury buildings on the Upper East Side. She had a lot of preparations to attend to. Tomorrow, a group of the Bingo ladies were coming to lunch and she wanted to do some baking.